SERPENT QUEEN

ANGEL SWORN

WALL STREET JOURNAL BESTSELLING AUTHOR

JEFF WHEELER

OLIVERHEBERBOOKS

Cover Art by Drazenka Kimpel

Published by Oliver-Heber Books

0 9 8 7 6 5 4 3 2 1

Also by Jeff Wheeler

Your First Million Words

Tales from Kingfountain, Muirwood, and Beyond: The Worlds of Jeff Wheeler

The Last Harbinger Series

The Last Harbinger

Angel Sworn

Queen Mother

Tyrant Queen

Dark Queen

Serpent Queen

The Invisible College

The Invisible College

The Violence of Sound

The Alchemy of Fate

Master of the Royal Secret

The Dresden Codex

Doomsday Match

Jaguar Prophecies

Final Strike

The First Argentines Series

Knight's Ransom

Warrior's Ransom

Lady's Ransom

Fate's Ransom

The Grave Kingdom Series

The Killing Fog

The Buried World

The Immortal Words

The Harbinger Series

Storm Glass

Mirror Gate

Iron Garland

Prism Cloud

Broken Veil

The Kingfountain Series

The Queen's Poisoner

The Thief's Daughter

The King's Traitor

The Hollow Crown

The Silent Shield

The Forsaken Throne

The Poisoner of Kingfountain Series

The Poisoner's Enemy

The Widow's Fate

The Maid's War

The Duke's Treason

The Poisoner's Revenge

The Legends of Muirwood Trilogy

The Wretched of Muirwood

The Blight of Muirwood

The Scourge of Muirwood

The Covenant of Muirwood Trilogy

The Banished of Muirwood

The Ciphers of Muirwood

The Void of Muirwood

Whispers from Mirrowen Trilogy

Fireblood

Dryad-Born

Poisonwell

Landmoor Series

Landmoor

Silverkin

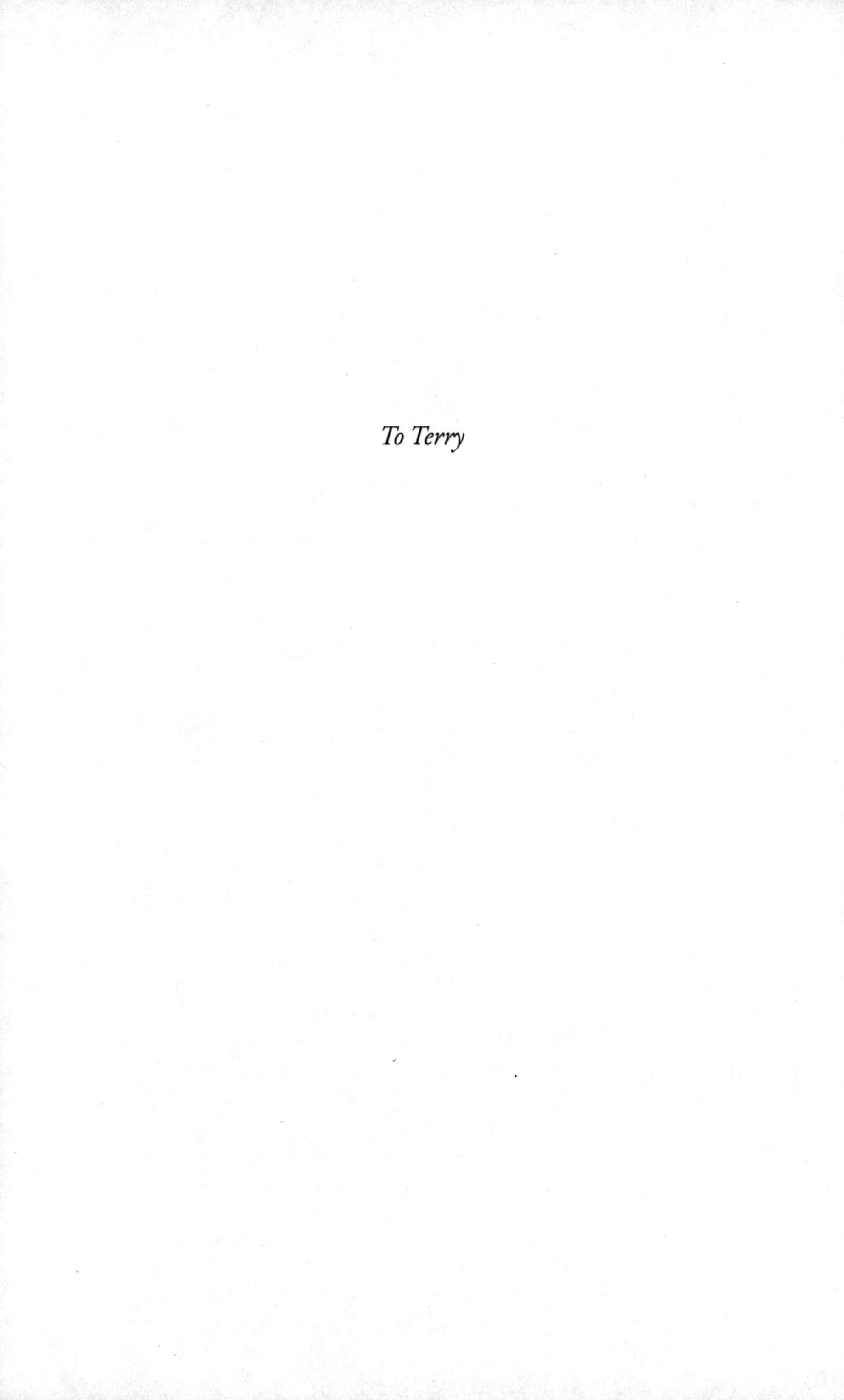

To Terry

Metamorphistry rests upon four pillars—philosophy, astronomy, alchemy, and ethics. The first pillar is the synthesis of knowledge of earth, water, and salt. The second supplies a full understanding of all that is fiery or airy in nature, how time, light, and distance weigh on perception; and how comets portend the future. The third consists of an adequate explanation of the properties of the four elements—that is to say, the entirety of the whole cosmos, including beings made of spirit and intelligence—and an introduction into the art of their transformations. Finally, the fourth shows the practitioner those virtues that are necessary up until his death to promote the transformation, and should support and complete the three other pillars. Every transformation of man into beast is a combination of the above. Thus knowing the properties, I theorize that any mutation can be reversed.

—The Hermetic and Alchemical Writings of Paracelsus

Prologue

The Coliseum of Vaud

The fall of Vaud—three months after the fall of Ecbatana

Theo walked hastily and quietly down the corridor, his heart in his throat as he passed blood-spattered corpses and claw marks gouged into the stone walls of the coliseum interior. He reached the door he sought and waved his ring over the iron handle, which began to glow. Theo gripped it and pulled on the heavy oak door to slip into the room beyond. When the door shut behind him, he leaned back against it, breathing fast and sighing in relief.

He pulled the druid stone from his pocket and commanded the entity held within to glow. The room smelled of various reagents and chemicals, but he saw it was undisturbed, thank the Maker. An assortment of books lined the shelves, each of which he had written. Theo was a prolific writer, and going back as far as he could remember, he had enjoyed spending countless hours summarizing his thoughts on the properties of magic and nature. One of the books was on the grafting magic of the angel sworn gleaned from his childhood living in one of the intermountain villages in the region once ruled by the Queen Mother.

Though he wasn't in his study searching for books, he couldn't help but pause to admire the gold inlaid on the spines revealing the various titles. *The Theoretical Imposition of Comets on Crop Health. A Study of the Transformation of Moth Beetles. The Pyrophoric Fruit.* He rubbed his forehead, memories of writing each one crowding his mind.

Theo went to the bookcase nearest his desk, where he secured the more dangerous ingredients in his study. He twisted a ring on his finger, revealing a tiny key, and slipped it into a lock hidden among the books. With a quick turn, a series of tumblers clicked and clacked. When it was safe to open, he pulled on the front, and the top half of the unit unfolded, revealing a series of glass vials… some filled with liquids, others with grains of deadly poisons. His fingers were jittery as he reached for the stoppered vial full of quicksilver. He tucked the vial into the pocket of his doublet and patted it. Then he closed the cabinet doors and reset the trap, waiting for the lead balls to slide back into place.

He was about to leave, but he paused, then went to his desk and opened it, drawing out the scionwood wand he stored there. He'd paid handsomely to acquire it years earlier. He slid it up his fur-lined sleeve and anchored the tip inside the cuff so it wouldn't be easily shaken loose.

Once he believed it was secure, he went back to the door, and his stomach gurgled with dread. He knew the coliseum was overrun with hideous wolf creatures. The gladiator games, which had attracted vast sums in revenue from gambling over the outcomes, were no more. The loud, raucous crowds that had caused the coliseum to shudder with the noise of their cheering had ended. The furnaces that had heated the majestic structure during winter were silent and cold with no one left to tend them. Few people remained at all, and all that loss had come from one source.

The first gladiator exposed to the metamorphic disease had been brought to Vaud weeks previously. He'd had a swipe of silver on his arm, a wound that hadn't healed right. And then he'd transformed into one of the vicious wolf-men and had torn through the ranks. He'd been subdued, of course, when the transformation reverted him back to a human form. Locked away in one of the many cages in the underground part of the coliseum. Only, all those he had injured, not killed, contracted the disease as well, and each had suddenly transformed and begun to maim and kill the guards. And the disease had spread again and again.

Theo paused at the door, summoning his courage. He licked his lips, as sweat trickled from his bald dome into the wreath of hair above his ears. He extinguished the druid stone and put it back in his pocket. He waited for his vision to adjust to the darkness again and blew out a held breath. *Patience.* Since no other light source was in the room, he waited the requisite time for his pupils to dilate.

Finally, he released the locking mechanism and carefully opened the door. The stink of rotting flesh intruded. He peeked out into the corridor, found no one there, and edged out through the smallest opening he could before he closed the door and locked it.

He'd walked perhaps ten paces when a low growl behind him revealed he'd been discovered. Theo steadied himself. He slipped his hand into his pouch attached to his belt and grabbed a handful of powder.

The wolf-man charged at him, slavering and snapping its jaws. Theo whirled and flung the gray powder at it, then extended his other hand and summoned a blast of blue flame from his fingertips. He gritted his teeth in concentration, trying to subdue his instinct to flee, and soon the gray powder burst into white-hot combustion. The wolf creature shrieked in pain as the fire engulfed it and the light blinded it.

Theo raced away, knowing the noise and the light would draw

other creatures there. In fact, he heard the skittering of claws on the stone flooring ahead of him. He hurried to the archway leading to the stairs and began to take them two at a time, his heart pounding like a hammer as he ran. The light and the cries of the monster behind him drew attention. He made it to the next level and raced upward.

He heard one of the monsters pursuing him up the stairs and huffed even harder. He didn't want to waste another handful of the magnesia dust—a supply he would not be able to restore since all the caravans had ceased.

His left knee throbbed with pain from the run up the stairs, making him wince. But he managed to reach the door at the top, pushed his way through, and shoved it shut just as the wolf creature crested the final stair. His eyes widened as he listened to its claws savaging the wood. He backed away, gulping air, and then turned to rush down the corridor in case it managed to open the door.

Theo made it to the next doorway and once he had touched its different trigger points, the door opened. He slipped in, and as he started up the steps, he heard groans of pain from the man trapped above.

Theo was mopping his sweaty head with a handkerchief he'd snatched from his pocket when he reached a once opulently furnished room with a private balcony. The interior had been thrashed and upended by the man chained to an iron ring in the middle of the floor.

Glancing at the dove in its cage suspended from a rafter, Theo saw that the rope was still and the dove was calm, which meant a transformation of the man was not imminent.

"What took you so long?" the man—a nobleman, with a proud olive-skinned face and unruly hair—demanded angrily. His shirt had claw marks in the front, revealing a set of four silver scars that maimed the skin of his chest. His pants were ripped as well.

But the damage didn't end there—his pants were in tatters from his own struggles against what he was becoming, his well-made boots had been carelessly kicked off, and his stockings showed the wear of his constant writhing on the floor.

"I was nearly disemboweled," Theo cried, as he hurried to one of the tables at the side of the room. He used a napkin to deliberately wipe away the magnesia dust from his hand and recaptured as much of it as he could before returning it to the pouch tied to his belt.

"Did you bring it?"

"I did." Theo removed the vial of quicksilver.

"Give it to me."

"A moment, if you please." He walked over to the window and checked outside. The landscape was pale with snow as a blizzard raged, explaining the shiver-inducing temperature in the room. Theo went to the fireplace, but the man scolded him.

"Stop! I already feel like I have a fever."

"But I don't," Theo answered. "I'm cold."

"You don't understand what I suffer."

"You are right. I don't." Theo knelt by the grate, scooped a few heaps of coal onto it, and then used the flame from his hand to ignite it. Soon the little glowing bricks were emitting an amiable quantity of heat.

"Give it to me," the man pleaded.

The noise of an owl hooted from the roof outside. That was a new sound. Another one, farther off, repeated the call. With the gladiator games over, how long before the coliseum reverted back to a state of nature? When the man-made pillars and halls would become the lair of jackals and screech owls?

Theo walked over to the man whose name he didn't know or care to know, who groveled for the flask of quicksilver.

"Please. Anything...anything to end this madness."

Theo handed over the vial, then retreated to a chair, pulling out his little notebook as he watched. The nobleman uncorked the tiny vessel and grimaced at seeing the liquid metal inside. Quicksilver was quite toxic. No one had drunk it willingly before.

The man stared at it, a grimace twisting his mouth. "We never suspected this would occur when that beast was brought in a cage."

"Hmmm?" Theo grunted questioningly.

"They took it to Ecbatana for the revenant to play with."

"I heard the golem killed the revenant. But isn't that impossible?"

"Who knows? All we understand is that it learned. It learned metamorphistry. And it created these abominations that plague us. But what will happen when every last man and woman is ripped apart and destroyed? What is the result when you cannot die and cannot bear the taste of meat? When only blood will satisfy?"

Even intense heat, like that from magnesia dust, couldn't destroy the wolves. They still regenerated and became whole again. The nobleman was wise to consider the possibility of what would take place when all the prey was gone, and the predator couldn't die.

Theo kept a little cyanide pill in his necklace for just such an emergency. He'd rather kill himself than risk such an end.

The man lifted the vial to his lips and began to swallow the quicksilver in hasty gulps, groaning at the taste. Theo wondered what the globs of liquid metal felt like on the way down his gullet.

The man finished quaffing until all was gone, then tossed the glass aside, shattering it.

"How do you feel?" Theo asked.

"Like I've a lead weight in my belly," he said with a wrinkled nose.

Theo observed the man as he became increasingly agitated. "My throat is burning," he groaned. "My thoughts...my thoughts are muddled. It hurts to breathe."

"Anything else?" Theo asked after inscribing the symptoms in his notebook.

"Nnngggbhh." The nobleman moaned, holding his stomach. He began to writhe and convulse.

"Interesting," Theo murmured, jotting down more of the symptoms. It was an incredibly high dose of quicksilver. Breathing the fumes of quicksilver was often fatal, but ingesting it? What would that do? But nothing had killed these creatures so far. No poison had worked.

"Aaahhhh!" the main wailed, thrashing on the ground. Theo had continued taking notes while watching the man in his torture. He guessed it had been a half hour or so.

Spasms began next. Violent, rocking spasms. He twitched and groaned, his legs pumping uncontrollably. And then he sighed and lay still. Not even breathing.

Theo leaned forward eagerly. He rose from the chair and cautiously approached. The man's chest hadn't moved. The silver claw marks were gone from his skin.

He knelt down and touched the man's wrist, feeling for a pulse. He found none. Giddiness began to churn inside him. He couldn't wait to draw his scalpel, to cut the fellow open and examine what had happened internally. How would his organs look? Would the quicksilver still be in his stomach? Was there a property to quicksilver that had countered the curse? Theo was anxious to study it further.

The balcony window suddenly shattered, and a man in angel sworn armor marched inside.

Theo gaped in shock at the sudden arrival. Fear surged inside his chest. He hadn't seen an angel sworn since he was a child.

The man grabbed Theo by the fabric of his tunic and cloak and dragged him to his feet.

"I've been watching you," the angel sworn said with disdain shining in his eyes. "Archangel Jodocus will want to meet you now. You're coming with me."

"But we can't leave. We'll be torn apart!" Theo exclaimed.

"I summoned another owl," the angel sworn sneered. "We'll be flying there." He lay a drawn sword against Theo's neck. "Try that fire on me, and I'll make you repent it. There's a creature Jodocus wishes you to kill. Another abomination."

ONE
THE GOLEM

PRESENT DAY

Cimree approached the kneeling statue of Khaf, who had turned to stone in the crouch he had assumed when he went to reach for her inside a pit. Yet the statue was no longer in the deserted gardens of Ecbatana. Uorsin had situated it at the entrance to the tunnel leading to the waterfall cavern where they'd trapped the golem.

Cimree studied the face, remembering when she'd met Khaf in Ecbatana. He was one of the Watchers, a group who had been hunting the revenant. He'd helped her against the machinations of Lord Roque. And in the end, he was the first of her many victims after the golem had used its magic against her, transforming her into a creature with snakes for hair and the curse that turned to stone anyone who beheld her full face.

She knelt, pulled her carving tool out of her belt, and began to etch the runes of the Qodes Adonai into the stone effigy at one of the stone ripples of his shirt. In each statue she'd incised with the symbol, she'd hidden it so that it wasn't obvious where to find the engraving. After she'd inscribed the runes, she rose, put her hand atop the statue's head, and thought about what powers to endow it with. Some statues were meant for defense. Some generated heat to warm the caves in the mountain tunnels.

The idea of water came to her. The long walk to that part of the tunnels would make people thirsty after their journey. She bowed her head and asked the Oldknow to grant the statue the power to summon water. She immediately felt a ripple of magic pulse from her hand to the stone, and the statue's eyes began to glow. Water pooled like tears around the stone orbs and began to run down Khaf's face, dripping from his chin to splash onto the floor. She cupped her hand to gather some of the water and then drank from it.

It is from the Silver River.

The whisper brushed through her mind simply, unobtrusively, even tenderly. She'd come to rely on these whispered thoughts and the information they communicated. The water happened to be from the valley of Clairvaux. The statue was an intermediary, a connection between one place where water was plentiful and another where it was needed. But she understood that the source of the water was a gift, a little mercy to her and to the angel sworn. That, even though they could no longer live in their cherished homeland, a part of it was still available.

She bowed her head and offered a prayer of gratitude. Then she quenched the statue's power. The light faded and the flow of water ended. She had taught the other survivors how to trigger the statues to produce heat, light, or protection. A simple thought command was all that was required. An expression of a need. The statues that Azra, Andrin, and Uorsin brought from Ecbatana had been put in place, one by one, over several weeks.

Cimree walked past the statue and went down the final corridor toward the rushing sound of a waterfall, which told her how near she was to the place in which they'd caged the golem. By a locked iron gate, she found the statue of Wegner. His eyes were constantly glowing, although more dimly at the moment, indicating that the golem wasn't as near. Wegner had been attacked by one of the golem's latest creations, a malformed bat that thirsted for the blood of the angel sworn. It had spread an incurable disease to him, which had caused a bloodlust to build inside him that would have driven him to kill. Azra had stabbed him in the chest with the fated blade before his transformation was complete, capturing his knowledge and skills while ending his life. But as Wegner lay dying, he'd stared at Cimree and had become the first of her silent guardians of the caves of Tirich Mir.

Cimree was overwhelmed with tenderness at seeing the calm smile on Wegner's mouth as he'd died. Her statues all had different expressions, depicting the subtle and not so subtle range of human emotions. Most had died in terror. Some in surprise. And a little boy named Chuq had died with a look of wonder suffusing his face.

Her leg began to ache, and the statue's eyes suddenly flared with light. When she was near the golem, she could tell its proximity through the pain in her leg, which the golem had healed after the bone had been shattered from a trap in the catacombs of Ecbatana. It had given her part of itself, a new bone to replace her broken one, a new muscle to mend the mangled one.

The golem approached the bars, reaching through them with its clawed hand.

"Cim-reee," it sighed at her with a forlorn tone. She didn't sense an intention to grab her or destroy her.

"I brought you some food," Cimree said, unslinging the package she'd carried through the tunnels and kneeling on the stone ground. She had five fish, caught by digging through the ice at a nearby pond. The practice of ice fishing had been taught to them by the villagers, and it provided a daily store of fresh meat. After she opened the fold of the waterproof sack, the smell of the fish met her nose. She reached inside, grabbed one, and tossed it to the golem.

It snatched it with hooked claws and hastily devoured the offering.

"More!" the creature groaned enthusiastically, beckoning. She tossed it another, and another, until the five were gone.

"More!"

"That's all I have for you," Cimree answered.

"More!" the creature demanded more persistently.

Cimree opened the mouth of the bag wider, upended it, and shook it. "All gone."

The golem hissed at her rudely.

The cavern provided plenty of water for it to drink, from the waterfall and the little lake that trapped it. The bats had all fled, driven out by the Oldknow's power manifested in the statues. Sometimes the golem raged at its imprisonment. It regularly shook the bars. Cimree didn't know if it was trying to weaken them or just expressing its frustration.

She crossed her arms around her knees and studied it. In the few months since they'd captured it, she had learned that it knew more words than her name. In fact, by her count, it knew several hundred but could only speak a few. It was highly intelligent. And highly temperamental. The golem's tantrums could last for days on end.

"More?" the golem pleaded again, changings its tone to something more plaintive.

"I don't have any more," Cimree answered. "Later."

"Later," the golem answered. It leaned against the bars, stroking them.

She marveled at its muscles and blood vessels seen through its translucent skin. Its large eyes swiveled beneath invisible eyelids that bore no eyelashes. She knew it could become invisible; could adopt features of other animals, like wings, only to discard them with a flick of its claws; and its power to heal was impressive. Sometimes it hurt itself, but the wounds closed quickly. A bow and a quiver of arrows made with flint arrowheads were propped against the wall beside her. Azra said the precaution was necessary. But Cimree wondered whether the arrows would actually kill it.

What should they do with such a creature? If they set it free, it would use its power to create more monsters. The golem was obsessed with the angel sworn, but when Andrin had arrived to check on it, the golem's demeanor had changed to indifference. Wegner had said, before he died, that he believed Asmodeus had created the golem to be the bane of the angel sworn and to destroy them and their creations. That seemed to be the primal instinct driving it.

"Do you have a name?" she asked the golem once again despite knowing the response she would receive.

"Cim-reee." That was always its answer.

It hated Azra. Whenever he came to take a shift watching over the golem, it brooded and snarled and stayed away from the gate. It appeared the golem had its favorites. What, if anything, did that mean?

What were they supposed to do with it? Would it die if they withheld food? Could they fashion a weapon that would kill it? The idea of torturing it to death made her squeamish. It lived as it had been created to live. So she had no illusions about its behavior, knowing that if they let it go, there was no end to the harm it could do.

She heard no whispers about this dilemma. On that topic, the Oldknow was silent.

Through the bond of the Tanaquil amulet, she sensed Azra approaching up the tunnel. Once he was near, the golem sniffed as if catching a scent. It began to growl, then rose and paced back and forth. Azra rounded the corner, and the golem bared its teeth and tromped away, calling her name as it went.

Azra sat down by her.

"You slept restlessly last night," Cimree said, touching his shoulder.

"I couldn't fall asleep because I was designing a way to expand the kitchen," he answered helplessly. "I had no idea Wegner's mind was so relentless."

Since Azra had dealt his friend a mortal blow with the dagger, all of Wegner's strengths and instincts had been inherited. Azra had been skilled at catching fish before, but he had gained Wegner's affinity for them and could lure them closer without even using bait. His gift designing inventions and his knowledge of machinery were added benefits.

"Is that all that's made you restless?" Cimree asked.

"I'm nervous about your mission as well."

"We need to warn the other angel sworn," Cimree said pointedly.

"I agree. I don't think Jodocus—I don't think my *son*—will let them go willingly. I have this nagging feeling that when spring comes, it will be too late to persuade him."

"If he's anything like his father, then he'll be stubborn," Cimree teased him playfully.

Azra was staring blankly into the cave but that earned her a smile. "There are so many things that can go wrong."

"We believe they're wintering in the city of Koa," Cimree said. "And that other angel sworn have paid homage to him as the archangel. No more of our people have been lost to him, though. That's good news."

"But I think we still have a spy with us," Azra said. "I have personally watched each angel sworn, looking for evidence of treachery. I've found nothing."

"So maybe the spy isn't an angel sworn," Cimree suggested.

"I've considered that, but that doesn't make sense to me either, strictly from a loyalty standpoint. Jodocus was captain of the Morgarten. None of whom defected with us. In fact, we killed some of them when we left Clairvaux. Would Andrin or Perreta be secretly loyal to those people? There isn't a motive. I've thought about every single person who came with us. The captures all occurred when we had two guards for the caves. Once we made it three, then no more were taken. It had to be someone who was already here, who knew where the guards were and which of them were vulnerable."

"And then there's the missing leaf from the Gallows Tree," Cimree said.

"Yes," Azra said. "The leaf went missing before Chrys bonded with the tree and became a Dryad. It wasn't until she regained her power to speak that she was able to tell me that a leaf had been torn off. So it's possible Jodocus knows where the tree is. That he has people watching it from afar."

"He's going to lay claim to the tree," Cimree said. "Or do you think he'll want to destroy it?"

"He won't destroy it," Azra said with certainty. He reached over and touched the curve of her shoulder. "What if he knows that you're coming? We've been very careful not to share that information. Not even the entire high council knows. I have a fear you're walking into a trap."

"It's possible," Cimree agreed. "But I have the Tay al-Ard. I can get out."

"We have to assume they know you have it," Azra said with concern. "I was able to get it from you."

"Are you saying we shouldn't warn them? I can't just let them all die."

Azra frowned. "I don't want to lose you again."

She rubbed the beads on the fringe of her tunic. "You can't lose me, Azra."

Two

The Spider

The entire high council had gathered in their meeting chamber to discuss for the first time the mission Cimree was about to embark on. Secrecy would mean the difference between success and failure. If a traitor was amongst these trusted members, would it finally be revealed? The light from a single druid stone was dimmed to the point that all they could see were the shapes of the figures in the room. Cimree wore her veil as she usually did when they met together.

"I've chosen Avari, Trinati, and Uorsin to accompany me," Cimree announced.

"Why not Azra?" asked Setara. She was the wife of the most prominent village elder. Cimree had chosen her to take Wegner's seat on the council. In the time of their acquaintance, she had struggled to learn their language but had made a concerted effort to do so.

"Azra will stay behind in case of trouble," Cimree said. He had, for the most part, recovered from his injury, but with their connection through the medallion, he would realize immediately if trouble arose, and with the spirit-infused beads that he had enchanted on her clothing—which no one else knew about—he would also be able to find her. "The purpose of this mission is to get to Koa, find out where the angel sworn are being held, and get as close to that place as possible. As I explained, we are trying to build a gate of sorts to rescue as many as will come."

"After Avari escaped Jodocus, I sent him to find Koa, based on his assumption that it was where Jodocus would end up," Trinati declared. "Avari is our way in. Cimree will guide him in using the Tay al-Ard to get us into Koa, and once she has been there, she'll be able to ferry us between here and the city. I might not be as deadly as Azra with a blade, but I am the strongest warrior among us, though hopefully I'll be able to influence others to join us."

"Uorsin is coming"—Cimree picked up where Trinati left off —"in case there are other obstacles. Gates that need to be opened. Or if anyone has chains that need breaking. He'll bring tools and his strength."

"Others could also be useful," Odeon said, his voice betraying a hint of worry. Even he had been left out of the planning. Only Azra, Trinati, and Uorsin had been part of the discussion with Cimree. Avari had been told prior to the council to be sure he agreed, and Cimree had tasked Andrin with watching him ever since, to make sure that he didn't speak of it to anyone afterward.

"Like yourself?" Cimree asked.

"I'm responsible for defending the caves," Odeon said. "I can tell why I wasn't included. What about Darcia, though? She knows people and is good at listening to concerns. She might be helpful in persuading people to come."

"No," Uorsin said firmly.

"We discussed her, Odeon," Trinati said. "We discussed every possible combination. Four allows us redundancy. It varies our skills. It also makes it possible to bring some back with us and not drain the Tay al-Ard too much."

"What about the language?" Setara asked. "Many customs of

the Pashmir are...what's the word. Subtle. Someone from our village should go with you."

"We hadn't considered that," Trinati said. "Setara raises a good point."

"An excellent point," Cimree agreed. "But this first mission is just to establish the way to get deep inside Koa. I have experience doing this. Avari's knowledge gets us close. The others will wait for me to infiltrate. We'll go at night to reduce the risk. We have Pashmir clothing and weapons at the ready. But the Pashmir also need to be warned. Our first obstacle is outwitting Jodocus."

"You speak wisely, Siyah Malkah," Setara said. "I will not share this information with my husband. He would insist that one of our sons go."

"The fewer who know about this mission, the better," Trinati said. "Azra will be watching here. Obviously, we'll come back directly if there's a problem, but we believe doing the mission now, in winter, will be the most unexpected time."

"The mountains are impassable except by air," Odeon said. "We could get a lot of people out before Jodocus could even do anything."

"Is there any other counsel before we go?" Cimree asked. "Anything else we haven't thought of yet?"

"Will we have enough food if many decide to come?" Setara asked.

"The Oldknow will provide what we need," Cimree said. "There will be enough."

She had pondered the mission, the food supplies, had considered every angle. So had Azra. A traitor likely still lived amongst the angel sworn. Unless the spy had already departed. Cimree had not felt any whispers of warning from the Oldknow. Her desire to bring more people to safety was her chief aim. That felt right.

"How long will you be gone?" Odeon asked.

"The plan is to return by morning," Trinati said. "Night is our ally. Avari has offered two suitable options. The oldest part of the city is called the Murad Khani. It's very crowded and the angel sworn have taken over some of the nicer homes. The other is the turquoise mine on the outskirts. Cimree will decide which one will be our entry point before we go. There are advantages and disadvantages for both locations, but out of all the options Avari suggested, these two were the most suitable for this type of mission."

"Even if someone grafted with a snow owl and flew directly to Koa," Odeon said, "they would not get there in time to warn them."

"And if we find where the captives are sooner, we'll return sooner," Cimree added. "If there are no other suggestions, we should make haste."

"Agreed," Trinati said. "We will depart soon."

"Do not tell anyone where we're going," Cimree said. "We will leave from here, from this chamber. Be on your guard."

The members of the high council wished them success on the mission, and Setara even gave Cimree a hug before departing. Cimree felt confident that they would be able to slip in and out of Koa before dawn. She trusted Trinati and Uorsin implicitly. Both had been easy choices. Azra would also be invaluable, but if she'd had any impressions at all from the Oldknow, it was that Azra should remain behind. Jodocus was his son. No one else from the high council knew that, nor was it the right time to divulge that information.

"I'll fetch Avari," Trinati said and left.

"I'll wait outside," Uorsin offered, giving Azra and Cimree a moment alone.

After he was gone, Azra lifted the veil from Cimree's head. He had subdued his nervous energy, for he trusted in her and her abilities. He grazed her cheek with the edge of his hand and then kissed her passionately. The joining of their feelings burned intensely. Knowing one another's heart and feelings had brought them a closeness that was overpowering. All their memories had been returned: of the time she'd persuaded him to abandon the Queen Mother and steal away to Tirich Mir. Of his encounter with the Dryad of the Gallows Tree, which had produced Chrys, his daughter. Cimree's memories of when she'd eaten an entire fruit, had become an infant again, then was handed over to Milena to be raised as a healer. All of her past lives were in sight. Getting in and out of Koa would be simple. Especially since they didn't know she was coming.

"I won't sleep until you're back," Azra said, after the fierce kiss ended. "And I'll make sure the golem stays put."

"There's something else I wanted to tell you," Cimree said, giving him a tender gaze. "Setara said we've waited long enough. She's convinced we should marry before the spring."

"It doesn't matter what Setara wants. What do *you* want?"

"I want you for my husband," Cimree answered promptly. "I want to explore this wide world with you. The only reason I haven't asked you yet is that I've wanted to make sure everyone will be safe. I think convincing the angel sworn to join us would be more difficult if they believe we violated the law of celibacy. That's the only reason I've held back."

"It's a thoughtful reason," Azra said, touching her chin. He kissed her again. "You are worth waiting for."

"And you're worth having," Cimree agreed.

She sensed the vibrations of the others returning and kissed him once more. Then they gripped each other by their hands. She had the Tay al-Ard in her belt. He had the fated blade in his. The voided key was hidden in his room.

"If you find Iddawc, don't tell him where I went," Cimree said lightly. "I don't think we'd need enmity to help on this mission."

"Agreed," Azra said. Then he lowered the veil over her head again.

Trinati entered with Avari, followed by Uorsin with his sack of tools.

"Have you decided on the place we'll go?" Trinati asked.

Cimree drew the Tay al-Ard. "Murad Khani," she said. "Let's go to the heart of Koa. The cellar you told us about, Avari."

"I was hoping you'd choose that place," Avari answered. "The turquoise mines will be much colder than these tunnels. Those statues that give off heat are very helpful."

"Is everyone ready?" Cimree asked.

"Yes," Trinati answered.

"I'm ready," Uorsin agreed. He sounded a little nervous, but that was understandable.

Cimree held out the Tay al-Ard, gripping it tightly. "Avari, you put your hand above mine. The others, grasp our arms."

They did so.

"Think of the cellar," Cimree said. "Picture it in your mind. It's past nightfall already. The streets should be quiet. The houses still. Take us there, Avari."

She sensed Azra's concern building, his natural worry. She tried to offer reassurance.

Then the magic gripped her navel until it felt like the floor had dropped away and they were plummeting, but the sensation ended quickly, and then they were on solid ground in a dark, musty place. No light source was present at all. She smelled old wood and olive oil.

Cimree returned the Tay al-Ard to her belt and lifted her veil. She looked around using her heat-sensitive vision and saw the outlines of the other three and no one else, then raised the cowl of her cloak to hide herself.

"Are we here?" Trinati asked.

"Can't see a thing," Uorsin said.

"I'll light the druid stone and face away from you," Cimree said. She did so, and the little glow brightened the place. They were in a storage room with vats of oil stacked on each other. Scuff marks marred the wooden floor. A ramp led up instead of stairs. The four of them fit easily.

"I don't remember there being oil here," Avari said then sniffed. "But this is Murad Khani. The angel sworn live in different places here, but those who rejected Jodocus were kept in a walled area north of here called the Mikrorayon. It's heavily guarded, which is why we didn't go there first."

"I'll find it," Cimree promised.

"Be careful," Trinati warned. "Come back here at once if there's trouble."

"I won't abandon you," Cimree said. "Thank you all for joining me. Just wait here. But keep it dark so if I need to return abruptly, I don't surprise anyone."

She then padded softly up the ramp and lifted the trapdoor at the top. All was quiet. She lowered the trapdoor back down behind her and slipped through the room to a door that led to the streets outside. With her hood concealing her, she left and entered the back street. A bright winter moon shone that night. The walls of the buildings were crafted from wood, but they were intricately designed. One pattern along the walls, she noticed, were beams with triangular notches in them both vertically and horizontally, which gave the impression of two offset squares. The beams had dried moss on them and were heavily weathered. The cold was omnipresent, but there was no snow, except in a few patches.

Cimree reached a wider street and found it empty as well. No one was out that night. The windows were all dark. She joined the street and walked swiftly down it, keeping to the shadows. The moonlight told her which direction was east, and so she made her way to a street that went north.

She'd walked less than a mile when she sensed the vibrations of someone walking behind her. Someone close enough that she felt them on the stones. Someone trying to be quiet.

If she lowered her cowl, the serpents would be able to spy whoever was following her, but she'd also risk turning them to stone. That would reveal her presence in Koa prematurely.

She pulled the Tay al-Ard out of her belt and shifted direction to the nearest alley. She could then use the device to reappear farther back down the street so she'd be behind the person stalking her.

But as she started to dart down the alley, the Tay al-Ard somehow flew from her hand and hurtled down the street behind her, caught by a cloaked figure standing forty steps away.

Three

New Eyes

"Thank you for coming, Cimree," said the cloaked man. "You saved me a visit to the mountains."

The voice was Jodocus's.

She didn't understand how he had wrenched the Tay al-Ard from her grip at a distance. She didn't know who else was nearby. He'd set a trap and she'd walked into it. And she also knew that one of the people she'd brought with her had been part of it.

"Well done, Jodocus," she said. "You've been planning this for a while."

"It was your mistake, your weakness, that brought us here, Cimree. If you'd killed me at Clairvaux, we wouldn't be here right now. I'm not going to make the same mistake as you. I have archers on the rooftops with arrows made especially for you. It's time we did away with the monster of Ecbatana."

Cimree lowered her cowl. With her serpents exposed, she could witness the heat coming off the archers who had risen from their crouched positions on the flat rooftops. She counted at least four. The serpents were agitated. Her fingertips produced venom.

Surprisingly, no taste of salt filled her mouth. Surely they were looking at her but maybe they were at a far enough range not to be impacted?

The moon was bright enough to see her clearly. Others had been killed glimpsing her in moonlight. They expected her to flee like a frightened animal.

"You've lost," Jodocus said triumphantly.

Cimree rushed toward him. Maybe her charge would disorient them, but she changed direction after two steps and launched herself to the right, diving into a forward roll as the bowstrings twanged and arrows clattered against the street.

Jodocus vanished, using the Tay al-Ard to disappear. She heard an arrow whistle by her head and shifted direction again, becoming an erratic target. With a bit of luck, none of those arrows would hit her. She had to get out of that street.

One of the angel sworn leaped from the rooftop, clearly grafted with a bird, and flew toward her while loosing another shaft. She ducked into an alley just as it struck, and it stuck in the wooden beam right where she'd been a breath earlier.

As soon as she was in the shadows of the alley, she climbed up the wall of the building with the ability of a snake and then stopped, using the natural camouflage of the serpent to blend in with the wooden slats on the walls.

She spied the flying angel sworn in the sky above the street she'd left. "I can't tell where she is!" he shouted.

"I'll take the far end," another cried out.

She waited, her heart thudding, but she forced herself to calm down. She needed to elude these enemies, then get back and warn the others. When Azra had questioned Avari on his capture, Cimree had dosed him with nightshade, and he hadn't revealed anything about a dual allegiance. He'd escaped from Jodocus. He'd revealed the locations of where they could go, but he hadn't chosen the destination. Cimree had.

That meant it was either Trinati or Uorsin.

"Where is she? Do you see her?"

An angel sworn had reached the far end of the alley and was approaching on foot. Two were above with their bows, hovering in the air on invisible wings. The fourth entered below her, bow in hand, arrow nocked. They were skilled hunters, searching for any movement, any sign of her. She noticed the heat from their bodies, but they couldn't see hers.

Cimree waited until the angel sworn passed beneath her and then dropped onto him.

The sudden weight of her body slammed him down. She used her fingernails to scratch his face, which would send the venom into his bloodstream. Her action knocked something from his face that landed on the street like a piece of rounded glass.

She kicked him hard in the ribs and then raced back through the alley head she'd entered from, dashed across the street, and fled down another one. An arrow slashed her arm as she fled, causing a sting. An instant later she plunged into the shadows again.

What had she knocked off the man's face that had sounded like glass?

She heard yelling from the alley opposite her.

"She got me! She got me! The wound burns!"

That was the venom at work. The gashes she'd cut into his face would sting terribly. That left three to deal with since Jodocus had fled.

"She went down the other alley, across the street!" shouted one of them.

As Cimree kept running, she used the vision of her snake-hair to observe the two airborne angel sworn flying after her from above. She reached a corner and rounded it, increasing her speed once more. Then she saw a wooden railing jutting from the second story of a building and leaped up to grab it, pulling herself up to the balcony it enclosed and hiding beneath the overhang of the roof.

"Where'd she go?"

"I can't hear her either."

"She stopped running."

From where they'd started, she could hear the injured one moaning in pain.

Beneath the eave, she couldn't see the two in the sky, but they couldn't spot her either. In the dark, she'd be able to evade them in the streets, but then she would be lost and lose track of where she'd been. Without the Tay al-Ard, she couldn't transport herself back to the cellar.

Could she take out three members of the Morgarten? They were some of the Queen Mother's most skilled warriors. She had to learn why they hadn't become stone. How had they seen her but not turned to stone?

Jodocus had been overconfident. He was expecting the Cimree he knew about, the one who had become a monster. He didn't realize she had all her past memories and lives again.

She jumped to grab the edge of the eave and pulled herself up, vaulting up to the flat roof in a single tug. Farther along the same roof, she noticed one of the angel sworn had landed on the edge and was searching the dark alley for her. At her movement, he lifted the bow, turned, and sent an arrow at her, all in one motion.

Cimree leaned to the side and twisted. The arrow sailed past her. She rushed toward him, and he began to fly upward while reaching for another arrow from his quiver. Cimree drew a dirk and threw it at him. He blocked it with the bow as he continued to rise, but she jumped and grabbed him by the boot, then by the belt.

The sudden weight brought him lower. She saw light glinting off something embedded in a fabric band at his eyes, two disks polished like glass. His distaff was lodged in his belt, so she pulled it out and dropped back down to the roof. As he arched away from her, she snapped the distaff in half, severing his grafting to the bird. The angel sworn bellowed in surprise as he struck the rooftop hard. She rushed to him, jumping on him, then rolled him onto his chest. The remaining aerial angel sworn was aiming his bow at her, but she pulled on the cloak of her captive so that his chest was facing the other fellow. If he shot the arrow, he'd risk killing his own comrade.

Holding the angel sworn upright, Cimree groped at his face and found the wrapping covering his eyes. Not just a strip of cloth but two glass circles, bound together by metal rims.

He drew a dagger from a scabbard at his belt, so she seized his wrist and bit it before he could plunge the dagger into her, evoking venom from her saliva. He grunted in pain as he continued to struggle, but she knew more subduing maneuvers than he did and effortlessly disarmed him of the dagger while putting him in a choke hold. She managed this while shifting to keep his body as a shield against the other angel sworn poised in the sky.

"Let him go!" the airborne one yelled at her. He was aiming at her, but with all the commotion on the rooftop he could not get a clean shot.

Cimree ripped the device from her captured foe's face with her free hand.

The splash of salt came into her mouth, and he turned to stone.

A twang of a bow sounded. The angel sworn in the sky was struck. He snorted in pain and began to fly off, but another arrow struck him from behind and he plummeted to the ground. Dead.

Cimree gasped to catch her breath. The statue she'd made lay in contortions of stone, a grimace on his face, his mouth wide in revulsion at seeing her.

She studied the fabric, like a headband, but woven into it were two glass lenses that had covered his eyes.

"Cimree!"

The voice was Trinati's.

"I'm on the roof," Cimree called down.

"Should I come up?"

"No. There's a balcony below me on this side. Go inside and see if anyone is there. We need to hide."

"We killed one and captured another in the alley," Trinati said. "The one you injured."

"Jodocus has the Tay al-Ard," Cimree said.

Trinati let out a curse that was very unangelic.

Cimree revived the man with a drop of smelling vapor. Uorsin had struck him on the head, so the fellow was still dazed. They'd bound his eyes with a blindfold.

"Who's there?" the captive snarled, wincing in pain. His wrists were tied behind his back and his legs bound tightly. The dried blood from the gashes on his face contrasted against his inflamed skin, still ravaged by Cimree's venom.

"I recognized you," Trinati said. "You're Lyander."

"Trinati," said the captive hatefully. "You are the archangel no more."

"That's true. I hear Jodocus bears that title now."

"Jodocus was faithful to her until the end," Lyander said spitefully. "You are traitors."

"I've been back to Clairvaux, and all is ruined. They broke down every hut, every hamlet. Every trough. And the Queen Mother is dead, so whoever pretends to take her place no longer matters."

"It matters to some of us, Trinati," Lyander growled.

Trinati, Uorsin, and Avari all had their eyes bound as well. Cimree put her hand on Trinati's shoulder and squeezed.

"Where did you get these contraptions?" Cimree asked. "Who made them?"

"Paracelsus made them," Lyander answered without hesitation. "To help us defeat *you*."

"And who is that?" she asked.

"Ardigus found him at the arena of Vaud," the angel sworn said. "Paracelsus is the last one who knows metamorphistry. We brought him here. We knew arrows wouldn't kill you permanently, demon spawn. But there's a poison that will."

That didn't make sense to Cimree since a bolt had broken her leg and severely injured her. She did not have the rapid healing of the gévaudan. But how would Jodocus know that?

"Oh?" she pressed.

"It's one of Paracelsus's secrets," Lyander said. "Our duty was to capture you and bring you to him. He's the one who will put an end to you."

"Where is this man?" Trinati demanded.

"He's at Jodocus's palace," Lyander said. "Now that you can't escape, it's just a matter of time before we hunt you down. None of you are leaving here alive."

Cimree noticed the tightness on Uorsin's mouth, the fury in his eyes. Avari looked troubled.

"We came here to save *you*," Cimree told Lyander. "To provide the other angel sworn an opportunity to escape before the end comes. All those monsters that drove us from Clairvaux are coming here. And the golem has made even more."

"It's true," Trinati added. "We've established a new Gallows Tree."

"We know." Lyander chuckled. "Jodocus knows where it is. It belongs to us now."

Cimree tried to quell the pang of dread in her chest. Angel sworn were not known for being dishonest.

"You have a spy among us," Cimree said. "Who?"

"I am too lowly to be trusted with that knowledge," Lyander said. "But know this. Those caves will be ours before the winter snows melt."

Four

Qodes Adonai

The sky on the horizon had begun to transform, night shedding its skin to reveal day. Cimree knelt on the flat rooftop, using the tip of her dirk to carve the rune of the Qodes Adonai on the statue before her. Her serpents spotted the heat signature of several angel sworn heading her way in the sky. The hunt had started afresh. She finished the last of the rune and wiped the dust from it.

Cimree rested her hand on the statue and thought about what kind of protective ward she could put on it. Perhaps it could protect the dwelling and offer some refuge from the Morgarten searching for them. But staying sequestered in that building wouldn't be helpful. She needed to find Jodocus and take the Tay al-Ard back. Her best chance of doing that would be at night.

Summon a bane on this city.

The thought whispered into her mind. That idea had never crossed her mind before. To use the Oldknow's power to curse Koa. A feeling of uneasiness twisted in her stomach. She had ventured to Koa to try to save the angel sworn. Not to punish them.

Summon a bane.

The thought triggered a second time, producing feelings in her that made her shudder. Not as a punishment. As a warning. The wild creatures the golem had created would attack Koa, just as they had Clairvaux and Ecbatana. Time was running out.

Cimree wasn't sure what the bane would do to those who were residing in the city, but she knew she needed to follow what the Oldknow was encouraging her to do. She put her hand on the statue's brow and bowed her head, trying to think about the sort of bane she could summon. A drought? A storm? A disease?

And then the answer struck her like a thunderclap. Her own affinity. A pestilence of serpents. In her mind, she thought about the streets overrun with serpents, biting anyone who wandered about. It would keep people indoors. It would keep the angel sworn in the skies.

Iddawc would have approved of her plan.

But winter was an obstacle. Serpents went into a state of dormancy triggered by the cold. They gathered in dens below the frostline and waited until spring or until they needed to drink. In their low-energy state, they could last all winter. But on days when the sun was shining and warming up rocks, they would venture out and bathe in the light and warmth.

That was what she needed to do to the statue. To create light, warmth, and heat. And to draw the rousing serpents to Koa.

Cimree closed her eyes and thought about what she needed. *Warmth, heat, early spring. Bring the serpents from the surrounding area to Koa. Be a torment to the inhabitants, angel sworn and mortal alike.* Another thought flickered to her.

Do not bite anyone near the rune of the Qodes Adonai.

A pulse of warmth emanated from her hand into the statue. When she opened her eyes, the statue glowed like the others in the caves. But with her heat-sensitive vision, she could also see that heat emanated from what should be a cold stone form.

The approaching angel sworn would spot her soon. Cimree covered herself with the cowl, crept to the edge of the roof, and slithered down to the balcony. She wondered how long it would take for the serpents to arrive.

She rapped on the balcony door to announce herself.

Uorsin opened it, his eyes closed. "We bound him down in the cellar."

"Is he gagged as well?" she asked.

"Yes. They won't be able to hear him. Come in."

Cimree entered, spying Trinati and Avari waiting for her as well, also with closed eyes. "There are angel sworn flying this way. I set a rune on the statue on the roof that might make them curious. It will make heat and light and will draw serpents to Koa that will attack anyone wandering about."

"You've summoned a horde of serpents?" Trinati asked with a tone of revulsion in her voice.

"I felt it was the Oldknow's will. A warning that time is running out. No one is safe here."

"We need to find another place to hide," Trinati said.

"I agree," Avari said. "There are some warehouses in the Taimani district. I can lead us there."

"No," Cimree said. "Please. Sit down. We need to talk."

"Do you think that statue with the glowing eyes is going to protect us from them?" Trinati demanded.

"I believe the Morgarten expect us to flee and find another place to hide. Years ago, when the Queen Mother had all Clairvaux searching for me, I hid right in front of her. In her inner sanctum. She's the one who found me, ultimately. They're going to search the rest of the city first before they get the idea of backtracking. They'll start here and search for a trail. They won't find one."

"They'll find us," Trinati declared. "We're just sitting here in the open!"

"You forget, Trinati, about my affinity. I can graft all of you with my serpents, and we'll all disappear. They'll overlook us. It's a serpent's best defense. Camouflage."

Trinati fell silent for a while. "I forgot you had all your memories back."

"I'll help you with the graftings when or if they arrive. But before that, we need to talk."

"About what?" Avari asked.

"Sit by me," Cimree coaxed. "Knee to knee."

After she sat cross-legged on the ground, the other three gathered nearby until they were all touching. Trinati was on her left, Uorsin on her right, and Avari directly across.

"We came here together. No one else knew the plan in advance except the four of us and Azra. Jodocus was waiting for me. He knew which building I would emerge from. And he had some sort of magic that yanked the Tay al-Ard away at a distance. No one else could have gotten word here that fast."

"It has to be one of us," Trinati said. "I had the same thought. Once you were gone, Cimree, I left the cellar and stood guard by the door. That's how I knew you were in trouble. So I told Uorsin and Avari to help. We walked into a trap. A carefully laid one, like a fly hitting a spider's web."

"It wasn't me," Avari said defensively. "For certain I'm the newest one here, but—"

"Avari"—Cimree interrupted his worried rant—"we used nightshade to learn that you were trustworthy. We did not use nightshade on Trinati or Uorsin. It has to be one of the two of you."

Trinati sighed. "Which brings us to an impasse. Because I have trusted my life with all of you. I swear by the name of the Oldknow that I have not betrayed this mission. I have no reason to ally myself with Jodocus of all people. I always found him to be pretentious. But he is skillful and loyal."

"I trust you, Trinati," Cimree said. "You've proven worthy of it so far."

She'd been watching Uorsin's face as Trinati spoke. He frowned deeply, his brow mottled with wrinkles. He had worked tirelessly when they'd reached Tirich Mir. Not once had she suspected him of being a deceiver. It didn't seem in his nature to dissemble.

"Uorsin," Cimree said solemnly, "I would like to use the nightshade on you. I need to know."

"I have not betrayed us," Uorsin said resolutely. "I will do anything to prove I'm innocent."

"Thank you," Cimree replied, patting his knee. Through the Tanaquil amulet, she could tell they were all sincere, which only perplexed her further.

She drew out the little pouch with the powder and emptied a small bit in her palm. Then she shifted to get closer and blew the dust into his face. As he was a large man, the effects would not last very long.

Uorsin sneezed after the dust struck his face. He wrinkled his nose and then wiped his beard. Then his shoulders drooped and relaxed.

"Uorsin, did you tell anyone where we were going?" she asked him.

"No."

Disappointment wriggled inside her.

"Did you tell Darcia where we were going?"

"I told her that I'd been chosen for the mission. But I did not tell her where or when we were going."

Trinati glowered in frustration.

"Did you tell her goodbye?" Cimree asked.

"No. She talks...a lot. I didn't want to risk it."

That matched Cimree's experience as well. Darcia was loquacious and friendly to everyone.

Another thought prompted her. "Do you know of Darcia's affinity, Uorsin? What is it?"

"Her affinity is with spiders."

"What?" Trinati snorted.

This was new information. "How do you know?" Cimree pressed.

"She loves needlework," Uorsin said. "And I've seen her graft with spiders. She can make them spin webs."

A painful stab pricked her heart. Nightshade loosened the tongue and it also made the person forget. Uorsin might have revealed the plans for the mission inadvertently.

"You've seen spiders around her?" Cimree asked with foreboding.

"She keeps it private," Uorsin said simply. "People are afraid of spiders."

"I thought spiders were solitary," Trinati murmured.

"I think some breeds are social," Cimree whispered. "Uorsin, hold still. I'm going to search your clothes. Keep your eyes shut everyone."

She drew out the druid stone and lit it so she could see better. Then she removed his cloak clasp, carefully drew the cloak away from his shoulders, and held it up. There were flecks of soot clinging to it. Stone dust as well. Cimree laid it down and held the druid stone closer, peering across the folds.

When she was kneeling down and peering close, she noticed the little orange-and-red spider on the fabric of his cloak. It instantly turned to stone. Then she spied another. Lifting herself up, she shone the light on his back. Another one scuttled across his tunic before the same fate. A fourth was on his sleeve. They were all very small and nearly inconspicuous. How much could these little creatures communicate? They were stealthy and quiet. Spiders had many eyes. But this would make them exceptionally vulnerable to Cimree's power.

Cimree had wondered why the Queen Mother had sent Darcia on the mission to Montheron. In fact, hadn't Darcia offered to bond with Azra through the Tanaquil amulet?

Uorsin hadn't betrayed the mission.

Darcia had.

Any transformation requires a harmony within nature. Among the angel sworn, for example, a distaff made of scionwood allows the joining of power, but not every angel is adept at bonding with every creature. They call this natural predilection affinity, and I have yet to study it in depth due to their predictable reticence among those not bound to their covenantal lifestyle. But as I intuit the facts insofar as I understand them, someone with an affinity for wolves might find it troublesome bonding with a hare. In a different way, metamorphistry also requires a matching. Trying to force a lodestone against a version with the same polarity will always result in a repelling response. It will not remain. But fix together two lodestones of the opposite polarity and they will cleave to each other permanently. This is important to study, for it is the meekest and most harmless 'hares' of humanity that transform into the most savage beasts.

— The Hermetic and Alchemical Writings of Paracelsus

Five

Blindness

Azra watched the sunrise over the snowy peaks of the Tirich Mir from the entrance of the cave leading to the village. He hadn't slept all night, worried about Cimree and the dangerous circumstances she'd found herself in on reaching Koa. Soon after the Tay al-Ard had taken her there, he'd experienced the vicarious emotions of danger and threat. It had taken a significant measure of self-will not to tear after her in haste. But she'd succeeded so far and for that he had to give her credit.

What problems she'd encountered, he didn't know. Had there been someone waiting for them in the cellar? That seemed unlikely since the danger hadn't arisen immediately but shortly after. What did that imply? All night his mind had raced to find answers. It felt similar to groping in a dark tunnel without a druid stone or fire-blood. He was blind to the causes of Cimree's distress.

He drew his grafting wand and bonded with a snow cock, a breed of pheasant that lived in the Tirich Mir Mountains and didn't migrate to warmer climates in the winter. It readily accepted him, and Azra lifted up and began to fly down from the cave toward the village, enjoying the frigid air on his cheeks. Lazy plumes of smoke drifted from the village rooftops and carried with it the smell of cooked palaw, a mixture of rice, carrots, raisins, and lamb.

After the brief flight down, he landed at the dwelling of Setara's family. He found her cooking the morning meal while her youngest was dressing to take the goats out for forage.

"Azra! Is Cimree back already?" Setara asked, using a wooden spoon to move the food around in the pan. They always spoke in the Pashtun tongue when he visited.

"No," Azra answered tightly. "There's a problem, but I don't understand what it is."

"Oh, no," Setara said with sadness. "We should have sent more to help."

"She is all right." Azra assured her. "But I am nervous she hasn't returned yet. There must be a good reason."

"Of course there must be. Have you had any breakfast yet? Let me get you a bowl."

"Thank you."

She added some extra spices to his and he gratefully wolfed down the meal.

The youngest wrapped his in naan and took a bite as he left. The other sons were still sleeping. He spied them bundled in blankets, and a few were snoring.

"Did you tell anyone?" he asked Setara, dropping his voice lower.

"Of course I didn't," Setara answered. "Not even my husband, the one who is snoring the loudest. If there was trouble, it must be the traitor among you."

"But who?" Azra said, mostly to himself. He had spent time with every single angel sworn in the caves. While not everyone was as committed to their new life as to the one they'd left behind, they all knew that Clairvaux was destroyed and that the new Gallows Tree had been planted somewhere. No one had tried to find it or asked about it. No one stood out. It frustrated him that he hadn't been able to reason through it yet.

"I can't tell you that," Setara answered sympathetically. "In the village, I know that Barbour and Fatima are unhappy in their marriage. That Kouda and Shilla's new baby won't sleep at night and cries all day. I know this because these are my people, their concerns are my concerns. But I will give you this advice, Azra. Ask the women. If there is something wrong, one of them will know."

Darcia would be a good person to speak to, then. Azra avoided talking to her because she was so talkative that it made him want to run away. But she was good with people and had made connections with nearly everyone.

"Thank you for sharing your wisdom," Azra said.

He cleaned his own bowl, even though she offered to, and then went outside the dwelling. The winter meant that the sun rose later and set earlier. The view of the mountains choked with snow was a dazzling sight to see. Avalanches were a risk, but the villagers all knew the signs and the conditions that led to them. They were safe in the caves, of course. The villagers were the ones at risk.

The bleating of goats sounded as the men began to take them out of the pens for grazing. Many offered him the traditional greeting, a nod with one hand touching the heart, which he responded to in kind as he walked through the village before slipping past the outer edge. His shoulder blades tingled from holding on to the grafting so long, but he used it to fly to some boulders and disappear amongst the slopes. Every time he went to see Chrys, he was careful to approach from a different location, just in case anyone was watching him. Only he and Cimree knew where the Gallows Tree had been planted. Maintaining that secret would mean their survival.

He paused at the half-frozen waterfall and cupped some of the icy water in his palm to drink. Then he flew to the tree, not having left a single set of tracks to reveal the location of the sapling. He touched down on a boulder overlooking the area and searched for any signs of intrusion before sitting down.

Chrys appeared next to him on the boulder. As a Dryad, she

had a certain radius from the tree where she could simply materialize without needing to approach.

"Good morning, Father," she said, wrapping her arm around him. Although the cold caused mist to emerge from his mouth, none came from hers. She didn't need to wear cloaks or thick tunics to stay warm.

He hugged her back and kissed her hair.

"You're anxious about Cimree."

Azra nodded, saying nothing in return.

"She's important to the Oldknow," Chrys said. "You both are."

"Will you tell me how?" he asked gently.

"If you'd known all that you would endure before this moment, would you have ever left Clairvaux to travel to these mountains? Or would you have hidden from your fate?"

What a poignant question. With her kiss, he could remember his entire life. The depravity of the city he'd run away from as a child. The painful training he'd suffered to be part of the Long Patrol. His past life in the village when he'd adopted the way of the Pashmir. The wrenching loss of his family. Cimree's coming to the village. There were joyful memories among the painful ones. But had he known all he would suffer, would he do it over again?

"If it took losing Delara to make me who I am today," he answered, staring at the little sapling of the new tree, "then it was worth it. But I don't think I would have wanted to learn the whole story. Not in advance."

Chrys took his hand in hers. "And that's why I can't tell you what will happen next."

His heart clenched with foreboding. "But you know?"

"I walk with the All Father," she said brightly. "He knows *all.* All that was, all that is, and all that will be. This is not the first creation. Nor will it be the last."

He kissed her hair again. "I'm glad you're my daughter. I'll protect you and your tree."

She touched his cheek tenderly. "I know you will try."

Again the premonition made him uneasy. There were many questions he wanted to ask her. But that moment felt sacred to him, so it would be inappropriate for him to press for more.

She stared at his cloak. "A spider came with you." She studied the little insect and set her finger before it. The spider climbed onto her. Such a tiny thing, a reddish-orange variety that was smaller than her fingertip.

"It's a cave spider," Azra said. "Some of the others are much bigger than that one." When they'd first come to the Tirich Mir, some of the angel sworn had to get over their innate fear of spiders.

"I'll take it to the garden with me," she said.

He knew that when she wasn't in the mortal world, she was at a place where the Oldknow dwelled. A wondrous garden full of trees and different fruits. It was never winter there.

She vanished, taking the spider with her.

He sat on the boulder top until the cold began to get to him and the snow cock began to feel impatient at him being connected for so long. Carefully he flew back, using yet another different route. He needed to talk to Odeon about defending the caves again. The stone statues Cimree had empowered would keep evil creatures away. But what about other angel sworn? What about one who was so subtle they didn't reveal themselves in any way.

Someone clever. Cautious. Deliberate.

He needed to talk to Darcia. Maybe she would have ideas about anyone acting abnormally. It would require a lot of patience, and he was only just getting better at that. But with his ability to remember details, maybe something Darcia said would reveal the truth later.

Azra sensed Cimree worrying about him. Not just about her situation, she was also expressing unease for his well-being. She was the one in Koa, in danger. Yet she was harboring cares for his safety.

He wished he knew why.

Six

Heartforge

Cimree, Trinati, Uorsin, and Avari pressed against the walls in the corner of the room, unseen by the angel sworn who were searching the dwelling. Cimree had grafted her companions with her serpents, whose natural camouflage allowed them to blend in with the wooden walls. Though Cimree didn't know his name, she could tell the leader of this band of scouts was part of the Morgarten based on the style of his leather armor, the mirror blades strapped to his back, and the heavy cloak. He was also exceptionally handsome, as were all the men the Queen Mother had chosen to defend the Gallows Tree.

Shouts spurted from below, making the leader's face twist with consternation until a few moments later when one of his underlings entered the room.

"Kaelis, we found Lyander in the cellar, bound up," said the newcomer.

"Was he turned to stone?" the Morgarten, Kaelis, demanded.

"No, he's alive. He's arriving soon."

"Good. That's news we can report to Jodocus, then."

The angel sworn Cimree's group had captured and spoken to

was brought up to the room. He appeared relieved to be among them again.

"Lyander," said the Morgarten stiffly. "You were captured?"

"I was, Kaelis," he answered. "Trinati is here. So is Uorsin and that hag. There's someone else with them, someone I didn't recognize. But there are only four."

"Where are they now?" Kaelis demanded.

"I have no idea. They interrogated me and then bound me and put me in the cellar."

"Where is your matia band?"

"They took it from me and asked about it," Lyander said. "I told them about Paracelsus. They can't have gone far, Kaelis. Not in the daylight. And they broke my distaff."

"We're searching every street, but we need to be careful," the Morgarten said. "There are only so many pairs of matia bands, and not everyone is trained to use them. But you are, so you will join in the hunt."

"Of course," Lyander said. "But tell Jodocus that Cimree is not what he thinks. She is more skilled than I anticipated. Azra has trained her well. She won't be easy to catch."

Cimree smiled to herself, thinking that it was true to a point, but they also didn't know about her restored memories.

"But she's still in Koa now that Jodocus has the device."

"Is Paracelsus going to study it?" Lyander asked. "He might be able to make more."

"Jodocus doesn't trust him enough to allow Paracelsus to touch it on his own because he has yet to earn that trust. He could use the artifact to escape." Kaelis gave a frustrated sigh and growled, "We must make sure she's still here, so we can begin attacking the caves!"

"I would go," Lyander said vehemently. "The apostates all deserve to die."

"But you're needed here. Report back to Jodocus. You can get another distaff and a matia band and then rejoin the search. We must search every dwelling until we locate her. Find her and bring her to Paracelsus. More statues will come, I fear. But we must rid the world of her curse once and for all."

The angel sworn left out the balcony and began to fly away, Kaelis having used his grafting wand to provide Lyander the ability to fly. As soon as they had departed, Cimree lifted the cowl over her head to keep the others safe, then released the graftings to her serpents, and she and her companions all became visible.

"One of us needs to go back and warn the others," Trinati said.

"My affinity is with bears," Uorsin said angrily. "Although I wish it were birds. I want to be the one to go. If Darcia did betray us, I would like to confront her."

"What is your affinity, Avari?" Cimree asked.

"I'm a Beesinger," he replied. "I can fly easily but not quickly."

That really left only one choice.

"You're the fastest of us all," Cimree said. "But let's be realistic. They're expecting one of us to head back and warn the others. They're going to try and stop you."

Trinati's voice was determined. "None of them can fly faster or longer than I can, especially if I graft with a swift. There might be an injured one nesting nearby that didn't migrate with the others."

"You're right," Cimree agreed. "It must be you. But caution should be your watchword. Many of the Morgarten also have affinity for raptors. It will not be easy to elude them."

"It won't be easy to catch me either," Trinati quipped. "None of them will outfly me. Be assured of that."

Cimree reached for Trinati and put a hand on her shoulder. Trinati followed suit.

"Be careful," Cimree warned.

"Trust me. I'm going to join the hunt for you first. Act like I'm searching the streets while getting to the edge of Koa. I need to find a swift to graft with."

"Thank you, Trinati," Cimree said, giving her a brief hug. "Tell Odeon to defend the caves. Bring the villagers in for protection."

"I will," Trinati said. "If you get the Tay al-Ard first, you'll beat me there. But best to be going on anyway."

"What are you going to do with Darcia?" Uorsin asked brusquely.

"If we can cage a golem, I'm sure we can trap a spider," Trinati answered.

THE SHADOWS in the room thickened as the sunlight began to fail. Uorsin sat with his back against the wall. He'd hardly eaten anything that day. Cimree wasn't hungry herself, for her body had not required a constant flow of nourishment since the golem had transformed her. Avari was out on the balcony, communing with bees in Koa as their spies. The search had reached far beyond where they were resting. It was part of human instinct to flee dangerous situations. By curbing that inclination, they'd found an easy shelter.

"I'm tempted to ask you for a favor, Cimree," Uorsin said, breaking the stillness.

He'd always been a taciturn fellow, someone who preferred to stay busy all day in his forge, using his talents to benefit the community. Idleness was not a trait she'd ever associated with him.

"You only need ask," she said.

"The amulet you wear…does it reveal the truth about emotions?"

"I don't understand your question."

Uorsin's eyes lowered. "I've believed for a long time that Darcia cared for me. At least I convinced myself it was that way. I would have done anything to make her notice." Cimree could hear the pain in his voice. His inner turmoil. "Now I can only think the worst. That she used me. That her friendliness…her shyness even… was just a disguise. I want to know the truth, but I'm afraid of it.

Can your amulet tell you whether any of what I experienced was real?"

Cimree's own heart ached for him. "If the two of you were bound together by it, then you'd understand for certain, without any doubt. She couldn't have deceived you if you wore it. You'd know the truth of her heart. But without that bond, without that union, I can only use it to alter your feelings."

"I wish you would just take them all away," Uorsin said bitterly. "I'm the one that led us into this trap. It's my fault."

"It's not your fault," she replied sincerely. "Human feelings are very complicated. I never even suspected her. She was always so talkative it made me believe she was in earnest."

"I as well," Uorsin said. "But she changed when we were alone. She would say little compliments, admiring my handiwork. Praising my concentration. Was it all just flattery? I wanted to believe her. That someone as pretty as her would want to be with a man like me."

"To be with you in what way? As a companion...or a husband?"

"As a husband, I think," Uorsin said, sounding wretched. "She asked me if I'd considered forsaking the law of celibacy. You can imagine what *I* imagined she meant by that."

"And what did you answer?"

"I told her I couldn't imagine anyone wanting me. In that way. Flames, I understand. Hammers, I understand. Her question created a heat inside me that my imagination took to with a bellows. Was it all just a trick? I wish I knew. But I'm afraid of the truth now."

"I'm sorry, Uorsin," Cimree said earnestly. "Based on what you said, it does seem to me that she was manipulating you. She gave you attention. She showed you kindness. Maybe some of it was real."

"Maybe I'm just a fool."

"She deceived us all," Cimree reminded him. "Even Azra, and you realize how clever he is."

Uorsin chuffed and fell silent.

"Thank you for talking to me," Cimree said. "That wasn't easy."

"In my forge, I can quench a red-hot piece of metal to cool it down faster. Oil, water, or brine will do. I wish I had a trough I could put my heart in while it cools down."

"I could take your feelings away," Cimree replied. "But that's like numbing a wound. The numbing doesn't heal it."

Based on the approaching tremors on the wooden floor, she knew Avari was returning from the balcony.

"What have your bees found out?" she asked.

"There are no angel sworn in the vicinity," Avari answered. "The search has expanded beyond this area."

"Are there people roaming about?" Cimree asked.

"Yes. But you can see the tension in their faces. They go from place to place. It's surprisingly warm outside. Feels nice actually. Like spring is coming."

Had her statue caused that? The Oldknow's power was truly beyond comprehension. The warmth would bring snakes. A feeling of warning came into her heart. Danger was approaching Koa. A curse.

"I need to warn the others," Cimree said anxiously. She needed to find Jodocus. If she told him about who his father was, how would he react? Would he, like Uorsin, be troubled in his mind and heart? Would it open him to understanding more about his past, about the people he was subjugating, who had once been his own people? Or would it only harden his heart more?

Her plan before had been to go to where the angel sworn were being held captive. That way, she could use the Tay al-Ard to bring them back to the caves of Tirich Mir. But circumstances had changed, and she needed to find Jodocus himself. To surprise him so that she could take the Tay al-Ard back.

He'd be waiting for her. He'd be expecting it.

"I think I should go to the captive angel sworn first," Cimree announced. "Their grafting wands were taken away, but they need to be told the truth. We can assume some were abducted from the caves and would help us."

"But we'll still be trapped here," Avari said.

"One step at a time," Cimree responded. "Spread the warning. Rally supporters. If I knew where Jodocus was, that would be helpful."

"You'll need to get one of his allies to tell you," Uorsin offered. "That fellow we captured, Lyander, he seemed to think he was at a palace somewhere. Others would as well."

"How long until sunset do you think?" Cimree asked.

"It'll be dark in an hour," Avari answered.

"I think it's dark enough," Cimree said. "I'm going out now. Like I'm trying to run a final errand. I want to get to where the captives are after dark."

"What do you want us to do?" Uorsin asked.

"Cause a disturbance," she said. "Draw their attention away from me. Then get back here. This is where I'll come for you."

"What if you don't return?" Uorsin wondered.

That was a realistic question to ask. And a frightening one. "If I'm not back by morning, get out of Koa."

"I'm not leaving you, Cimree," Uorsin said forcefully.

"They want to kill me," Cimree replied. "If they capture me, Azra is the only one who will know where to get to me. He'll come if I'm in danger. I'll feel better knowing you both are safe. Please do as I say. In a day or two, it won't be safe to walk these streets. There will be serpents everywhere. I'll give you a rune to protect you from them, but if I'm not back by morning, I want you to escape."

Her words were met with silence.

"If I return without you," Uorsin said, "Azra will kill me. I'm not afraid of serpents. We will get this done. No matter what it takes. If you don't arrive by morning, I'm coming after you."

Seven

The Forgotten Ones

The encampment was exactly where Avari had said it would be. That section of the city appeared to have once been a bazaar, a trading hub. There were stalls with wooden frames covered with multicolored canopies sewn together instead of rooftops. All the entrances to the encampment were guarded by armored angel sworn with mirror blades. Cimree had no problem sneaking in, for she could squeeze through the barred fencing with her serpent powers, and had begun wandering through it without detection.

The survivors of Clairvaux, those who hadn't knelt in obedience to Jodocus, huddled in small groups within the stalls, using broken fragments of wooden structures to burn for warmth. Cimree kept to the shadows and walked swiftly, hood pulled up, seeing faces she vaguely recognized from her homeland. Not a single one had a distaff. And the canopies revealed nothing of the city beyond. She could feel the festering resentment as she passed by them.

She spied two guards roaming the streets with their weapons sheathed, and she paused at a gap between stalls, using her camouflage to hide herself until they passed. The guards peered in on the huddled forms with disdainful expressions. As she held her position, she breathed in the smells of bread and the flavors of Pashmir cuisine. At least they weren't starving.

After the way was clear, she continued going from booth to booth. The floor was made of dirty stone paving blocks, which dampened the sound of her steps. As she peered inside each stall, she used her affinity's vision to discern the heat from their bodies and the metal braziers that provided warmth. She searched for anyone who had traveled with Cimree and Azra's group or had been in the caves of Tirich Mir. After a thorough search, she found one.

Her name was Salisha. Cimree recognized her instantly when she passed by. Salisha had been in Ecbatana before Cimree's group arrived. They'd stayed at the manor together in the blue quarter. And Cimree had broken Salisha's nose when she and a couple of other angel sworn confronted her at breakfast one day. That cohort, from the Long Patrol, had been in favor of Trinati ruling the angel sworn. That they were inside the encampment meant their loyalty wasn't to Jodocus.

Cimree continued down the flank of booths and then circled back to sneak around from behind it. The ropes and stakes for the canopies had to be navigated, but Cimree was adept at seeing in the dark. She counted back to the booth she'd passed with Salisha and crouched by the tarp that formed the walls. A little eavesdropping would aid in the situation.

"Overpowering two guards isn't a problem," one of the women muttered softly. "But that only gets us two distaffs. We need more."

"What if we overcame one of the perimeter pickets?" asked another.

"Those are more heavily guarded," Salisha said. Cimree recognized her voice. "And even if we succeeded, they're armed and we're not. They said they'd kill us if we tried to escape."

"What do you make of all that commotion this morning? I

spoke to Jara an hour back. He said the Morgarten are searching the whole city."

Jara was another familiar name. He had also gone with them to Tirich Mir. A friend of Azra's who had been on guard duty and then disappeared. It was obvious that the captives were plotting together. Because of Jara's friendship with Azra, she had more trust in him than in Salisha who might still bear a grudge for having her nose broken.

If *she* could get grafting wands and provide them for the captives, then it would be another way to escape en masse. If all these angel sworn had their distaffs taken away, then Jodocus would be keeping them somewhere protected.

Should Cimree trust Salisha by revealing herself? It would save time, and that was more important. Cimree drew her dirk and slit the fabric wall.

"Someone's there," one of the woman hissed.

"It's Cimree. I wanted you to know I was here."

"Cimree!" Salisha whispered eagerly.

"We're working on a way to get you out of here," Cimree said in a hushed voice. "Do you know where the others are from Tirich Mir?"

"Yes," Salisha responded. "They haven't tried to separate us. I can't believe you're here!" She sounded thrilled.

"I'll try to bring you some distaffs," Cimree said. "Where does Jodocus keep them?"

"I'm not sure," said another angel sworn. "We went to the palace once and were offered the chance to swear fealty to him. We were brought here when we refused. They took our distaffs."

"Cimree," Salisha asked, "are you the reason for the disturbance earlier? I've heard reports all day that the Morgarten are searching for someone. I'm assuming it's you? Did anyone else come with you?"

"I came with Trinati, Uorsin, and a man named Avari."

"Yes, he escaped months ago," Salisha said. "I remember him from the Long Patrol."

"Do you know who betrayed us?" Cimree asked.

"Darcia," Salisha answered vehemently. "She showed up when I was on guard duty with Rithia. They were in league together. Darcia poisoned me with a needle. It happened so fast. I couldn't move; I couldn't scream. It felt like my heart was going to stop. Then Rithia took me away while I was helpless. There are Morgarten hiding in the mountains near our caves."

"Rithia is one of them," said another woman. "She was at Jodocus's palace in arms."

"I never suspected Darcia," Salisha said firmly. "She was always so friendly, but it's an act. She knew I'm loyal to Trinati, but she asked about my loyalty to you, Cimree. More than once."

"And what did you tell her?"

"It was because of you and Azra that we made it to Tirich Mir. Even Trinati got duped by the Ecbatanans. You even stayed behind rather than risk our lives. I'm loyal to you. Soon after that conversation was when I was poisoned and removed. I think Darcia is trying to get the best defenders away from the caves. The Morgarten are going to attack. Soon, I fear."

"Then we'll need all of us back there," Cimree replied. She was grateful to understand that Salisha had come around.

"I'm loyal too," said another woman.

Two others agreed as well.

"I'm going to go now to try and steal you some grafting wands," Cimree said, thinking to herself, *And hopefully the Tay al-Ard too.* Then she could transport herself back to the tent and get them out. "When I return, I'll use this rip to deliver them. Stay awake. Wait for me."

"We will," Salisha promised. Her voice sounded so relieved.

"Warn the others. Don't all gather here or it will be suspicious. But tell the others I'll return. I won't leave you here."

The palace Jodocus occupied sat atop a hill in the south part of the city. Cimree had found it by following some guards who had left to make a report. Round stone turrets provided strong defenses along with ledged walls that rose over the hillside. Triangular crenelations kept the ridge secure. Cimree gazed up at it in the moonlight and could see the mountains of Tirich Mir in the distance. The fortress appeared formidable, but it wasn't as extensive as Ecbatana's walled protections had been, and even those walls had succumbed. With her heat senses, she watched angel sworn fly up to the hilltop and enter, delivering whatever news.

Cimree climbed the steep hillside easily, clambering over protruding boulders on the way up. She reached one of the walls and then undulated up the stone to an arrow slit and peered inside, seeing only a stairwell. So she continued to the top, where she spied a single sentry standing guard on the rampart, bow in hand. She waited until he rotated and faced the other way before slipping over the crest of the wall and wriggling down the other side.

Turf and dirt were on the other side, leading to the minimal design of the fortress. Lowering her cowl and checking the position of the moon and stars, she estimated that it was already nearly midnight. Grateful for the long winter night, she stalked forward toward the citadel.

She crossed the earth swiftly, her serpents acting as eyes around her so she could spy the guards patrolling the walls. When she reached the walls of the palace, she crouched in the shadows. After a brief wait, she glided up the wall so she could enter from one of the upper balconies protruding from the front edifice. One balcony was as good as any. She climbed over the railing of one at random and went to a door made of wood with an offset square symbol designed in it. She tested the handle and found it locked, but it was easily undone.

Cimree lifted her cowl and gently opened the door. No lamps

burned inside. She slipped in and shut the door behind her as soundlessly as she could. She saw a bed with several people asleep on it, and when she stilled, she could hear their breathing. Moonlight came in through the upper windows. The perfumed smell in the room and the elaborate couches and garments indicated that it was inhabited by women.

She cautiously crossed the room and went to the door. After an assessing pause, she opened it and went into the corridor. The marble hall had no vibrations at all, but the stone would make it easy to sense if someone else arrived.

She'd infiltrated the palace easily enough, but finding Jodocus was her first priority. If she got back the Tay al-Ard, that would improve her options. She could always use nightshade on him to get him to reveal where the distaffs were stored.

Jodocus would be in the most prestigious room, which was typically on the highest floors of a palace. A little throb of self-doubt struck her, but she persisted. The lavish interior would still provide a way to hide herself against the stone pillars. The tall upper windows could also provide a way to escape. She roamed down the hall until she found a staircase going up and took it until it went no higher.

Down another impressive corridor with massive pillars on each wall, she found an ornate door. No angel sworn guarded it, which made her hesitate. Were there no guards because they were still searching Koa for her and her companions? Were there guards inside instead? Or did Jodocus feel he did not need any?

What would Azra do? She sensed he was awake still. Thinking about her. Worrying. He might not know what she was doing, but he could no doubt comprehend she was taking a risk.

Not a single tremor or vibration.

Maybe Jodocus wasn't there at all. The sooner she knew that, the better. He might have gone somewhere else with the Tay al-Ard. She was wasting time, then, if her goal was to find him.

Cimree walked the rest of the way down the corridor and listened at the decorative door. All was still.

She tried the handle and it twisted easily.

The snakes were getting restless beneath her hood, but she didn't want to turn someone to stone inadvertently. She looked back down the moonlit corridor. Nothing. No tremors.

Cimree finished twisting the handle and pulled the door open. A light source illuminated much of the room within. A druid stone.

An opulent bed with hanging curtains blocking sight of the sheets had been positioned in the middle, and large cushioned chairs sat together off to one side. It smelled like cedar and musk. She quietly entered and gently shut the door so it wouldn't make a noise when it closed.

Her pulse had quickened.

On the side of the room opposite the comfortable chairs was a desk with a contraption on it, a vertical jeweled box with mirrors and a druid stone lighting it. She noted the Tay al-Ard inside the contraption. On display. Jewels glimmered along the edges of the ornamental box.

All Cimree's instincts screamed that a trap was ready to go off.

Eight

The Taste of Quicksilver

Cimree parted the curtains of the bed to see if someone was sleeping there, even though she'd heard no sounds of breathing. The bed was vacant, the sheets and blankets all made up. It was inviting, but she could not rest. She was there to find Jodocus and the Tay al-Ard, and though she had succeeded at the latter, seeing the device in such a contraption did not entice her to reach for it. Turning back, she examined the druid light emanating from the box containing the Tay al-Ard.

A flicker of salt flashed into her mouth. Just a small dash of the taste. She whirled, yet saw no one in the room. The light from the druid stone diminished slightly.

Chairs and couches emphasized the hospitableness of the place. But no clothing hung in the wardrobe. No evidence suggested that anyone lived there.

Another taste of salt.

Cimree spun around again, trying to determine what was being transformed by her power. Her heat sense revealed nothing. Glaring in frustration, she approached the druid stone and Tay al-Ard device, watching as the stone's light dimmed again. She sent a thought to it, willing it to shine brighter, but it did not do so. Another mind, or previous orders, compelled it.

If someone was already aware of her, it meant that others might be coming for her. She'd felt no vibrations signaling arrival, but angel sworn could float and thus approach undetected.

Part of her was tempted to snatch at the device. But that course of action would be the one most likely to result in her capture. So she decided to abandon the room and search for Jodocus elsewhere. She walked to the door and gripped the handle.

Pain stung her hand. In the dimness, she saw a black spot on her hand and instinctively swatted it, smashing the insect that bit her. Vibrations of pain continued to pulse.

A feeling of nervousness thickened inside her. Pulling out her own druid stone, she tried to light it to see what had stung her, but the stone would not respond to her thought command.

Brighten! she ordered again.

Nothing. She winced in pain and twisted the handle, but it was frozen in place. Locked. She knelt, spying a keyhole beneath the handle. The pain in her hand grew more intense.

A spider bite. It was no accident.

She struggled with the knob for a few moments, then crouched down and peered into the lock. More light was required. Cimree rose and struck the door with her boot, but the door was solid and didn't crack.

She went to the nearest curtained window and when she opened it, she found out that thick panels of wood had been nailed in place to block the potential egress. She hurried to another and found the same.

The pain in her hand was still worsening. She wished she had some of the salve Azra had used on her that could dampen pain significantly. Methodically, she searched each window and found them all boarded up. A feeling of nausea penetrated her stomach, bad enough that she wanted to vomit.

Continuing her search for a way out, she discovered another

door on an adjacent wall. It too was locked. A round aperture beneath the handle seemed to be the stub of a locking mechanism, but it had been removed.

The entire room was the trap, not just the Tay al-Ard. Frustration mounted inside her. Then the noise of a wooden object hitting the floor sounded, followed by the mewling of a cat. Turning, she saw it appear in a small gap in the wall, formed by a fallen panel that was lying on the floor. The cat glowed in her thermal vision, hissed at her, and fled. But it did not alter.

The hole in the wall was no higher than her knee and wide enough to squeeze a cat through, but not herself. The painful pulses in her hand redoubled, as did the gut-wrenching spasms in her stomach. Her heart beat more erratically. Dizziness swelled her thoughts.

She stooped by the hole in the wall and spied through it into the next room, which was darkened.

Using her serpent abilities, she started to squeeze through the gap, her body contorting to fit the space.

A man crouched on the other side, glass fragments shining in his face. He reached down and pressed a cloth against her mouth before she could react.

It had a sweet smell, like freshly cut hay.

Cimree blacked out.

Another smell roused her, this one a horrible concoction that stung her nose. Involuntarily, she jerked her head away from the horrid stench.

"That roused her," Jodocus said smugly. "What is that smell?"

"Volatile salts," replied another man in a voice Cimree didn't recognize.

Her serpent hair was sluggish, the creatures bonded to her drowsy still. She was sitting in a wooden chair, her wrists tied together behind her. Her ankles were bound to the legs of the chair.

The connection to Azra was gone. The amulet had been removed.

Startled surprise battled with a surging fear.

The room was still dark, although she saw the dim glow of a druid stone from an open doorway. This was the other room, a bathing room, she surmised when she noticed a stone tub. Across from her was the cut in the wall she'd tried to squeeze through.

"Are you awake, Cimree?" Jodocus asked.

Lifting her head, she noticed he too had glass facets strapped to his brow. The angry welt on her hand was still agitated and the queasiness had not faded.

Her weapons had been stripped from her.

"Yes," she answered tightly.

"Theo said you would come," Jodocus mused. "He's quite clever."

"I live to serve you, Archangel," murmured the other man. He stood to Cimree's left. Jodocus was straight ahead.

"Now that we have *this*," Jodocus said, dangling the Tanaquil amulet by its chain in front of her, "it will make overwhelming the caves even easier. As you no doubt feel, your unholy connection to Azra has been severed."

"There was nothing unholy about our connection," Cimree countered. "Jodocus, time is running out. We need to bring all the angel sworn and anyone else wishing to survive to the caves of Tirich Mir."

"That sounds perfectly reasonable," Jodocus taunted. "I will accept any who bend the knee and swear obedience to me. I'll even forgive Trinati if she begs for it. But there are a few exceptions. You and Azra. The two of you will die. And unlike you, I will fulfill my threat."

"Jodocus..."

"Your entreaties are pointless!" he snarled at her. "How I've been waiting for this moment. For my sweet revenge."

"I let you live," Cimree shot back.

"And that was your mistake. For some reason, you've inspired a rather fierce loyalty among some of your followers. Once you're dead, there will be no other choice but to transfer their allegiance to me and the new Queen Mother."

His words rattled her. "The *new* Queen Mother?"

"I was named the archangel," Jodocus said. "Darcia was named Queen Mother. Surely you realize that plans were set in motion after your betrayal and before before Clairvaux fell."

Cimree struggled against the bonds, but they were knotted tightly.

"Your rebellion has ended," Jodocus pronounced. He rose to his full height. "Make her drink it, Theo. I want to watch her die."

"As you command, of course," said the other fellow patiently. She sized him up. He was shorter than Jodocus, with a spare frame and dark clothes that were indistinguishable in the dark room. He produced a stoppered vial from his pocket.

"Jodocus, you must heed me," Cimree warned.

"There is no reason to heed you," he countered with contempt. "You betrayed the Queen Mother. She told me, before she died, that you succumbed to the fruit of the Gallows Tree on your own volition. That instead of facing her judgment, you became an infant. Her compassion prevented her from harming a child. But you've harmed children, haven't you? That little boy in the cave. Chuq?"

Darcia had told him. Cimree's anger was provoked, but she remembered that enmity was not the solution.

"Did she also tell you that *you* are Azra's son? You were born in these mountains, Jodocus. Your mother was slaughtered on the Queen Mother's orders."

Her words struck him mute.

"Shall I proceed, my lord?" Theo asked submissively.

"She'd say anything to spare herself," Jodocus answered, a slight tremble in his voice.

"I speak the truth," Cimree said fiercely. "Bond us together through the amulet and you'll realize I'm not lying. I can prove it to you in other ways."

"Do it," Jodocus snarled.

The feeling of helplessness made her panic. She believed she could slip her wrists from the bond ropes, just as she could slither through bars in a gate. But as soon as the instinct arrived, she heard a calming whisper in her mind.

Be still.

Her feelings were anything but still. But she recognized the impulse that cut through her distress. An urging to trust the Oldknow.

She relaxed her shoulders and stopped struggling.

"Azra is your father," Cimree said.

"I doubt it, Cimree. He tried to kill me when you were leaving Clairvaux."

"He didn't know it then. He does now. I came here to *tell* you."

"You came here to rescue your fellow traitors," Jodocus answered. "Make her drink it, Theo."

"Yes, my lord." Theo unstoppered the vial.

"What is that?" Cimree demanded.

"A liquid metal called quicksilver," Theo answered. "I've used it to kill one of the demon wolves. The gévaudan as your people call them."

Again the instinct to squirm and resist developed into an overpowering urge.

"And now that we can finally *kill* them," Jodocus sneered, "we can return and redeem Clairvaux. The new Gallows Tree must stay here, but with the Tay al-Ard, we will have access to its fruit in time. We'll destroy all those idols you've made with your curse. In the future, no one will remember your name. Your reign has ended, Serpent Queen. Tonight."

He motioned to Theo, who brought the vial to Cimree's face and gripped her behind the neck with a firm hand.

She pressed her lips closed, holding still.

"If you'd squeeze her cheeks, please," Theo said calmly.

Jodocus wasn't gentle and forced her head back. Her neck arched painfully as Jodocus pried her mouth open. The vial was tilted and emptied, and she gagged on the heavy clumps of quicksilver going down her throat. Theo clamped his hand on her mouth to prevent her trying to spit it out.

The metallic taste and sensation of it trickling down her throat was horrid. It made her shudder.

Jodocus stepped back, folding his arms. "How long does it take to work?"

"It killed the gévaudan almost instantly," Theo replied.

They both stared at her.

Cimree was nauseated, but it might still have been the result of the spider bite. She began to tremble. Convulsions rippled through her. She groaned and twisted her torso.

Jodocus grinned in triumph.

"It won't be long now," Theo said in awe.

Cimree began to gasp. More than anything else, she was thirsty. Her breathing calmed and lessened. She slumped forward in the chair, lowering her head. Then she shut her eyes. And stopped breathing.

"It worked," Jodocus said in relief. "Have her buried on the steepest edge of the slope. Do not mark it. I don't want it becoming a place for her followers to reverence. She deserved this ignominious death. I'll go to the caves and meet with Darcia."

"May I…study her first?" Theo asked plaintively.

"Must you?"

"It would be a waste of an opportunity."

"You have until dawn," Jodocus commanded.

In an instant he was gone. Cimree didn't hear him leave or sense the tremors from his boots. But he had the Tay al-Ard with him. Of course he had.

"He's gone now," Theo said with a charming voice. "That was a suitable performance."

Cimree lifted her head. "How did you know I was pretending?"

She could hear the smirk in Theo's voice. "Because I suspected the quicksilver wouldn't kill you. I've deduced that your curse is very different than the gévaudan's. A different form of metamorphistry. A unique variant. I'm glad I have until dawn to study you."

Nine
Paracelsus

Being separated from Azra's emotions was deeply unsettling. How was he reacting to the breach in the medallion's magic? When would Trinati get there and be able to warn the rest about Darcia and her schemes? Cimree had to crush down all her worries and focus on her own danger—strapped to a chair with a man intent on studying her.

"Is your name Paracelsus?" she asked him, seeing him standing, back to her, at a small decorative table with a bowl, tools, and an assortment of vials.

"Actually it's Theophrastus von Weissenau," he answered, lifting a vial with one hand and flicking it with a finger from the other hand.

"Weissenau?" Cimree replied, astonished. "Isn't that a village on Lake Beatriz?"

"It is, in fact—or *was*. Nothing but ruins now, or so Jodocus has said."

"You are from the lake country."

"I was born in a house next to a bridge over the Einsiedeln River," he replied with a huffing noise. "My parents had too many children. They wanted me to join the angel sworn. I was curious, naturally, but I had no desire to swear all those oaths."

"How did you end up here, Master Theophrastus?"

"You may call me Theo. I was an apprentice to an apothecary in Turicum and was equally fascinated by the merchant caravans who brought different spices and oddities to trade. All roads lead to Ecbatana, as they say, and my road led me there. And that is where I earned my new name."

"Were you in Ecbatana when it fell?" Cimree questioned.

"No," he said curtly. "I was at the coliseum in Vaud. Where the gladiators fight."

Cimree knew of Vaud, from her past lives. An arena of death, where the wealthy and others addicted to gambling wasted their fortunes betting on and watching blood sports. It drew sizable crowds. Cimree had been there on assignment before and had been deeply disturbed at how bloody the events were.

Theo approached her chair. "If you would tilt your head back for a moment, I'm going to apply this to your eyes."

"What is that liquid?" Cimree asked.

"Hogweed oil," Theo answered. "I'm trying to blind you... temporarily."

Her stomach clenched. "Theo—"

"I'm testing to know if your power can be subdued, at least for a little while. There are several oils I would like to try out. I've already experimented with light levels, and this amount of darkness renders sighted creatures immune to your gaze. As may blindness, I think. But now that I have you, I want to find out if we can quell the effect originating from *you.*"

"Hogweed oil causes burns," Cimree said warily, straining against her bonds.

"You're knowledgeable about plants? Interesting. But burns only occur when the oil is exposed to sunlight. It is phototoxic. I have more rats, you see, which I'll use to test against your power but only in dimness. I used the cat after I was certain."

"So I was turning rats into stone?"

"Yes, of course. I wasn't going to test it on *myself.* It took only three to determine a suitable level of shadow to nullify the effect of looking at you." He stood over her. "It may sting a little. I'm sorry for that. But I don't have as much time as I'd like to study you."

She was about to use her serpent powers to slip her hand free of the bond. But again she had the distinct impression to be still. She didn't understand why.

"Lay your head back, please," Theo coaxed.

She did so and kept her eyes open. The snakes writhed listlessly, although several wanted to strike at him. She suppressed them with her will.

"Interesting," Theo murmured. He uncorked the vial and, with a practiced hand, tipped a single drop into her right eye. As soon as it struck her, the feeling of warmth and burning began to irritate her. And it itched. Cimree screwed up her face, enduring the discomfort. Then he tipped another drop in her other eye.

She squeezed her eyelids shut, her eyes watering against the foreign oil's irritating effect. The itching was unbearable and she sighed in frustration.

"Let's bring a little *ratgen* back in here, shall we? Open your eyes, please. Is your vision blurry?"

"Yes," Cimree said through gritted teeth. Her vision was mottled, and the fiery sensation in her eyes made her want to rub them, but the bonds prevented it.

"I'm sorry it's so uncomfortable," Theo said. "But there hasn't been one like you in a very long time."

"There have been others?"

"You are the first of *your* kind. Some breeds of ogre turn to stone if touched by raw sunlight. There are the basilisks as well, and catching their gaze will turn someone into stone. But their gaze can be conquered by reflections, which is the lore I've used against you. I've never heard of a maiden having this affliction, so you are the first. Which is why I need to study you before it's too late."

Her perception of Theo was just a smudge against the shadows. He stooped and picked something up and then the room brightened. It made her eyes sting even more, and before she could cry out in agony, the taste of salt flicked to her mouth again.

The light dimmed once more, and Theo clucked his tongue. "That didn't work unfortunately. Poor little *ratgen*."

He then produced a washing bowl and crouched by her chair to wash away the oil with soapy water. It stung as well, but in a different way that became soothing. Her vision remained blurry, but she could see better.

After drying her face, he brought the bowl to the table and stood there silently, deep in thought.

"Will you let me go, Theo?" she asked him.

"I'm afraid I can't do that, Cimree," he answered. "I'm as much a prisoner here as you are."

"We can escape together."

"Jodocus took your grafting wand. And he has the Tay al-Ard. You can't get out either."

"Why don't you pretend to bury me, as you said you would, and I'll leave instead. I want to save as many people here as I can."

"Save from what, exactly? An angelic civil war?"

"Theo, that is not what this is about."

"It's very much what this is about," he said with a hint of bitterness. "Asmodeus was once an angel sworn. He was cast down to this world. The Ecbatanans had their own traditions, their own mythology about him, but I grew up where we learned the dogma. The perennial struggle between good and evil. I'm just trying to survive this latest skirmish. So if you please, I need some quiet to think. Blindness did not stop you from making the *ratgen* into stone. What if we blindfolded you completely? I could try that."

"I could *help* you, Theo."

"I'm sorry, but I really don't believe you would," he answered with a chuckle. "I do have to kill you, Cimree. That was part of the deal with the archangel. I only bargained so I'd have some time to study you *alive*."

"But I can help you."

"Why would you want to do that?"

She wasn't sure why. He intrigued her. He reminded her a little of Wegner. His mind, his reasoning powers, his knowledge—these were attributes that would be useful in the future. She thought it an odd coincidence that this man, Paracelsus—Theophrastus—was there in Koa. That they were alone together.

"Whenever someone transforms, I experience a salty taste in my mouth," Cimree said, not answering his question. "When I was made like this, I had a coptic fruit with me."

"A coptic fruit?" Theo said with interest. "I've studied that fruit. I believe it grew as part of the royal gardens in Ecbatana. They kept many different kinds of fruits there that held extraordinary powers."

"Do you know of the Watchers?"

"I do," Theo said. "They're an order seeking to destroy the revenant and the lychgate. They'd infiltrated the nobility in Ecbatana. Whenever one was caught, they typically preferred suicide to revealing information about their band."

"One of the Watchers taught me about the coptic fruit," Cimree said. "Maybe it was one of the poisons they used. But I had the fruit with me when I transformed. And I have an affinity for serpents."

"An angel sworn with *that* affinity?" He sounded incredulous.

"Rare, to be sure. But where I was captured, Lord Roque had used serpents to incapacitate his prisoners. He didn't realize it wouldn't work on me."

Theo began to pace, rubbing his chin in thought as he walked back and forth. "Coptic fruit. I wouldn't have thought of it. Tell me of your transformation. Which of the Grand Wizrs cast the spell on you?"

"No person did this to me," Cimree said. "The golem made me."

Theo fell silent and stopped. "The creature?"

"The one that destroyed Clairvaux. That has caused all these devilish monsters to appear. It has power to create new life. We have it captured in the mountains."

"Oh dear," Theo muttered anxiously.

"What?"

"Cimree. That thing...that abomination cannot *stand* imprisonment. From what I understand, and this I've only gleaned in fragments, it began as a foreign creature brought from a distant land to join the arena at Vaud. The games were getting too predictable, you see. The people wanted a spectacle unlike any other. The revenant, the true ruler of Ecbatana, would fashion monsters in its lair. But something went wrong. A creature was formed that outwitted the revenant. That *destroyed* its bones. Lord Roque found pieces of it strewn all about the chamber. The cage broken. This golem had the revenant's power of creation somehow. And it has a hatred of all men. It was tortured in its captivity. It will do anything to escape."

Cimree listened intently, her heart shuddering with fear. She realized the golem was very patient too. Very cunning. It would lie in wait for an opportunity to escape. It would find a way out of the cave they'd trapped it in.

In her mind, she could hear its mournful voice pleading with her. Freedom. It wanted its freedom again.

"You could study it, Theo," she whispered. "I could bring you to it."

She heard his brief intake of breath.

"You truly are a serpent," Theo said, half chuckling. "What a temptation you've unleashed in me."

"Bring me the Tay al-Ard," Cimree said. "And I can take you there."

"Jodocus would *kill* me. He doesn't trust me with it. Not even to touch it."

"You helped him take it from me, didn't you?"

"Of course. A subtle spell of attraction. A powerful one. I made a ring for him that summoned it to his hand."

"But how did you know to make such a ring? How did you know it would come?"

"That's why they call me Paracelsus," he said smugly.

An apple seed contains a fatal toxin. But it would require eating the pulp of over one hundred seeds before a normal person would sicken and die. Simply ingesting that many apples is impossible. All things are poisonous, for there is nothing without poisonous qualities. Even too much water may kill. It is only the dose that makes a thing poison, and the matching of the right cause with the right effect that will result in the death of any creature.

— The Hermetic and Alchemical
Writings of Paracelsus

Ten
Unknowable

"The bond between us is broken, Odeon. I can't sense her at all. I feel nothing."

Azra struggled in vain to keep his voice neutral. He was worried, and that emotion was tainting his words. It was after midnight. What should have been a brief journey to Koa had already taken far too long with too many complications. He'd paced the tunnels for nearly an hour—waiting and hoping that the connection would be restored. Until finally, he'd awakened Odeon. Azra needed to counsel with someone before desperation drove his actions.

Odeon paced as well, his hair askew from lying on the bed restlessly, his eyes bleary. He hadn't slept either. He was worried about someone too.

"Do you think she severed the connection again—like she did last time?" Odeon asked with a scowl.

"No, I don't think that. She was knocked unconscious somehow. I could feel that she was concerned. Agitation was the strongest sense I had from her. And then the connection was broken. Not severed, like with the cut of a knife, but pulled at until it broke. In the lore of the medallion, the power could be broken temporarily if the medallion was taken away from the person bonded to it. That is what I think took place."

"It sounds like Jodocus has her, doesn't it?" Odeon exclaimed. "Do you think she surrendered herself?"

"No," Azra shot back. "The Tay al-Ard was taken away somehow. Otherwise she would have ended the mission. I could sense her, throughout the day, feeling safe. I think she was with the others until tonight. It's difficult describing the emotions of the connection. After dark, she had a firm purpose. And then...confusion? Worry? Something shocked her and her senses began to fade."

"It sounds like poison," Odeon said thoughtfully.

"It does," Azra said. "A poison that incapacitated her. It's like they knew she was coming."

Odeon approached and put his hand on Azra's shoulder. "I'm concerned too."

"I want to go after her," Azra snapped. "I was the destroying angel. They have no idea what I'm capable of."

Odeon gave Azra's shoulder a squeeze. "That's what they're expecting you to do. And it would leave us vulnerable without you if they chose to attack."

Azra closed his eyes. He believed Odeon was right. But the anguish of uncertainty was gnawing at his stomach.

"Trinati is relentless," Odeon said, lowering his hand. "She won't take defeat without doing everything she can to help. And Uorsin is reliable too, although I wonder about his emotional state."

"He has been more sullen," Azra agreed. "His diligence is unwavering, but he's tormented."

Odeon offered a thoughtful look. "Darcia is on his mind."

"I spoke with her earlier today," Azra said. "She didn't appear all that concerned, to be honest. When I told her the mission had gone wrong, that Uorsin was at risk too, she didn't betray any look of concern."

"It's possible that he feels more strongly than she does," Odeon suggested.

"I pity my friend, then," Azra said. "I asked if she'd noticed anyone acting strangely. Someone carrying heavy troubles. She mentioned quite a few actually, which was tedious to listen to." He rubbed his forehead. "None of the people she mentioned were connected to the high council at all."

"Do you think someone has betrayed us unwittingly?" Odeon asked. "What if you or I did, and we didn't even know?"

Azra snorted. "That would be the most difficult kind of treachery to detect. The unknowable kind."

Odeon pursed his lips, his wrinkled brow implying a deep trepidation. He walked over to the druid stone giving light in his room. His chamber was not out of the way like Azra's but in the thick of things. His mirror blades leaned against the wall. His armor was fastened to a metal stand Uorsin had forged for him.

"Back in Ecbatana," Odeon said in a low voice, "guilt tortured me day by day. I justified what I'd done because I believed I was serving a higher cause. I believed that my actions would have saved the Queen Mother's life. My loyalties were conflicted, Azra. I esteemed and respected Trinati. But duty required me to serve Lilith. Losing Montheron had broken me. That I aided in its demolition..." He breathed out slowly and shook his head.

"We all justify ourselves," Azra said. "I carried a grudge against her for far longer than I should have because of what she stripped from me here, in these mountains. It took Cimree to help me learn the truth about myself. To finally understand who I truly was and who I wanted to be. The same happened to Trinati."

"It did," Odeon agreed. "She did her penance. Even though I disagreed she even needed to, I wouldn't stand in the way of her trying to heal her conscience. Whoever is acting against us is either suffering with guilt or they believe they're in the right. They've convinced themselves of moral superiority or some other nonsense. We are struggling for survival, Azra. We're fighting against extinction."

Azra blinked, an idea forming. "We are."

Odeon appeared bemused. "I recognize that expression. You just had a thought."

"I'm tired of playing their game," Azra said. "We are reacting to *their* schemes. We're playing into *their* hands. It's time to seize the advantage. To make them react to *us*."

"I don't think you should go to Koa, Azra."

"I'm not planning to. You're right, that's what they're expecting. I'm still not fully recovered. Logically, it doesn't make sense."

Odeon's eyes twinkled. "We could send someone else. Who?"

"More like *what*."

Odeon frowned.

"We release the golem."

Odeon looked aghast. "No," he said, shaking his head.

"Hear me out. The golem is drawn to Cimree. After she was injured in the catacombs, it healed her. When she fled the mountains, it bonded with an albatross and flew after her. Then it came for her here. I believe that if we set it loose, if we *let* it escape, it would go to her. It knows where she is. And it would get past all the Morgarten to reach her."

Odeon's expression remained dumbstruck. "Why does it pursue her?"

"I don't know," Azra said. "I just know that it does. If it wanted to harm her, it's had plenty of opportunities to. Instead of healing her in Ecbatana, it could have killed her. It nearly killed *me*. And we can use it to our advantage. It cannot enter the caves, not with the statues protecting us. But if we open the gate by the waterfall, it could get out."

Odeon touched his mouth, with a bewildered wrinkle to his brow. Then he lowered his hand. "The risks, Azra."

"Letting it out would not be without risk," Azra said. "The

gate by the waterfall is held by hooking pins at the bottom. The gate swung down from the ceiling."

"Whoever opened the gate would get attacked. And even with distaffs, it can break the bonds, which would make escaping it problematic."

"I'm glad we're talking about it, then," Azra said. "You're right. The golem is cunning. And vengeful."

"It would probably attack whoever let it loose," Odeon agreed.

"Then we just show it how to get free. We break one of the pins. Rattle the gate so it knows it's broken. Let it destroy the other one. I've seen it yank on the bars. It wants to get out."

"That is true," Odeon said. "Your plan has merit, Azra. But I feel wary unleashing that monstrosity again. I can't forget what it did to Montheron."

"It will go after Cimree," Azra said with certainty. Undeniably, some connection existed between the two of them.

Odeon nodded but looked like he was still not convinced. "When the kobolds brought me to the Queen Mother's palace, when I saw Lilith bound, I still remember the golem saying Cimree's name. It can only say a few words, and her name is probably its favorite."

"So do you agree?" Azra asked.

"I'm not sure this is a decision we can make on our own," Odeon said. "We summon the high council in the morning."

"Cimree might not have until morning," Azra said impatiently.

"Be prudent, Azra. I'm nearly convinced. But let's hear what the others have to say about it. Let's decide together. Maybe we should evacuate the village into the caves before we set it loose."

What a sensible recommendation.

"You summon the high council," Azra said in agreement. "I'll go inspect the gate. It will take some work to undo Uorsin's handicraft."

"Fair enough. Meet us in the high council room at dawn."

Azra clapped Odeon on the back and departed to fulfill his task.

THE MOON SANK on the horizon, and the brisk winter winds buffeted Azra as he flew over the mountains to the secret valley on the other side. He'd bonded with an owl for the night vision and the magical warmth linked to comfortable downy feathers, which kept him warm against the frigid night. The glare of the moon against the snow made it feel bright as day. He soared down through the crags and snow-pregnant slopes that could, without warning, break out in avalanches.

There was nothing in his heart but determination to rescue Cimree. Since he had access to all of Wegner's memories and knowledge, he knew how the gate worked and had already decided on a course of action to remove the hooked pins that kept it closed.

As he flew down to the cave fed by a mountain stream, he paused and wreathed his hand in flames, using the light to examine the snow for marks of passage. It wouldn't have been surprising to find animal tracks, but the snow was undisturbed. The few trees nearby had branches laden and drooping.

With the fire swirling on his hand, he walked to the cave entrance, listening to the trickle of water passing beneath the layers of ice underfoot to feed the little waterfall inside the cave. His breath came out in puffs of mist.

Echoes of moaning rumbled from the cave. The golem was distraught.

He extinguished the flame in his hand so as not to reveal his presence. Once inside the tunnel, he stepped past where the wind could extend the reach of the snow. The burbling waters of the brook masked the sound of his steps. He carefully maneuvered his feet, trying not to betray the sound of his arrival. The silky strand of a spiderweb brushed against his face, and he pawed it away. Then another.

He didn't remember there being any spiderwebs the last time he'd passed that way, but admittedly it had been quite a while. Without the bats in the caves, some species of spider or other had taken refuge.

Azra squinted, grateful for the owl's keen vision to see in the darkness. Something hazy blocked the path to the gate, like a veil of silk.

Curious, he stepped farther in and felt wisps against his hair. He reached out and cleared away a giant cobweb. Little insects danced along his hand.

Azra summoned the fireblood and gaped in shock. The entire interior of the tunnel was sheathed in spider silk. Hundreds of spiders scuttled along the strands. The web at his hand ignited and the little insects shriveled and burned.

A sting on his wrist. Another on his neck.

Fear twitched in his heart. Then he heard the crunch of boots in the snow behind him.

Azra shifted, holding up his hand, and saw Darcia blocking the way out, her hair covered by a cowl but her serious face illuminated by the flames.

He glimpsed the bulb of a spider suddenly on his nose. Pain stung there instantly. Then the pain struck his other hand. His neck.

Tiny painful bites.

ELEVEN
MIRRORS

"What are you grinding in that bowl?" Cimree asked, observing, from her position strapped to the chair, the methodical way Theo used an implement to grind seeds. The scraping noise sounded like the bowl was made of stone.

"This is a mortar," Theo answered. "The cone-shaped rod is called a pestle. I'm breaking down seeds from pears."

She already knew the names of the objects but didn't want to give away anything unnecessarily about her background as a healer. "What do you need the seeds for?"

"Certain fruit seeds contain properties that will only be unleashed if pulverized. If you ate the seed, it would pass through you."

"I'm going to be eating seeds next, am I?"

"It's nearly dawn, Cimree. I've learned a great deal from our conversation. Knowledge that will be useful to the future. Just as the writings from the past helped me conquer your power. Knowledge should be collected, written down, and preserved."

"Where are your writings now?" Cimree asked.

"I have a library at the arena in Vaud," he replied, scooping some more seeds from a pouch at the table and dumping them into the mortar. He began to grind them into the mix.

It is poison.

The thought drifted through her mind like a breeze. A warning that she needed to leave or he would kill her.

"I've learned a great deal from you as well," she said. "We could still learn much from each other."

"I wish we had more time, truly I do."

"What about the contraption with the Tay al-Ard that was in the other room? It lured me in."

"I didn't actually think you'd be foolish enough to try and grab it," Theo said with a chuckle. "It was to draw your attention. I enchanted some mirrors, you see, with the reflection of the device. An illusion of it only but one powerful enough to trick the senses. If you'd reached out for it, your hand would have struck nothing but air. It allowed me to control the amount of light in the room so I could test the level of darkness required to nullify your power on the rats instead of myself."

Cimree twisted her wrist in the rope around her right arm. Her skin stretched, and it pulled out easily. She did so with the left as well.

"Jodocus grafted with the spiders, naturally. Isn't it amazing how potent the toxin of spider venom is at paralyzing prey? Did you know that a bird can be killed swallowing a spider if it bites while it's in the gullet? It's quite fascinating."

"You have a prodigious memory, Theo."

"Thank you. I've spent years gathering the knowledge of others. I knew that darkness was a protection against you and so were reflections, hence why I fashioned that particular eyewear. It takes some getting used to, of course, but that refraction is enough to counteract the power. I didn't guess that on my own. That knowledge was a lesson learned from the past."

Cimree focused on her right foot, and it slid out of the boot strapped to the chair. Then her left.

Theo paused his work suddenly and Cimree held still. Had he heard her freeing herself? She watched him closely. He set down the pestle, reached back into the pouch, and dropped about five or six more seeds into the bowl.

"That should be sufficient," he muttered to himself.

Cimree rose from the chair on silent stockinged feet and grabbed his wrist as he reached for the pestle again, wrenching his arm behind his back and shoving his belly into the edge of the worktable. He grunted in surprise.

"Maybe you'd like to eat some of your own concoction?" she said in a warning voice.

"Oh dear," he groaned in surprise.

"Sit in the chair, Theo. I could break your neck if I wanted to."

"I believe you could," he said, a shudder rippling through him.

"If you try to shout for help—"

"I w-won't. I realize that would be very foolish. I am not trained in the various martial prowesses. I'm utterly inept at them in fact. I beg you n-not to kill me. There is too much I haven't transcribed, and I don't want my life to be forfeit quite yet."

"Then sit down in the chair."

She eased the firm grip on his arm, and he instinctively massaged his shoulder. Head down, he went to the chair and willingly submitted as she undid the knots and used the same bonds to secure his wrists. She then untied the ropes that still held her boots and tugged them back on.

"How did you escape if you don't mind my asking? The knots were still tied, and I'm certain they were sufficiently tight."

"I'd rather not share all my secrets with you, Theo," Cimree answered. She went back to the workbench and peered into the shadowed mortar bowl.

"I was going to steep that into a tea," Theo said. "I'm certain that dose would have killed you. It would have made you very sick regardless. But it felt more...humane instead of...well..."

"Instead of what?"

Theo swallowed. "B-Beheading you. It is possible your power might remain intact after you are dead. Since your eyes don't even need to be open for it to work, I thought saving your head to study later might be prudent."

What an awful confession. But Cimree did not sense any malice in it. Theo was not as socially astute as others. But his mind was certainly full of useful facts.

"Is Jodocus still in the fortress?"

"I believe so," Theo replied. "There are tunnels and chambers dug into the hillside. He's belowground. The upper rooms are where he's keeping his harem. Interestingly enough, they're more his hostages than actual concubines. He still adheres to the law of celibacy, from what I've observed. Although one tribal princess seems to fascinate him. I've seen her in his company more than once this winter, so there's a marked preference for her."

"You're trying to help me?" Cimree asked.

"Being useful serves many purposes."

"What is her name?"

"Spozhmay. Daughter of the Eagle Clan chieftain."

"I'm going to gag you, Theo. If I didn't, it would be suspicious."

"Please d-don't. I have a terrible aversion to having things stuffed into my mouth. I'm certain I'd vomit and choke to death. I'd much prefer a faster, efficient solution. I've a tonic that will render someone unconscious very fast. It's on the table, the tall vial with the cork."

Cimree walked to the table and pointed to one.

"That's the one," Theo said. "Put it on a rag and cover my face with it, and I'll be asleep until they find me."

"Won't they suspect you cooperated with me?"

"I find the angel sworn rather naive when it comes to artifice. You seem to be an exception."

Cimree lifted the vial and twisted off the cork stopper, careful to keep it away from herself. She took a rag and doused it with the liquid and stood behind Theo. His shoulders were slumped in defeat.

She held it against his nose, and Theo slumped forward, the weight of his body making the ropes stretch a little. His eyelids were partly open in a daze.

Cimree put the cork back and slipped the vial and the rag into her pocket. Uorsin had promised that if she didn't return by dawn, he would seek her. She paused, studying the table, and then flung the powder from the mortar onto the floor and scattered it with her boot heel.

An angel sworn passed Cimree in the corridor, totally oblivious that she'd blended with the wall. As soon as he was past, she stepped silently behind him, using the cloth and tonic to smother him, and he toppled listlessly, but she caught him before his armored body could clatter against the stone tiles. She removed his grafting wand first and then armed herself with a curved dagger from his hip.

She'd discovered one of the underground passages when she noticed tremors from it and had located the entrance after following the rumbles from beneath. By hiding in the shadows and observing, she located the trapdoor used to come up from below, similar to the kind the Ecbatanans employed. She hunkered down near a large decorative vase and watched as several angel sworn went through the hatch, waiting until only the tremors of one man remained, and then seized the opportunity to disable him and hide the body.

Sensing no nearby tremors, Cimree went back to the trapdoor and hoisted the rope handle, revealing an inconspicuous alcove. After pulling on the handle and lifting the door, she went down the steps. The growing light from the approaching dawn would have made lingering in the palace more difficult and dangerous, but in the darkness of the tunnels, she was more assured. For all she knew, Theo was still bound to the chair, for no alarm had been sounded.

With catlike grace, she padded into the alcove and began to search. There were vibrations aplenty on this level. She kept the cowl of her cloak down so she could use her roused serpents to spy in all directions at once.

The tunnels were a maze of doorways and aisles splitting in different directions at expertly cut angles in the stone. Venturing down one, she saw no markings on the floor or near the ceiling to identify location or direction. She backtracked the way she'd come, but the thrum of passage came from the stairs.

She slipped into a nook and summoned her natural camouflage to disguise herself. An angel sworn in cloak and hauberk stormed down the passageway at a determined pace, sword held in hand. As he left Cimree's location, she ventured after him. It seemed to her that the fellow was a messenger and might lead her directly to Jodocus.

Lifting her cowl to cover her head, she followed at a discreet distance, able to match her speed to the trembling sense in the stone his passage made, although there were other conflicting vibrations as well.

The angel sworn turned down two different intersections before reaching an unguarded door. The keystone at the top of its rounded stone arch bore no symbol. The angel sworn did not even knock but burst into the room.

"Archangel, she's escaped!" the fellow said with a snarl.

Cimree held off briefly, but when the person entered and tried to swing the wooden door shut, she intervened and stopped it from latching with the toe of her boot. She gripped her dagger handle expectantly. Light from a fire blazed in a brazier full of steaming black stones. The heat from it blinded her vision momentarily, but she promptly made out the occupants. Jodocus in a tunic and belt, the Tay al-Ard tucked into the front.

"She was dead earlier," Jodocus answered with a tone of confusion. "I saw it myself."

"My lord, it was no doubt a ruse on her part," the angel sworn said. "Paracelsus was trussed up in the chair in her place, drugged. And I just found Helios sprawled out in the corridor above. His distaff is missing. And an empty scabbard at his belt."

"No!" Jodocus exclaimed.

"There were three reports of snake attacks in the city last night."

"Snake attacks? Who was attacked?"

"The locals. In three different sections of the city, the night watch was disturbed by people hurrying for healers to treat the injured. I was suspicious at the second report. When the third arrived, I was dispatched at once to find Theo and discovered him unconscious. My lord, she is free! And I believe she's *here* in the fortress still."

Jodocus's fingers closed around the Tay al-Ard. "I've already sent the advance force to attack the caves."

"What about Trinati? Did they catch her?"

"No," Jodocus said with fury. "She had the advantage in the dark, but there's no question she's heading back to the caves to warn them. We're short on soldiers right now. I thought the threat was over."

"The threat has only begun, it appears. What are your orders?"

"Double the guard on where we're keeping the prisoners," Jodocus said. "If they knew our numbers, they'd revolt. Even without distaffs, they'd be a threat. If anyone tries to escape, order the archers to shoot."

"What about the reports of the serpents?"

"It's her, I tell you. She's causing it. Have them kill all the snakes. She'll use them against us."

"As you will, my lord."

"I'm going to evacuate the concubines from the fortress. If any of them become stone, the chieftains will revolt."

Cimree smirked, grateful that Jodocus was so talkative when he was stressed.

"I'll tell them myself," said the messenger.

"No, I will."

And Jodocus was gone, dashed away by the magic of the Tay al-Ard. Silence fell.

She sensed the messenger returning to the door and hid herself to one side. He didn't even glance her way when he left.

A moment later, he was on the ground, stunned, and Cimree dragged him back inside Jodocus's room.

Twelve
Cornered

The sun burned in the sky by the time Cimree made it to the corner and reached the street she sought, a bag hoisted over her shoulder, full of distaffs. She had gathered thirty of them from a trove in the fortress. Getting off the rocky mound had proven tedious and slow, but the camouflage of the surrounding talus had allowed her to blend in and sneak away despite the brightening sky. With the cowl covering her head, she slunk back into the city.

The closer she came to the street, the more snakes she sensed. The variety was new to her but seemed common in the mountainous area. They were a breed of viper with serrated scales and a bronze-and-gold pattern. Instead of hissing in warning, these vipers coiled tightly, and when they got agitated, the sawtooth scales caused friction and a sizzling sound. A few streets back, she'd seen one leap at a frightened passerby to strike. The townsfolk were using staves as they made their errands for food, but these serpents were aggressive and didn't shun the people. The warmth in the air from the sun was unusual, and serpents were sunning themselves on every street.

Cimree ventured down the final street, searching for signs of being followed, but there were none. She could feel the power of the statue on the rooftop radiating its summoning signal, gathering the serpents to Koa like some invisible draw.

When she reached their hideout, she knocked the code to alert Uorsin and Avari that she'd returned. The door handle twisted and the door opened, revealing shadows.

Cimree entered, careful to avert her face from them and unslung the bag from her shoulder.

"I was about to head after you," Uorsin said gruffly.

"Better that you didn't. There are snakes everywhere," Cimree said. "But even more here, so close to the statue on the roof. I'm sorry it took so long to get back. They had a trap waiting for me, but I managed to escape."

"So you didn't get the Tay al-Ard?" Uorsin said with a disappointed tone.

"Jodocus still has it. They sent a host of angel sworn to attack the caves last night."

"We'd better get back ourselves, then," Uorsin replied.

"I agree," Avari said. "There's little good we can do here."

"Actually, there is some good. I went to the area where they're holding the prisoners. We have allies here. Without grafting wands, they'll be unable to escape. I made contact and promised to help."

"How many are we talking about?" Avari asked.

"Dozens, maybe more," Cimree answered. "They deserve a chance to escape the destruction."

"Do you know where Jodocus is?" Uorsin wondered.

"I came very close to Jodocus. But he disappeared before I could reach him. He's leading an evacuation. He knows I'm still in the city," Cimree answered. "And he's doubled the guard over the prisoners with orders to kill anyone who tries to escape."

"Doubling the guard will make freeing the prisoners even more challenging," Uorsin said.

"Jodocus is overreacting because he hasn't left enough people to defend Koa," Cimree explained. "With distaffs, the captured angel sworn will at least stand a chance. And escaping will be easier if so many have already fled."

"So do we hunker down here and wait until nightfall again?" Uorsin asked.

"No," Cimree said, setting down the bag. "We need to get these distaffs to the prisoners and urge them to fight their way free. They outnumber the ones guarding them. I can get back into the camp easily enough."

A creak sounded from a floorboard above them. Cimree froze. She hadn't sensed any vibrations to warn her that danger was near.

Uorsin reached for his hammer and slowly picked it up. Avari drew a scimitar. Cimree held her breath, straining to hear any further signs of movement.

Another creak from a different location in the dwelling sounded.

Then the noise of a crashing door from the back of the house. Wood splintered and broke.

"They found us!" Avari gasped in shock. He sped to the front door, grabbing the handle.

"No!" Cimree warned, but the panic had overrun Avari, and he rushed outside. He made it two steps before multiple arrows pierced him. Groaning in pain, he fell backward, and another arrow struck him in the heart, killing him.

Cimree grabbed Uorsin by the tunic and pulled him against the wall, enveloping them both in her serpentine affinity, making them blend in with the woodwork pattern. Thrums came from the floorboards above and from the back of the house on their level. Cimree lowered her head and tried to calm her racing heart. Had someone followed her back to the building, then? Someone she hadn't seen because she'd covered herself so as not to injure anyone else? Frustration mounted inside her.

Three angel sworn burst into the room from the lower floor,

mirror blades at the ready. One wore the armor of the Morgarten and had two blades, one in each hand. They all had the wrappings over their eyes and the glass to protect them from seeing her.

"Callum!" shouted the Morgarten angrily.

"No one upstairs!" came a loud reply.

"They're here," the Morgarten said menacingly. "One tried to flee."

A shadow appeared in the doorway. Another Morgarten with a bow and arrow had landed deftly at the door. "One fled. Wasn't her," he said.

"She's in here."

"There's the bag!" cried out another, kneeling down by it and pulling open the mouth. "It's full of distaffs!"

Cimree felt Uorsin trembling with rage. His muscles went taut. She had her hand on his arm, connecting them by touch, warning him to stay still.

Both of the Morgarten were suspicious and careful. They moved slowly in the room, their weapons poised. Soon another joined. Then another. Cimree's stomach began to shrink.

"She's in here," one of them muttered. "Hiding. Search the walls."

They began dragging their weapons across the planks. It was only a matter of time before their concealment was lost. The venom surged into Cimree's saliva and beneath her fingernails, a visceral response to the danger they were in. Part of her wanted to hiss in warning.

Uorsin lunged into the room, swinging his hammer at one of the Morgarten's skulls. The warrior reacted and evaded the blow, countering with a savage sweep of his mirror blade, which cut deeply into Uorsin's side.

The formidable blacksmith roared in pain and outrage and swept his hammer around, catching an underling in the shoulder so hard that Cimree heard the bones break. Yelps and cries burst in the room. Uorsin was outnumbered, but still he fought them off, using his hammer to bruising effect. One of the Morgarten stabbed him again, another angel sworn piercing him from behind. The one with the bow backed to the door to block the escape.

Cimree slowly moved toward him, and she summoned the serpents on the street to come join the fight.

One of the angel sworn had grabbed Uorsin's arm, the one with the hammer, but he used his fist as a weapon and punched the fellow in the jaw, stunning him.

The Morgarten at the door did not give way, even when serpents began striking him from behind. His leather armor protected him from their fangs. She could hear the sizzling sound the serpents made. Then one of them leaped and flew up at the Morgarten, biting him in the hand that held the bow. The serpent hung from his hand, and the man's face twisted with revulsion and pain. He smashed the serpent against the doorpost, killing it, but another jumped at him and bit his cheek.

"Cimree!"

She spotted Uorsin on his knees. The Morgarten gripped the blacksmith by his hair, holding his neck up. The mirror blade was an inch from his throat.

"Surrender, or I'll cut off his head!" the Morgarten shouted. "His life is worth more to us than to die in so petty a way. And I recognize his friendship means a great deal to you and Azra."

Cimree saw the determination on the warrior's face. Several others had fallen and were convulsing on the floor in agony. The Morgarten who'd been bitten twice flung the serpent on the floor and crushed it with his boot. But the toxin was working. She noticed the mottled signs of pain on his face.

"Cimree," warned the one holding Uorsin. He brought the blade right up to Uorsin's neck, and she saw the razor-sharp edge depress his skin. If she lunged at him, he could finish the stroke.

"I've made my peace," Uorsin said resolutely. "Just kill me, then."

The look on Uorsin's face wrenched her heart. The grief at

Darcia's betrayal, the anger at his attackers, his willingness to sacrifice himself so that she might escape. She was confident she could fight her way clear. But it would mean losing Uorsin. Azra's friend.

Her friend.

"Spare him," she pleaded, stepping forward.

"Cimree, no!" Uorsin pleaded.

She watched a drop of blood trickle down his throat. The Morgarten seemed on the verge of slaying the blacksmith in front of her.

"No more bloodshed," Cimree said, holding up her hands.

"Wise choice," the Morgarten said coldly. "Now send away the serpents! Do it now, or I swear on the Oldknow that I'll finish him."

Cimree rebuked the serpents and sent them away from the dwelling. Two had perished in the fight. More had gathered in the street outside the door. The bitten soldier leaned against the wall, his breathing hard as he endured the venom's painful wrath.

"Cimree," Uorsin gasped, crestfallen. He'd been willing to sacrifice himself. But she wasn't willing to accept such a high price.

"Let him go," Cimree said. "Let them *all* go. What reason can you possibly have to keep the angel sworn imprisoned? We have enough enemies to last a lifetime."

"The first law of heaven is obedience," said the Morgarten with a sneer. "You never learned that. Not truly. I remember when you betrayed the Queen Mother. When you stole a piece of fruit and turned yourself into a baby. A coward's move. You will face justice for what you've done. Justice that is long overdue. Kneel so we may bind you."

She paused, wishing she knew whether what she was doing was right or not. Should she fight?

Nothing. No whispers warned her.

"Quickly, Cimree. Only my strong forbearance has spared him thus far. I *will* kill him."

Would Azra have done the same? Or would he have already anticipated that they'd been followed and planned for escape earlier on? She missed him fiercely.

Cimree knelt on the wooden floor and crossed her hands behind her back.

Magic is natural, for nature itself is magic. Is it not magical that all our nourishment becomes ourselves? Do we not eat ourselves into being? Every bite we take contains in itself all our organs, all that is included in the whole person, all of that which we comprise. Do we not eat bone, blood vessels, ligaments, and entrails? Bone does not make bone, nor brain make brain, but every bite contains all these. Is that not magic? Therefore, can we not, through metamorphistry, connect joint and bone, blood and brain?

— The Hermetic and Alchemical Writings of Paracelsus

Thirteen
Cavern Webs

Azra awoke gradually, the pounding in his skull drumming with the beat of his heart. His head felt swollen and tight with pressure, and it took a moment for him to realize he was suspended upside down, his arms and legs lashed so tightly he could scarcely move.

Nausea and body aches riddled him. He'd never been so sick before. When he tried to move, his body swayed, which brought dizziness. His eyeballs felt the pressure even worse. Opening his eyelids, he could hardly see past a filmy skein covering his face.

"You're awake, Azra?"

He recognized Darcia's voice. Memories pulsed along with his heartbeat. Since receiving the Dryad's kiss, he had become able to recall events perfectly. He had ventured into the tunnel to consider how to free the golem, where he'd been bitten by spiders before the venom had robbed him of awareness.

"Where are we?" he asked, his voice thick. Thirst added to his weakened state.

"Inside the mountain still," she answered. Her voice had a muffled quality to it, an absorption of some kind. Not the echoes of a large cavern. Squinting, he tried to find her in the dark. A little light could be seen in the distance, but not much.

"I didn't know your affinity was with spiders," he said, deducing this through several details, including how he'd carried a spider on his cloak to Chrys and the Gallows Tree.

"The Queen Mother knew," Darcia said slyly. "Many breeds of spider are solitary, but my affinity is with the kind that are social. That work together to build vast webs that can trap larger prey. Now, just to clarify, Azra. You have the fireblood and can easily burn yourself free. The spiders guarding you will bite you if you try. And in your weakened state, any more venom will kill you."

He realized that the stickiness on his exposed skin was webbing. How long had he been unconscious? He was encased in webs.

"I also have your distaff and weapons. In a fight between us, I think I favor my chances since the venom is weakening you right now. I'd like to keep you alive as leverage with Cimree should she unexpectedly return."

Uorsin. Azra felt a gut-wrench of disappointment for his friend. Had he been duped or a willing accomplice?

"Why reveal yourself now?" Azra asked. He wanted a drink, but even if he could get one, how would he manage to swallow when dangling this way?

"You forced me to."

"How?"

"I had to stop you from unleashing the golem," she said in disbelief. "That's a very bad idea. I've tried killing it, but it's impervious to all venoms and poisons."

"I'm thirsty," Azra said.

"You've been trained to suffer deprivations. You'll manage somehow."

"You surprised me, Darcia. I've never suspected you."

"Thank you for being honest, at least. The others were easy to deceive. But I've had to be especially careful around you."

"Your talkativeness has always been off-putting to me."

"Especially to *you*, Azra. It is my nature to be inquisitive, social, and friendly. When the Queen Mother assigned me the mission to Montheron, I had to play more than just one role. Trinati never knew that I was the Queen Mother's instrument. Nor Wegner. Why was I chosen, of all people, to accompany Cimree to the island fortress? I had to play my part well."

"You did so flawlessly," Azra said. Pieces fit together in his mind. Her purpose was to use him against Cimree, which meant that she was still alive. Thank the Oldknow for that.

"I enjoy praise as much as anyone does, but I also realize you're biding your time and trying to figure out a way to escape. You are the most dangerous of my foes, Azra. Even more dangerous than Cimree. I won't hesitate to kill you."

"That seems reasonable. If I were free right now, I'd probably kill you. I'm surprised I'm still alive."

"I'm not vicious, Azra. But I cannot have you lingering about either. I'm willing to allow you and Cimree to be outcasts. You can be the first parents of a new race of snakelings. Now that we're safe from all the golem's minions, the angel sworn can weather the storm while the new Gallows Tree grows. I'm a little confused about the girl, however. Chrys. I'm not sure what to make of her. She doesn't live in the village. She lives near the tree. I can't track her."

"You don't expect me to tell you, do you?"

"No. But I do like conversation. You have an interesting story as well. The Queen Mother told me all about it. It must be painful being back here where you lost Delara."

"I didn't lose her. She was murdered." Azra said it tonelessly.

"What, no resentment? Bitterness? Anger?"

"I wasted too many years with those festering emotions," Azra said. "They were poison to me. Venom in my blood."

"And gentle Cimree has healed you," Darcia said. "Well, not so gentle now. I wish you hadn't brought her back, Azra. But what's done is done."

The aches throughout his body had not lessened. The toxin from the spiders had thoroughly weakened him. "So if I understand things, Jodocus was named archangel simply to replace Trinati, not because he is going to rule the angel sworn. You are."

"Indeed. Do you really believe she would have allowed a *man* to dominate? Or even be her equal?"

"I don't know what she was thinking in her final hours. She'd been betrayed by those she'd trusted."

"Trinati's betrayal hurt her the most," Darcia said. "And then she betrayed Cimree in Ecbatana. Clearly, she wasn't fit to rule."

"And you are?"

"I'm more like the Queen Mother than Trinati was. Able to notice subtleties. Willing to do the hard tasks that need doing."

"I was the same way," Azra said. "I was her destroying angel. How many deaths did I needlessly cause because she didn't value a mortal's life?"

"That's too simplistic, Azra. Mortals quibble and bicker and start wars with each other. They embrace the lures of Asmodeus and fall under his sway. Generations have come and generations will go. We'll survive this and begin anew."

"If we'd stayed in Clairvaux, we'd all be dead. Cimree had enough courage to act. Courage that brought us this far. She never wanted to lead."

"That is where you and I must disagree," Darcia countered. "She has a defiant spirit."

"That is where you and *I* must disagree," Azra shot back.

"I watched her blunders in Ecbatana. So painful. So embarrassing. She's inexperienced. She depends on everyone else to help her make up her mind."

Azra wanted to laugh. So Darcia didn't understand how Cimree had transformed back into her old self, regaining her past memories.

"And you consider that a sin, a weakness? Or are you jealous you weren't asked to be on the high council?"

"You think jealousy is my motive? Please, Azra. Have a little more faith in me. Leadership is meaningless without a way to enforce commands. The Morgarten have pledged their loyalty to me, the Queen Mother's successor. They are coming—now—to conquer the tunnels. Those who are not angel sworn will be expelled."

That meant Andrin and his entire family. Ramesh and Yasmin. Of course. It was precisely the kind of action that Lilith would have taken. The relationships forged meant nothing compared to the edicts of faithfulness.

"And instead of forming your own community, you take over ours," Azra said with disgust.

"You planted the Gallows Tree, Azra, not I. It wasn't my choice to put it in Tirich Mir. You condemned the others with your actions. But as I said, I'm not vindictive. Those who are not willing to swear fealty will be free to leave."

"Free to be destroyed you mean."

"If that is their choice, Azra."

"What you are doing is unjust, Darcia, and you know it."

"And did everyone get a say to allow a stone-changer to live amongst us? Were we permitted to object to summoning the golem and caging it? Or to unleash it on Koa? You were so desperate to have your companion, your helpmeet, that you were willing to risk all of our lives because of selfishness. Be honest with yourself for once, Azra. You forsook the ways of the Oldknow to fulfill your carnal desires. And we're all being punished for it."

Azra's body swayed slightly. He listened to her rebuke, her scorn. Anger churned inside him. But he quenched it. Of course Darcia had attributed his motives this way. He and Cimree had wanted to save as many lives as possible. The angel sworn were the insular ones. The close-knit tribe granted immortality and disdained lesser mortals for being weak and easily beguiled.

"Let me go and I'll leave the tunnels now," Azra said.

He heard the soft scrape of her boots as she approached and then crouched so she was level with his face.

"If I've learned anything about you, Azrael, it is that you are relentless. You're my hostage in case Cimree returns. And if she dies in Koa, then at least I'll remember that you can always fall in love again with someone else."

The painful words were intentional, but Azra didn't feel it. Her boots skittered as she stepped away, and then she leaped and all fell silent. Was she traveling along the spiderwebs? Who was her next target? Odeon?

Azra shut his eyes, settled his feelings, and summoned a spirit messenger. In an instant, the chamber's murky darkness was expelled. A blue flickering light hovered by his head, sending inquisitive thoughts to him, asking how it might help. The cave he was in was swathed in cobwebs. The black shapes of spiders scuttled along the network of silk. Some smaller animals had been captured and bound and were the object of feasting. Some larger shapes too, all cocooned and unrecognizable. The veil of webs made it impossible to tell what part of the underground tunnel he was in. Clearly Darcia had been exploring.

The light danced eagerly, drawing his attention to it. Even if he could have escaped his bondage, he was too weak to walk.

Seek Andrin. Bring him here. Be patient until he follows you. Guide him to me.

Azra watched the glowing whorl dash through the tunnel, taking the light away. He thought he felt the tickle of spider legs across his cheek and held very, very still.

FOURTEEN
WARNING

The angel sworn gripping Cimree's arms clenched harder, and she could tell they were ascending ever higher from the sense of weightlessness. She dangled between them as they were buffeted by the wind. Her head was wrapped in linen to protect them and others from her. A lump of fear had settled into her abdomen. The rising must mean they were flying up the hill that held the fortress at the edge of Koa. Escaping a second time would be even more difficult, if not impossible.

The sensation of falling made her stomach squirm, and then her boots scraped against the ground. The angel sworn settled her but maintained their sturdy hold on her arms. The tips of their fingers dug into her muscles painfully.

"Come with us, demon," one of them muttered savagely. She nearly tripped as they began walking.

Blinded by the fabric covering her eyes, Cimree didn't know where they were going, but the clip of their boots against polished stone was joined by echoes. She smelled food, although she wasn't hungry, a familiar dish made by the tribes in the region. What was it called?

"You caught her?" asked another voice from ahead of them, one she didn't recognize.

"Uorsin as well," replied one of her captors.

"Excellent news! The archangel will be pleased."

"Where is he?"

"He just returned from safeguarding the concubines in another palace. All but Spozhmay, that is. She refused to leave. They're at the audience hall."

Cimree remembered the name. She was the one Theo had told her about, the Eagle chieftain's daughter.

"Tell the archangel we have her."

"I'll return shortly," replied the newcomer, and she felt the vibrations of his steps fading.

"Where is Uorsin?" Cimree asked. "His wounds are serious."

"That's why he's being tended by a healer. That's all you need know."

Soon after, the fellow returned. "Bring her to the audience hall."

They tugged on her arms again and she kept up with their pace, remembering her visit to the palace during the night. How would Jodocus respond to her? Would he execute her? Every urge she had to free herself had been tempered with the impression to be patient. Ahead, she heard furtive voices, including that of a woman.

The captors brought her inside and forced Cimree to her knees.

"You were found with a bag of distaffs," Jodocus said smugly. "Instead of fleeing for your life, you tried to lead a revolt against me."

"I was trying to save their lives," Cimree answered. "That's why I came in the first place."

"You couldn't even save yourself."

"The end is almost here, Jodocus. Enough warnings have been given."

"The only warning I needed was the one the Queen Mother conveyed to me not to trust you. You have been treacherous from the start."

"The Queen Mother was warned and she refused to listen. Now you are making the same mistake."

"Do not speak to the archangel thus!" snarled one of her captors. He sounded angry enough to strike her.

"No, let her speak," Jodocus said with a tone of unconcern. "I'm not afraid of her lies."

"Unfortunately, you are afraid of the truth," Cimree said.

"Please enlighten me," Jodocus said with a chuckle.

"Your plan will not work."

"How do *you* know my plans?" he replied with disdain.

"I know that Darcia is your inside help. She's probably told you about the statues and how they keep the monsters out of the tunnels. She's also told you about the Gallows Tree and where we planted it. But there are secrets not even she knows."

"And are you going to tell me these secrets, Cimree? Are you bargaining for your life?"

"I'm trying to persuade you with reason."

Jodocus snorted. "So far, you are failing. But please. Go on."

"Many centuries ago, the Queen Mother was visited by a wayfarer from another world. By a messenger from the Oldknow named Ilyas, who warned about the evil times we live in. Have you heard this before?"

"The more appropriate question is how you learned of this?" Jodocus said.

"It is in the Sefer Raziel, the Book of Secrets."

"What does that mean?" Jodocus said. "Another trick perhaps. But please, do go on."

He sounded so doubtful and pompous that she wanted to scream at him. Patience. She had to be patient. "The statues will keep the monsters out. That is true. You will be safe in the tunnels. For a time."

"And?" Jodocus pressed.

"You will run out of food. And you cannot leave the tunnels. If you do, the golem and its creations will destroy you."

"I understand that Wegner stored ample provisions," Jodocus said confidently. "And once we expel those who are not angel sworn, there will be more than sufficient."

"There won't be enough," Cimree said. "Especially if you cast out the rest."

"You said you were going to reason with me, but your logic doesn't make sense. Honestly, I didn't expect it to. Darcia said you were planning to shelter the entire village inside the tunnels. What were you going to feed them with? Compassion?"

"The Oldknow will provide for us."

"Ah, that makes perfect sense now." He chuffed.

"Jodocus, listen to me."

"I am trying to be patient, Cimree. But you tax my long-suffering with your nonsense."

"The words that Ilyas gave her spoke of how we would survive the devastation. These are the words, Jodocus. Let me recite them to you from the Sefer Raziel."

"My lord," one of the angel sworn said warningly, "she is attempting to deceive you. Didn't she *steal* the book?"

"If I let you read it for yourself, would you believe it?" Cimree pleaded.

"Speak. I will listen," Jodocus said.

"My lord!" insisted the other angel sworn.

"I didn't ask for your counsel or warning!" Jodocus barked at the fellow. "Be silent!"

That was just how Trinati would have done it. Cimree bowed her head, feeling it was futile to persuade them. But she had to try.

"This is from the Sefer Raziel. I quote it word for word. 'And the Oldknow sent the servant of the covenant—the archangel, the messenger, the watcher—to Lan and to Havah and imparted wisdom on how to be restored into the presence of the Oldknow.

They were commanded to build edifices of stone of intricate make and of craftsmanship exquisite. To adorn these with beautiful ornaments as can be the best offerings of artificers in brass, copper, gold, silver, and glass. And to make a plate of gold alloy and engrave on it as a signet these runes—Qodes Adonai.'" She paused, catching her breath. Her shoulders were tingling. Heat had begun to sizzle inside her. As she continued, her voice throbbed with certainty. "'And the power of the Oldknow would descend upon the edifice and protect it from intruders, enemies, and the myriads of evil *so long as* those who bear this signet are one in purpose, one in heart, one in mind, and suffer no poor to dwell among them. And the servant of the covenant swore on oath that the Oldknow would abide gates to open, to restore their offspring to Idumea, the dwelling place on high.'"

Silence settled on the hall after her little speech. Then Cimree heard another voice. A woman's voice. "I believe her."

"Spozhmay," Jodocus murmured with derision.

"Is that why the Queen Mother failed?" one of the other angel sworn demanded. "Because she allowed the poor to live among us at Clairvaux?"

"No," Jodocus said. "It means not to allow anyone to be poor. Not to have classes of people. Rich or poor. And we did not have that in Clairvaux. All who were willing to accept the oaths were welcomed. The prophecy you speak of, Cimree, obviously failed, for Clairvaux was destroyed."

"It was destroyed because the Queen Mother followed the actions, but she did not accept it in her heart."

"You judge her worthiness based on some ancient script." Jodocus snorted. "I've listened to you, Cimree. You act out of fear. We will survive this, and we will restore Clairvaux to its former glory."

She spoke more forcefully. "You will starve to death in the caves or be killed by the gévaudan."

"I don't believe you," Jodocus fired back. "You lost. Your

gambit failed. You are a curse and an abomination. And just like the serpent in the valley, you seek to deceive us."

She remembered Iddawc and what his name truly meant. *Enmity.* That was the feeling she sensed from these angel sworn. But Iddawc's power had not roused it.

"Jodocus, we need to gather all of the angel sworn to the caves. And everyone else who is willing to come. We can feed them all. I promise you. If you take over, it will mean extinction."

"That's enough," Jodocus said. "Take her to Theo. And stay there until she is truly dead."

"My lord husband," Spozhmay said. "Do not treat her thus. Her words are an omen."

"That is a superstition," Jodocus retorted.

"I feel the truth of her words," Spozhmay declared.

"You suffer with fear," Jodocus said. "And I will end the serpent queen's reign. Take her now."

"No!" Spozhmay yelled, and Cimree felt the magic of the Tanaquil medallion surging. Gasps sounded from the others. Cimree tried to remove the swath of linen around her head, but one of the captors kicked her in the back violently and dropped her on her stomach. He knelt on her spine, causing spasms of pain.

"Release her!" Spozhmay shrieked.

"She has the amulet!" someone shouted.

A rush of magical wind roared through the room. The man kneeling on Cimree's back scuttled away, driven by the mental terror blasting them all. Cimree felt protected from it, encased in a shield that blunted its force. How had the chieftain's daughter managed to get the medallion?

Azra was still connected to it, she realized. The bond between him and the amulet had not been severed, merely suspended after they'd removed it from Cimree's neck. He was controlling Spozhmay with it. Azra was trying to protect her.

A hand gently settled on Cimree's, and someone tried to help her rise. A feminine hand. The exotic fragrance she wore made

Cimree believe it was Spozhmay. She helped Cimree bring a knee up, despite the pain flaring in her back, and to stand. The roar of feelings, of both terror and command, thrummed in the room. The angel sworn were stunned by it.

Spozhmay gripped Cimree by the elbow and began to pull her away.

"N-Nooo!" Jodocus moaned in agony.

Suddenly Spozhmay went limp and collapsed. Cimree caught her, the magic quenching, the emotions guttering out.

Jodocus was sobbing. She knew exactly where he was. Some emotional toll had been dealt him. The medallion's magic had been unnerving and compromised him. The others were dazed as well.

Cimree lunged for Jodocus, trying to find the Tay al-Ard. He gripped her wrist, then caught her hand. Venom surged in her mouth, but her face was still veiled so she couldn't bite him. With her free hand, which was tingling with more venom and flushed the skin beneath her nails, she groped at his waist and found his tunic belt. Her fingers brushed against the Tay al-Ard.

Jodocus kicked her in the stomach, sending her sprawling. Two large male bodies tackled her to the floor and wrestled her into submission.

Jodocus gasped, his voice thick with emotion. "Take h-her out of my sight!"

Cimree kicked one of her attackers in the groin, and he choked in pain as he rolled off her. Blows rained down on her. A kick to her breast. A boot against her thigh. Her arm was torqued back until she cried out in pain and submitted. She'd touched the Tay al-Ard. She'd grazed it with her fingertips.

"Jodocus! Jodocus!" someone screamed, running into the audience hall.

All was mayhem. Pain exploded in her tailbone and her chest. She didn't cease her struggles, but they'd overpowered her.

"Jodocus! The serpents are everywhere! And they're flying now! They are flying at us!"

Cimree heard the words but didn't comprehend them. What had the newcomer said? The serpents unleashed on Koa had been attacking people. But what did he mean?

Snakes couldn't fly.

And as if in response to that thought, the bone in her leg began to ache anew.

Fifteen
The Coming

The familiar ache. Ever since the golem had healed Cimree's broken leg in Ecbatana, she had been able to discern its approach with an uncomfortable feeling that stirred beneath her skin and muscle. The golem hadn't just restored her bone; no, she suspected it had switched hers with one of its own, which meant it could follow her wherever she went. And the sudden resurgence of that pain meant the cage in Tirich Mir no longer held it prisoner.

The golem had arrived in Koa.

And just as it had in Montheron, Clairvaux, Ecbatana, and the caves of Tirich Mir, it would find a use for whatever creatures it discovered by twisting them into something even more deadly, even more lethal. The serpents she'd summoned were being transformed into flying ones.

The angel sworn who had subdued her were carrying her through the fortress halls, and she could only assume they were obeying Jodocus's orders to take her to Theo to kill her.

"The golem has come," Cimree said as she was jostled between them.

"Be silent, betrayer!" one of them barked at her.

"I can't be silent; you're all going to die!" Cimree warned.

"I said be silent!"

"You saw what she did to Jodocus," said another.

"What I saw was pure evil."

Cimree clenched her hands into fists. They'd lashed her ankles together and her wrists behind her back. She could get free of the bonds again. But not with so many of them. She wondered what had taken place at the caves. Had Azra released the golem for some reason? Had Trinati returned and warned them about Darcia?

Events were unraveling too fast.

She heard the opening of a door, and then she was maneuvered into a room.

"You brought her back," Theo said with alarm.

"Jodocus wants her dead," said one of her captors. "He said to try another poison."

"I d-don't have one ready," Theo said nervously. "She ruined the last batch."

"What you need will be brought to you."

"I need pear or apple seeds. About a hundred. Just the seeds."

"Talix, see that it's done," said a commanding voice. "Bring them at once."

"I obey!" came the prompt reply, and then Cimree felt the vibrations of him leaving. She judged that four other angel sworn had accompanied them.

"Set her on the chair, please," Theo said. "And keep watch. She escaped the bonds last time."

Her handlers deposited her on the chair. It felt like the same one she'd been on before. So she was back in the same room. If only she'd managed to get the Tay al-Ard from Jodocus.

"Our blades might not be able to kill her permanently," said the spokesman of her guards. "We could never slay a gévaudan, but we could stab them and weaken them. We'll do the same to her. You've been warned, Cimree."

Cimree did not have the regenerative abilities of the gévaudan or the grimalkin. The bone in her leg had stopped aching as they carried her farther from the audience chamber, but it began to hurt again. The rest of her body ached from the punches and kicks levied against her earlier.

"The golem is here in the fortress," Cimree said.

"What?" Theo demanded.

"Be silent," said her captor angrily.

"I can sense when it's near," Cimree said.

"If it was here, someone would have raised the alarm," said another man.

"It can move invisibly," Cimree said. "It could be right in front of you, and you'd not see it."

A sudden blow against her head stunned her. Her serpent hair began to writhe in anger, although the serpents were all still suppressed by the linen wrapping.

"Please, there's no need for violence," Theo said placatingly.

"You defend her? Be careful, slave. You do as we say."

"Of course," Theo said meekly. But she sensed a hint of resentment.

"Asmodeus created the golem to destroy the angel sworn," Cimree said, preparing herself for another blow. "That is its nature. It uses whatever is available and transforms it into a new predator."

"You summoned the serpents," said one of the others. "They were already killing people. This is your fault, demon!"

"The golem made me into what I am," she said. "I didn't choose this. I'm telling you that the creature is here in the fortress. It knows where I am. And it will find me."

"Where is Talix?" murmured one of her captors.

"Should I search outside for him?" asked another.

That was soundly rejected by the man in charge. "We have our orders from the archangel. And we stay to fulfil them. She will say anything to save herself."

"I'm trying to save all of you," Cimree urged. "If the golem is here, then fleeing is the only option. Fleeing to Tirich Mir."

"Will you not be quiet!" shouted the leader.

"Wait, did you hear something?" interrupted another. Silence fell.

Cimree's leg pulsed ardently. Pounding vibrations told her that the golem was hastening down the corridor.

"It's here," she whispered.

"What can we do?" Theo asked suddenly.

"The amulet I wore was the only thing that could stop it," Cimree said. "Spozhmay has it."

The door opened, causing a hiss of surprise.

"It's Talix," someone muttered in relief.

"I have the seeds," Talix said from the doorway.

"Bring them here, and I'll grind them up," Theo said.

A yelp of surprise sounded.

"Shut the door! Shut the door!"

Cimree heard the door slam shut and confusion reigned. She wriggled free of the bonds at her wrists.

"Talix! Talix! What took him?"

A heavy object struck the door. With her hands free, Cimree pulled loose the wrapping covering her head. As she did so, she discovered Theo kneeling before her chair, using a dagger to saw the bonds at her ankles.

He stared up at her, wearing the matia band over his eyes. The door splintered and burst open. The angel sworn had their mirror blades at the ready, but they gaped in horror as the golem stood in the doorway, filling it with its massive sinewy frame.

Theo grabbed her by the wrist and pulled her to the door on the adjacent wall that led to the room she'd been inspecting before she'd been captured.

The golem roared and reached in, grabbing one of the angel sworn by his head before dragging him out and throwing him away. She heard the sound of his body smashing against the stone wall in the corridor outside the room.

Theo unlocked the door, twisted the handle, and pulled as the rest of her angel sworn captors rushed the monster, their shining blades swirling as they attacked, but she knew it would suffer no injury from their celestial-iron weapons. The golem was impervious to them.

She and Theo fled through the door. She noticed the fake Tay al-Ard was still on display, glowing with the light of the druid stone. Otherwise, the room was full of shadows, even though it was fully day outside.

"Can it see in the dark?" Theo demanded, his voice fraught with fear.

"Yes," she answered. "And we can't outrun it."

"Cim-reeeee!"

Its otherworldly voice screeched at her from the other room, filling her with alarm. It sounded furious.

"Does it need to breathe?" Theo enjoined.

"I don't know," Cimree answered, still searching for a way to escape. When she'd tried the door earlier, that's when the spider had bitten her. "How do we get out of here?"

A mangled body struck the doorframe they'd just gone through, and the dead angel sworn landed in a heap on the floor.

"I need more time!" Theo bellowed in fear, standing in the middle of the room and spinning around in confusion.

As there wasn't much in the room besides the bed and luxury furnishings, they had little to aid them. Cimree's heart galloped furiously.

The golem hissed and approached the doorway, dragging the last dead angel sworn in its claws. The scrape of the body against the floor was chilling.

"Cim-reeee," it crooned but in a vengeful way. It tossed the dead man aside.

"Close your eyes or you'll be blinded!" Theo shouted.

Cimree did so, but the explosion of light seared her. The golem gave a roar of pain, which was accompanied by a loud sizzling, hissing sound, and Theo grabbed her wrist and pulled her away. A burning smell filled the air, a scent that was metallic and stung her nostrils. Whatever he'd lit on fire was burning in the middle of the room still. Theo pulled her with him, and she stumbled along blindly, then heard the twisting of a door handle. Then a booming explosion sounded from the center of the fire, spraying them with cinders and robbing her of hearing temporarily.

Opening the door, Theo dragged her outside before shutting it behind them. She found Talix in a broken heap on the floor along with another one of her guards. Both were already dead. Theo put a smoking cylinder on the ground, and his hand was suddenly wreathed in blue flames that he used to ignite what appeared to be a handle. Theo had the fireblood? She hadn't known. He yanked on her arm with his other hand and began to run. They had hardly gone a few steps when another flash of light erupted behind them, followed a few seconds later by a secondary boom, which was muffled by the previous damage to her hearing.

Frantically, Theo pulled her after him to a set of stairs heading down. The ripples from the explosions still vibrated the ground. Another taste of salt in her mouth, and Cimree turned to see a woman warrior, brandishing a sword, turned to stone.

Theo gaped at the sudden transformation, his expression one of awe. Then he composed himself, although it was obvious that he wanted to study it further, and continued to flee down the steps.

When they reached the lower corridor, she was amazed to see angel sworn everywhere, fighting against flying serpents. Bat wings had been appended onto their sinuous bodies, giving them the power of flight, and they were entering through open windows to attack the angel sworn. Some of the angel sworn warriors had already collapsed from their venomous bites.

The ache in Cimree's leg was increasing again. She furtively looked back and spied the golem scuttling toward them like a spider, racing along the ceiling above the stairs. A silver disk dangled from around its neck.

Theo pointed away from the battle between the angel sworn and flying serpents, and they hurried down another corridor. He ran to a wooden door and opened it, revealing a winding staircase going underground. His eyes were livid with fear, but he seemed equally determined to save both their skins.

Once through, he shut the door.

"This p-passage is too small for s-something of its size," Theo said, panting.

"Don't count on it," Cimree said, wincing as her leg throbbed violently of a sudden. Her hearing was finally returning. "Run!"

They hastened down the spiral stairs. The door at the top was instantly pulverized, sending fragments of wood clattering down the stairs after them. Though she could have run faster, she was stymied because Theo was taking the stairs as fast he could.

They reached the final level and entered a corridor lit by torches. The air smelled of sewage.

"Is this a dungeon?" she asked him.

"Yes. And there are more angel sworn down here. Allies of yours. I just hope the metal door at the bottom is sturdier than the other ones!"

They reached the bottom of the steps and, as Theo had said, a large iron door blocked the way. He pounded on it.

Cimree could feel the golem padding down the stairs.

"Give me your dagger and I'll force the lock," Cimree said, holding out her hand.

"It will take you an hour to figure out the mechanism," Theo said, continuing to pound.

"Just give it to me!"

He did so, and Cimree squatted by the lock, releasing it in seconds. She had penetrated many such prisons before, and none of the locks had the sophistication of a device only Wegner could invent.

Theo gaped in surprise and pushed open the metal door. Suddenly, one of the golem's arms came out of nowhere and grabbed him by the neck. The arm was not connected to the rest of the golem's body. The shoulder was open and exposed quivering raw muscles and bones, but even though the appendage was detached, the monster could still control it and squeeze Theo's neck in its grip. Theo's eyes rolled back in his head in terror as the arm throttled him.

Cimree grabbed the smallest finger of the golem's disembodied hand and yanked it until the bone broke. A hiss of pain sounded from the stairwell behind them. With some struggle, she freed the rest of the appendage from Theo's neck and then pushed him into the room. There were no guards at all inside.

Theo stumbled a few paces, rubbing his throat. Cimree entered and shoved the door to close it. Before the latch could strike, a heavier bulk hit it from the other side and sent her sprawling.

She had no time to react as the golem reached down with its other arm and picked up the fallen limb, quickly reattaching it to itself. Its body had condensed and shrunken into a smaller but still sizable version of itself.

The Tanaquil medallion dangled from its neck, its shiny silver surface blotted with blood.

Theo whimpered behind her, backing away in terror.

The golem advanced, and Cimree stood, blocking its path.

"Cim-reee," it crooned again.

Sixteen
The Chaining

"What do you want from me?" Cimree asked the creature. The golem hissed at her and removed the medallion from around its neck. It extended the amulet to her, holding it by the cord.

Fear rolled off Theo as he panted behind her, slinking as far as he could into one of the back corners of the room.

Cimree stared at the dangling medallion. The golem was offering it to her?

"You want me to take it?" Cimree wondered.

"Take," snarled the golem angrily. Its head bumped up and down and clicking noises emitted from its throat. One of its two bulbous eyes remained focused on her, but the other shifted, staring past her. Teeth bared, the golem started toward Theo.

Cimree blocked its path with her own body. "No," she said. "Leave him alone."

The golem snarled at her, and her leg quivered as if some worm writhed beneath the skin. She watched the creature's muscles ripple and stretch as it grew larger.

"By the Fates," Theo groaned in despair. He was on his knees, cowering in terror, wedged into the farthest corner.

"No," Cimree said forcefully to the golem.

It swatted her aside with its empty hand and charged at Theo. Cimree rushed to intervene, grabbing the golem's arm as it lifted its claws for a killing blow. Even with all her strength, she couldn't arrest its powerful limb, but it paused as it twisted its neck to face her. Every muscle in its cheeks and chin and jaw could be seen through the transparent membrane that held it all together in place of skin. Although the effect was horrifying, she'd seen it before, up close. Her initial revulsion had turned to bewilderment on why it had been created that way.

"No!" Cimree said forcefully, pulling ineffectually on the arm she still held. "Don't kill!"

The golem hissed at her and lifted the hand gripping the cord with the Tanaquil medallion to offer the silver disk to her again.

"Take," it grunted.

She reached out with one hand to grasp the dangling amulet and released the golem so she could hold the cord with the other. Theo had turned his despairing face away and was sobbing, surely expecting death at any moment.

"Take!" it growled at her once more, this time with some sense of expectation.

Cimree slowly slipped the medallion around her neck. Instantly, the connection with Azra bloomed in her chest, filling her momentarily with calm until she realized he was in a desperate situation. He was sick, violently so, his body weakened but his mind strong. She shared his surge of relief at being reconnected with her. He'd been so worried when he couldn't sense what she had been going through. And she understood, for even though he was in a bad state, she took solace in the fact that he was alive. What had transpired, she didn't know, since the medallion only allowed them to communicate with feelings.

The golem turned away and lifted its claw as if it were going to impale Theo.

"No!" Cimree shrieked as she raised her hand, summoning the

magic of the medallion and sending a blast of fear into the golem. The power rushed through her, the current racing along her bones. The blast of magical emotions struck the golem, who howled with fear and...with *pleasure*. It skittered away from her, then ambled around in circles as if delirious.

She lowered her hand, amazed and confused at the incongruous scene. The golem did not leave the room. It had grown too big to fit back up the stairs, its massive bulk filling up most of the space by the door they'd come through.

Cimree quenched the power and the golem became agitated.

"More!" it snarled at her. *"Cim-reeee!"*

"What...what does it want?" Theo whispered fearfully.

The golem studied Theo before growling and menacing him again.

"No!" Cimree yelled, standing up to block it again.

The golem advanced like it would swat her away again, so she invoked the power and sent another blast at it, a smaller one.

The golem began to croon and backed off once more, panting and writhing in some bizarre dance. Was it relishing the magic of the Tanaquil amulet? She couldn't understand why because she was using fear against it. Did it want to be afraid?

"Your eyes are glowing," Theo said hastily. "What is that medallion? What does it do?"

"It absorbs and releases emotions," Cimree said. "It is an artifact, a singular one. The Queen Mother had control of it in Clairvaux."

"The golem seems to enjoy what you're doing to it."

"I'm getting that sense too," Cimree agreed.

With the cessation of the magic, the golem began to whine, as if it desired more. Even though its form was grotesque, there was yet an aspect about it that made her pity it. This deformed and savage monster had been created by the revenant in Ecbatana. It had freed itself somehow and begun afflicting the angel sworn with its imminence. It destroyed things. But it was sentient. It had feelings.

The golem's whines began to shift to growls. It grew impatient.

"Can we outrun it?" Theo whispered.

"It's faster than we are," she answered, as she summoned another trickle of magic to feed into the distraught creature.

The golem barked with impatience. *"More!"*

"So you need a distaff, then?" Theo asked. "I have one."

"It has power over grafting magic. It can sever the bonding instantly. When we flew away from Montheron, it sliced our magic and we all fell into the lake."

"Goodness gracious," Theo exclaimed.

The golem snarled and advanced threateningly.

Cimree raised her hand and sent waves of fear into the creature. The golem began to howl, its cry rending her heart. It was suffering...but enjoying it. She couldn't understand why.

Using the Tanaquil medallion had a draining effect, and she was getting weaker. Her dilemma was that if she stopped doing it, the golem would kill Theo, but continuing to use the medallion endlessly was impossible. She'd faint and be unable to use it anyway.

Following those bleak thoughts, Azra's worry for her intensified, bringing her mind back to his with similar concern. She wished she understood the circumstances of how he'd gotten so sick. Had he been poisoned? The situation felt impossible. Not only did she agonize over Azra's predicament, but she couldn't escape the dungeon area even if she could then outrun the golem. In the past, the Tay al-Ard had saved her from it, allowing her to transport herself great distances. Without that, she was effectively trapped.

In the midst of using the magic once more to satisfy the golem's need, she sensed tremors on the stairs.

"Someone's coming," Cimree whispered to Theo.

"I'd wager it's the angel sworn," Theo muttered. "They should all be fleeing." His voice still trembled with suppressed fear.

The iron door groaned as it opened and the golem jerked and let out a fearsome bellow. Its bulk blocked her vision.

"Kill it! Kill it!" a man's voice shouted. A skirmish of weapons sounded.

Cimree watched in horror as the golem tore them apart. It charged at the door, sending bodies crashing into the walls. One was still alive when it struck the floor, and she realized when he noticed her because of the flash of salt in her mouth as he turned to stone before he perished.

If she could engrave him with the Qodes Adonai, the power of the Knowing could help protect her and Theo down there. Just as Wegner's statue in the tunnels had saved them from the creature.

Another man collided with the wall, dead on impact.

"I need a blade," Cimree demanded of Theo.

"None of the blades have harmed it!"

"Do you have one?"

Theo pulled a dirk from his belt, which had the same familiar style of those made in the mountain villages around Clairvaux. It was a precious sight to see, a reminder of their shared past. He offered it to her.

Cimree grabbed it, tucking it into her own belt, and scrabbled on her hands and knees to where the statue lay supine. The golem bellowed again as it charged at the iron door in a rage, more evidence of its wrath lying on the floor beyond the fallen angel sworn: an iron sword nearby and a broken spear next to it, inert and useless without hands to guide them.

Her mind was feverish at the intensity of the moment. From the yawning doorway, she saw the spiral staircase going up and she heard shouts and cries echoing down the well to her. How many more would die during the golem's rampage? But she already knew the answer.

Everyone in Koa would die.

Hurriedly she bent down to scrape the first portion of the rune as her mind tried to tame her own growing panic. She'd tried to rescue those imprisoned in Koa, but her arrival had brought devastation. Banishing that terrible thought, she continued carving into the stone of the angel sworn.

The golem must have heard the gentle scraping sound.

Suddenly it hissed in her ear and seized her by the arm, hoisting her off the ground. Snarling with anger, it shivered and condensed itself again, then yanked her along past the iron door, dragging her up the stairs. She bounced painfully along the steps as it went up the twisting circles, leaving Theo back in the room.

The golem burst through the upper doorway and went into the corridor, where Cimree heard shrieks of fear and tasted flashes of salt. The golem quickly shifted its grip to the back of her neck and lifted her above its own head, bellowing with a thunder of rage. She struggled to free herself from its iron grip as it rushed down the hall, but she was no match for its strength, and it used her as a weapon against the angel sworn.

In her helplessness, all she could think to do was blast out fear to warn everyone that they were coming. The golem trumpeted with glee as she did so, its cries echoing through the corridor. The weakness caused by the magic drained her until her head lolled, her vision quivered, and her sensed were benumbed.

At least Theo hadn't been killed. She'd saved his life at least. Just one life out of so many.

And that was her final thought before she passed out, exhausted.

Cimree awoke, confused to find herself lying on a stone floor. A familiar floor. It was cold in the room. Very cold. Her entire body hurt. She could feel bruises already. It even hurt to open her eyes. A metal bracket clenched her left wrist. A single shackle. She tried to lift her head to look at her surroundings, but dizziness washed over her. Snuffling noises sounded. The golem was near.

Cimree tried to make sense of what she could see. A large hall, one with a vaulted ceiling and light streaming in through the tall windows. It was the audience hall where she was brought before Jodocus. She turned carefully to the manacle that had been clapped around her wrist and tried to use her serpent powers to pull herself loose from it, but the powers were blunted. Like her arm was ordinary once more.

She reached up with her free hand to test her hair. The serpents were dozing, lulled into lethargy by the cold. So the golem had removed only part of the curse. Just on her left arm. The manacle was attached to an iron chain that had been driven through with a spike into the stone floor. She was in the middle of the room, bathed in the light from the windows, exposing anyone who looked inside to her curse.

"Cim-reeee," the golem crooned, its misshapen form appearing from the shadows, gaze intent as it leered at her. *"More. More!"*

A memory stirred in her unquenchable mind. Of Captain Odeon talking about the fate of the Queen Mother and how she'd been chained to the floor of her own palace.

Seventeen

Times of Need

Hanging upside down for so long had caused a massive headache in Azra's skull, along with increasing confusion and torment. Every thump of his heart was echoed in the pressure of the blood vessels in his head. In the agonizing wait, it was difficult to focus his thoughts on producing any logical plan. He had no grafting wand. The webs that shrouded him were filled with spiders that could bite him effortlessly, releasing more venom, if he used the fireblood.

He also knew that hanging that way for so many hours could possibly kill him. Hanging upside down was a torture that ruthless kings used against their enemies. In his many travels, he'd witnessed the brutal act and seen its consequences on the victims.

And then, impossibly, someone he didn't know had put on the Tanaquil amulet. It wasn't Cimree—that was clear from the varied emotions he received from the woman. With his muddled thoughts, it was difficult to sift through her feelings. But he discerned, after a time, that the woman was connected to Jodocus, his son, somehow. And that she was frightened of someone. The complexity of her feelings, combined with the thundering pulse in his skull, made sorting out his options vastly difficult.

A light flickered in the distance and brought with it the scrape of boots. A man's voice was muttering. Andrin? Was it Andrin?

"The webs are everywhere. How much farther must we go?" The familiar voice of Azra's friend sent a thrill through him.

"Andrin!"

"Azra! Are you in there?"

"I'm just ahead. Thank the Oldknow."

"What are you doing in this awful place?"

"Darcia captured me," Azra said, his heart surging with relief. "I need your help, old friend."

"You sound close."

"I am near. Do you have a cloak on? The spiders may attack you."

"Oh, Azra," Andrin said with a shuddering voice. "I loathe spiders."

"It's Darcia's affinity. She's been using them to spy on us. Is the passage blocked?"

"Not entirely. But the webs are everywhere. I don't see an easy way through."

"I n-need you to bring help," Azra stammered, his mind momentarily seizing up. "I need a distaff and my firavun faresi friend. They eat spiders. I'm wrapped up in webs right now and can't move."

"Can I cut you free?" Andrin pleaded. "You sound terrible."

"I'm very sick and hanging from my ankles. But if you try to free me, the spiders have been ordered to bite me. Darcia will be watching Odeon, so you can't go to him."

"Odeon is frantic," Andrin said. "We've been searching for you since before dawn. He ordered that the upper gate holding the golem be broken open. It fled in a rage."

"That's good news," Azra said, stifling a grunt. The golem would go after Cimree. It knew how to track her down in Koa. What havoc would it cause when it reached there?

"Odeon spoke to the chieftain's council, and it was agreed that all the villagers relocate into the caves before the golem was set loose. They're all inside right now."

"Good. My firavun faresi should be with Setara's family. They spoil it. You're not afraid of it, are you?"

"No. It's very friendly. How do I get a grafting wand?"

"I have an extra one in my cave. It's in the middle basket at the bottom." He groaned from the pressure in his head. "Hurry, Andrin. I don't know how much longer I can endure this."

"I'm glad you sent the light to find me. I'd seen them hovering around you, so I followed it. Darcia is the traitor. I never would have thought of her."

"Be careful, Andrin. Don't tell anyone what you're doing. Please hurry."

"I will. I promise. I'll be back as soon as I can."

"Thank you." Azra finally let out his breath. He communed with the spirit creature and thanked it for what it had done. It was eager to continue helping, and he sensed that it would trail after Andrin and guide him back again. Azra was grateful for that. Maybe the spirit creature understood that Azra was suffering. He resisted summoning fire to burn away all the webs. He had to be patient. He had to endure the torment.

While he waited for Andrin to return, Azra used the connection to the unfamiliar woman to focus on something else. He didn't understand how she had obtained the amulet, but once she willingly put it on, she could not take it off. The magic bound her to him. He didn't want to force her to obey him. What he did want was to persuade her to help. To help Cimree. To help soften Jodocus's heart.

So dangling in the darkness, he began to feed her his own feelings. To help her understand that love was his motivation. He loved Cimree. And he loved his son, Jodocus, loved that Jodocus had been born near the caves of Tirich Mir. He couldn't communicate facts. Only feelings.

And he hoped that would be enough.

ALL SENSE of the time or its passing became meaningless. Had it been hours or only minutes? He felt a closeness to the woman with the medallion. The raw sharing of feelings had turned her into an ally. He could sense her determination to act, but he would not command those actions, and she sensed that from him, that his intentions were not to force her. She would intervene somehow. She believed she could.

The whorl of light from the spirit creature rushed through the tunnel. It excitedly informed him that Andrin was approaching with an animal. The soreness in his eyes, his cheeks, the aching in his skull would soon be relieved.

"Azra?"

"I'm here," Azra said breathlessly.

The glow of a druid stone limned the skeins of webs, the spiders illuminated as black dots in the tapestry of silk. He heard the firavun faresi chitter at the sound of his voice.

"*Agh,* it's squirming to get free!" Andrin said with a laugh.

"You have the distaff?"

"Yes. It was just where you left it. There *are* a lot of spiders here."

"You need to slip the distaff through to where my hand is. I just need to touch it with my fingers. I don't have to squeeze it."

"This confounded pet...I'm *trying*, Azra. It wants to run to you."

Azra made a soothing clucking sound to calm it. He watched Andrin's shadow in the web. It took all his remaining dregs of patience to hold still and wait. What if Darcia returned? She'd kill Andrin without hesitation. An impediment to her plans. The thought of bringing on his friend's death would drive Azra mad. His old feelings of revenge began to sizzle in his heart. It took immense willpower to quench it.

Andrin ducked beneath the webs and appeared nearby, a welcoming grin on his fearful face.

"You look absolutely wretched," he said.

"However I appear, I feel worse. My hand is at my side. I think some of my fingers are poking through."

Andrin drew near, holding the light from the stone close to inspect the situation. The furry brown firavun faresi was cradled in his other arm. Its glassy eyes shone at Azra. He sensed its wild nature, but it controlled any impetuous actions at seeing him in such a predicament. As soon as they were grafted together, he'd be able to commune with the animal by thought.

"There's a big one right by your neck," Andrin said with disgust. "It's huge."

"Andrin. Just touch me with the distaff."

"What if the spider bites you?"

"Then it bites me. I've already been bitten many times."

"How awful. I'd be screaming if I—"

"Andrin. *Now.*"

His friend drew the distaff by the tip and brought the butt of it to Azra's fingertip. As soon as the scionwood brushed his skin, the grafting magic connected him to the firavun faresi. The joining was instantaneous. Their consciousnesses melded. He could feel the reflexes of the animal surge inside him. The queasiness of his infected state began to ebb as their strengths were joined.

Eat the spiders. All of them.

The mental thought was enough, and the firavun faresi leaped from Andrin's arm and landed on Azra, causing the restraining cocoon to sway. His little friend snatched the large spider by his neck and gobbled it up. It seized another, then another.

"That's utterly disgusting," Andrin said with a shudder.

But Azra felt the glee of the firavun faresi. It scrabbled up the length of him, quickly picking off the spiders one by one.

"Any more by my head?" Azra asked.

"No. They're clear!"

"What about my hands. Any exposed skin?"

"Wait...there's one. But it's running away. I think you're clear!"

Azra gave a mental command to jump clear, which the firavun faresi did just as flames erupted from Azra's hands and incinerated the webs holding aloft him by his legs. Andrin caught him before he crashed onto the stony ground and helped to clear webs away from his face and neck. Azra shuddered as he released pent-up feelings of horror.

His blood flowed properly once more, and the pressure in his temples began to subside. He rested a moment against Andrin, his heart swollen with gratitude.

And then surges of panic and fear came from the woman with the Tanaquil medallion. Fear for Cimree. Her life was in imminent danger.

Azra lurched to his knees, not strong enough to stand. He lifted his hands, and again flames rippled from his fingertips, scouring the corridor and destroying the network of webs and the spiders dwelling amongst several cocooned carcasses. The fire continued to spread down the tunnel. Apparently spiderwebs were intensely susceptible to it. He released the fireblood, but his hands were still warm with the heat.

The woman used the magic of the medallion against Jodocus. She was making him feel the things that Azra had shared with her. Was Cimree about to die with him unable to prevent it?

He would do anything to protect her. Scowling in helplessness, he pleaded with the woman to help Cimree. He shared with her the ruin his heart had been when Delara had been killed. How much it had pained him to have his children torn from him and sent to live elsewhere.

Please help her!

He anticipated with agony the impression that Cimree was gone. That he would never see her smile at him again.

Please!

The woman exhausted herself, the magic too strong for her.

He felt her faint and collapse. The connection was still there, but she was insensible.

Andrin squeezed his shoulder. "Are you all right?"

"Cimree's in danger," Azra said in anguish. He squeezed his hands into fists, trembling with fury and his own impotence.

"Let me help you stand," Andrin offered, hoisting Azra up until his knees wobbled. Azra leaned heavily against his friend. The firavun faresi stared at the burning webs, thrilled at the chaotic destruction, being an impetuous creature itself.

Surely Darcia knew he was free. And she knew he'd be seeking revenge.

Weakness had drained him. But he had a weapon still. A weapon she didn't realize he had. The fated blade. And he could take all her thoughts, all her memories, all her *plans*. He gritted his teeth and put one foot forward. Andrin helped him. Then another.

I'm coming for you, Darcia, he thought. He couldn't help Cimree. But he could help rid the tunnels of one last spider.

Thoughts are free and subject to no rule but that of the will. On them rests the freedom of man, and they either tower above to the light of nature and create a new heaven, a new firmament, a new source of energy from which new arts flow. Or else they plummet into the chasm, delve into darkness, wallow in blindness, until there is no more light or truth to be discerned. What we are, what we may become, begins with a seed of thought.

— The Hermetic and Alchemical Writings of Paracelsus

Eighteen
No Chains for the Mind

The heavy shackle on Cimree's wrist chafed against her skin. Had the golem ripped it out of the wall from one of the prison cells of the dungeon? What hammer had been used to drive it into the stone floor, with blows that had sent fractures throughout? She tried to pry the spike free, which Uorsin might have managed, but she lacked his strength. If she'd only had some oil she could lather against her skin, she might have been able to squeeze her hand through the cuff.

She stopped struggling against the unyielding iron and rubbed her eyes with her free hand, then sat still with her legs crossed beneath her and listened. Through the shattered windows, she heard screams coming from the people of Koa. It reminded her of Ecbatana when the walls had been breached. It reminded her of Montheron's fall. But this death arrived in the form of serpents that could fly. She could feel their presence in the city growing more strongly as their numbers multiplied. The continued shrieks pained her, yet no matter how much she wanted to help, she was trapped by the golem, who had ventured out and been gone for several hours.

She was grateful to be connected to Azra again through the

medallion, which once more hung around her neck. She was elated when he escaped whatever confinement had kept him, though she chuckled ruefully at their reversal in status, with her becoming the one who couldn't leave. He was still sick and very weak, but the determination inside him had never been stronger. Knowing him as she did, he would not cease his search for Darcia until he found her. And then he would put an end to her plans if he could.

Her freedom of movement was perhaps five feet in any direction because she could not move past the tether of the chain. It left her with time to think and remember. The sharp memory of when she'd discovered Azra in his cell at Montheron stabbed at her. She could feel the memory keenly, how she took notice of him without recognizing him. How he'd tricked her into approaching the bars so he could grab her, reach into her pack, and steal the fruit of the Gallows Tree from her. Such memories of his cunning made her grin. Like the time he'd snuck into her home in Clairvaux to find out where she lived and to spend a little time with her before they left for the Gallows Tree.

With the Dryad's kiss, every memory was clear and untainted by the intervening time. They'd gone together to the tree so she could deliver him to the Dryad that he might become the progenitor of the next Dryad to guard that tree. Chrys.

She remembered being back at the tree again with Azra when their memories were still shrouded. The Fear Liath had taken to haunting the place and had killed many of the Morgarten who defended it. Azra had fought valiantly against it, but the terrifying creature had savaged him and nearly killed him as well. Chrys had healed him before snatching away Cimree's memories. Was the Fear Liath still in Clairvaux?

Yes.

The whispered answer struck her forcefully. It had been a little while since she'd received such a communication. And rarely had one come from such an errant thought.

Or *had* her thoughts been merely rambling and roaming? She

concentrated her attention on the Fear Liath. A monster that had killed her mentor Milena and many others. It had hunted her as well, and even sitting on this floor so far from it, she could still feel the terror of being in its presence. Was it a creation of metamorphistry?

Silence.

Why had she thought about it? Why had her mind wandered that direction?

It was a creature the Morgarten all feared. They were the last defenders of the Gallows Tree, and the Fear Liath had decimated their ranks. Their weapons were ineffective against it. Their training useless. But like the golem, the Fear Liath also had a weakness. It was subservient to the Tanaquil medallion. She could drive it off. Perhaps even tame it.

The thought echoed inside her mind.

Even tame it.

Or set it loose.

Just as the golem had been released from the cavern with the waterfall. Its arrival had altered events. An element of chaos to add to the unpredictability of a fraught situation.

Her leg began to tingle uncomfortably. The golem had returned. She looked around for it, but it remained invisible. She craned her neck to look up at the broken windows. The daylight was strong, but many shadows covered the edges of the room.

A clicking noise sounded in the dark spaces. The spasm in her leg responded to it, and she massaged her muscle to ease the uncomfortable sensation.

The golem materialized right in front of her, making her heart jump, but she didn't flinch.

"Cim-reee," it whispered at her, holding three hen eggs in its palm.

It had brought her food. Why eggs? She didn't know, but she took them and set them within the circle of her legs.

"Thank you," she said.

It clicked noisily as it tried to speak. *"Ee-ee-ee-eat!"*

Although she didn't feel hungry, not with pangs anyway, she did feel she could eat. The thought of raw eggs didn't bother her. She remembered Iddawc telling her how he enjoyed swallowing eggs and cracking them inside his gullet. She wasn't going to try that technique.

Cimree took one of the eggs, tapped it on the ground to crack the head, and then broke away part of the shell so that the rest of it acted like a little cup. The golem watched her with its bulbous eyes and gyrated in anticipation of her swallowing it. She brought the little eggshell chalice to her lips and gulped down the yolk and the white.

The golem did a little dance as she swallowed them.

"More!"

She obeyed and swallowed the next two eggs, setting the broken shells next to her when she finished, but the golem snatched them up and devoured them in a single bite. In horrified fascination, she watched and listened to the crunching as its mandibles crushed the shells. It chewed and chewed for a long time before swallowing the pulp.

Then it extended one of its claws and tapped the Tanaquil medallion against her chest.

"More!" it pleaded.

So it wanted her to invoke the medallion's power again. It wanted to feel. Maybe she could use that to her advantage?

She began to invoke the amulet's power—gently, cautiously. The golem began to fidget with excitement and scuttle around her in a circle. She remained still, summoning a peaceful, lulling feeling.

The golem began to whine. It formed a fist and slammed it into the ground. *"More!"*

Cimree used her free hand to jiggle the chain. She tugged where the chain attached to the cuff and dangled it at the golem ardently.

"Off. Take it off."

The golem hissed at her angrily. *"Stay!"*

She jiggled the chain again. "Off."

The golem roared in fury and began to skulk around the room, climbing up on the throne and even throwing furniture until it splintered and broke. It raged and made all sorts of unimaginable sounds as it vented its fury at her disobedience. It came back to her, livid, its eyes moving in different directions at once.

"More!" It thundered at her.

She patted the ground in front of her. "Stay," she said. Then she patted her chest. "Stay." She faced it, not afraid of it even though she knew it was powerful enough to snuff out her life in a single swipe of its claws. She jiggled the chain again. "Take it off. I will stay."

The golem grunted, clearly displeased and doubtful. It paced back and forth, hissing and whining.

"Stay," Cimree repeated, patting the floor. "Sit. Stay."

The golem faced her. But it did not obey her. Either it did not understand or it refused to submit to her. It loped over to the throne at the edge of the light amidst the debris and rubble of the room. It picked up a spear from the clutter that she hadn't noticed before and sat on the throne and gripped the spear, as if it were some monarch at court.

"More. More! MORE!" It railed at her louder and louder.

Cimree jiggled the chain. "Set. Me. Free."

The golem broke the spear shaft in half and hurled the end with the blade across the chamber. It clattered noisily. Then the golem leaped from the throne, still holding the other half of the broken weapon, rushed at her, and began beating her with the spear.

Cimree cowered, trying to shield herself with her free arm, but the blows struck hard and furious as the golem shrieked at her. Pain stung her arm as it rained blows on her. She twisted away from the beast, and it began to hit her across her back next. Each blow would leave another bruise. How many strikes before she was knocked unconscious again?

Cimree felt the medallion ignite on its own before realizing that Azra was panicking, feeling every blow himself and in a frenzy that she was about to be killed. He'd use the medallion's power against the creature.

Realizing that refusing was pointless, Cimree summoned the power and blasted the golem with anger and fear.

Instantly the beating stopped. The golem tossed away its weapon of torture and began to moan with delight as the magic charged through him. It rocked backward, swaying with a sort of delirium. Her pulse pounded in her ears, and her skin reacted to the golem's attack. Pain riddled her in the places she'd been struck. Biting her lip to focus, she continued the flood of magical feelings, and the golem howled in triumph.

She cut it off and collapsed against the ground, feigning unconsciousness. The magic churned inside her, ebbing, but still demanding release. She lay supine, tethered by the chain, her legs slightly pulled in for fear of another attack.

"More," it bellowed at her.

She held perfectly still, hoping her deception would work. It knew she had limits to her strength. It knew she might be unconscious for hours. Did it even care? It hungered after feelings, especially those particular feelings. It took conscious effort not to groan in pain at the beating she'd sustained. Her body reacted to the shock with trembling.

The golem nudged her with one of its claws.

"More," it pleaded mournfully.

It had spared her life and chained her to the floor so it could use the medallion's power to feed its hunger for feeling. Whatever had happened to it in the past had scarred it. Possibly irrevocably. She'd tried reasoning with it, but that had failed. She'd given in to its demands in the end for fear of her life. And she knew that it would beat her again if she refused. It would teach *her* what it wanted. It would compel her to meet its demands.

The bubbling panic she'd felt inside Azra began to subside. The danger was over. She tried to comfort him, but he was aggravated. She tried to project a feeling of calm to him. She was all right. She would survive this, just as he had survived his many injuries.

What lessons did she need to learn from all this? Or maybe suffering was only pointless. When the golem had been caged, how had it been treated? And was it treating her the way it had been? Her heart was moved with pity for it. Had it eventually burst from its confinement and wrought vengeance on the being that had tortured it?

How much had it suffered? And how long would its vengeance last before its revenge had ended?

Not for long, it seemed.

Nineteen
Another Chain

As soon as Cimree appeared to revive, the golem insisted on draining her again. Its hunger or craving for the emotions she could provide was never sated. If she did not obey, it threatened to beat her with the broken spear again. The other half of the spear, with the tip still intact, was unfortunately out of her reach. Not that she could have killed anything with it, but she did have the idea of carving the Qodes Adonai on the floor near her in an attempt to create a magical barrier that could protect her from the golem's wrath. She wondered, if she stretched as far as she could, whether she might be able to snag it with her foot. But the golem had not departed, instead continuing to roam the hall and growl to itself while she pretended to have fainted once again.

Judging by the failing light, night was not far. The screams had become fainter throughout the day, although she did not understand the cause. Had more people died? Or had they run away?

She felt the tremors first, the cadence of steps arriving from another part of the fortress. Not heavy footfalls, but numerous. And a shushing sound accompanied that pattern; something was being dragged.

The golem became agitated with excitement and mounted the

throne again. It chuffed and snorted as the vibrations grew stronger. Cimree played her game still, feigning unconsciousness, but she alerted her serpents to keep watch for her. The golem gyrated in anticipation and began to pound its fist on the armrest of the throne.

Three kobolds entered, dragging a body with them. She'd seen the lizard-like creatures ruining Ecbatana, and Captain Odeon had told the tale of being captured by them at Montheron and then forced as a human slave to break down the fortress. How had the kobolds traveled all the way to the mountains of Tirich Mir so quickly?

It dawned on her that they hadn't. Lizards and salamanders were primordial creatures that had existed since the beginning, and she'd found them in nearly every location she'd ever visited. The golem had used metamorphistry and formed a new colony of them to fulfill the same purpose as the others. To break down evidence of civilization. To return the area to an unspoiled state.

The kobolds spoke in their guttural language and deposited their bloodstained victim before the throne. Recognition struck her. Jodocus. His weapons had been stripped away, his clothing was in tatters. The Tay al-Ard was gone. Had he expended its power too much? Had its magic failed and stranded him in Koa?

The golem clambered down from the throne and hissed at the body. Jodocus groaned in pain.

"Cim-reee! Cim-reee!" the creature hissed. It grabbed Jodocus by the back of his tunic and hoisted him effortlessly into the air. Jodocus wore no hood nor the crystal eyepieces. If he saw her, he would die.

Cimree faced away and tried to cover herself, but she lacked a cloak.

The golem cackled. A frantic feeling wormed inside her chest. She did not want to turn Jodocus to stone. Not Azra's son.

The golem carried the body closer to her. Jodocus was barely conscious, but she heard him breathing and rousing.

"Don't look, Jodocus!" Cimree warned.

The golem drew near and dangled the body in front of her, so she turned herself completely around to face the other way. It responded by circling that way too, so Cimree hunched herself and used her arms to try to cover her head, although concealing herself adequately was probably impossible. She dreaded the taste of salt that might suddenly bloom in her mouth.

"Cimree?" Jodocus murmured in confusion.

"Don't look at me!" she said forcefully. "The golem will try and make you."

"My eyes are closed. I was bitten by a flying serpent. I'm so sick."

The golem gave a throaty chuckle and set Jodocus down right next to Cimree.

"More!" it demanded.

She obeyed, summoning the amulet's power to feed the creature again with the twin emotions it craved. A delighted noise issued from its throat. It moved away, leaving Jodocus in a heap next to her.

"You need to cover your eyes," Cimree suggested in a low voice. "A blindfold. Something."

The golem groaned in relish at the renewed surge of feelings. Cimree wondered how far the whorl-like tattoos had spread over her, the effect of the amulet's power coursing through her. She'd been using the medallion nearly constantly since her capture, with only brief rests that weren't enough to restore her energy fully. But the golem didn't care about her mortal weaknesses. It would squeeze her for more until she died of it. The hopelessness of her situation weighed on her, but she drove those thoughts from her mind. She would escape. Somehow.

Through her serpents, she watched Jodocus rip off his torn sleeve and use it as a blindfold. The golem noticed this, barked in anger, and buffeted him with a paw, sending him sprawling, his body skidding across the stone floor. The creature ripped the blindfold off, tossed it away, and then dragged Jodocus back over to Cimree.

"*No!*" it ordered.

She thought she heard the kobolds snicker. Through her serpent eyes, she saw the shaking that looked like laughter. One of them stared at her balefully, to no effect. It made sense to her that the Golem had ensured its minions would not be harmed by her.

Jodocus moaned from the rough treatment and just lay on the ground, breathing heavily. The golem, seemingly satisfied, made some noises in a guttural language similar to that of the kobolds, and they hissed and gave sharp nods at whatever orders they'd been given and left the hall. As she watched them go, she felt the diminutive bodies leave and felt she would recognize it if they returned.

The magic of the medallion was taxing her body and mind. She diminished the flow, just a little to preserve her strength. She needed to learn what she could before she fainted again.

In a furtive voice she whispered, "Did the kobolds take the Tay al-Ard from you?"

"Theo stole it from me," Jodocus said bitterly.

"How?"

"He made another ring. Or enchanted another one. The same kind that I used to steal it from you. I watched him vanish. He's long gone now."

Disappointment stung her but not surprise. Jodocus had made Theo feel like a prisoner, and the golem had nearly killed him, so of course he'd fled. Where had he gone? Back to the arena where he'd lived before? But surely the kobolds would break it down as well, even if it took years of labor to accomplish it.

"Where were you when you were caught? What of the other angel sworn?"

"Everyone who can is fleeing. There weren't many left anyway. And the golem severed our graftings, so most are stranded here now. It's all ruined. Everything is ruined. And it's my fault."

He sounded miserable. But the confession he'd just ended with stuck out to her.

"What do you mean?" She kept her voice low, watching the golem while it was intoxicated by her magic. It wasn't paying any attention to them, lifting its face to the broken windows above and the failing light.

"Spozhmay made me understand. When she used the Tanaquil against me. Not to corrupt me, but to open my heart to the truth. Azrael is my father. And I never knew. The Queen Mother never told me."

She could sense his feelings through the medallion. He was broken inside, reeling from the knowledge that the Queen Mother had manipulated him his entire life. And he was grieving all of that and something more. The feelings of loss he carried were potent.

Jodocus continued, "It's caused me much reflection on the things she did to me. Things that didn't align with her previous words. How she used us to fulfill her ends. I began to see Azra in a different light. And you. All the sacrifices you've made, even after you were cursed by that wretched golem. And now it feels like my life has been cursed by it as well."

"The golem killed Spozhmay," Cimree said, reaching over and touching his shoulder. He was face down on the stone, head turned away.

A spasm of guilt and anguish rattled him. "Yes," he choked out. "I saw it. If I'd only listened to you. If we'd joined forces, we could have gone to the caves before the golem was set loose. It's my fault she's dead. It's my fault they're all dead."

Cimree knew what it felt like to be guilty. To carry the weight of someone's demise on her shoulders.

"You know the little boy in our caves," she said gently. "The son of parents I rescued from Ecbatana and brought to Tirich Mir. He was...fascinated by the thought of seeing me, even though he'd been warned. It was an accident."

"Yes," Jodocus said with sympathy. "Darcia told us about it.

And I thought when you left, it was a blessing to be rid of you. And my father. Only...you both returned before we could conquer the caves. We were about to strike. The Morgarten were poised to conquer. But we knew we could not if you were there. I was so frustrated. Now I feel like a fool."

"Will Darcia listen to you?" Cimree asked. "What if we joined forces now?"

"I think it's too late. She weakened Azra, but he's free again. And hunting for her. She, um, has affinity for spiders."

"I realized that," Cimree said. "But how do you contact her when she's so far away?"

"Theo has a way of sending messages through spirit creatures. So she's been communicating with us more easily now. She had him hanging upside down in a cave full of webs. He's destroyed it and is searching for her to kill her. She's going to order the Morgarten to attack the caves. And there's nothing I can do to stop it." The regret throbbed in his voice. "No way to call it off."

If Trinati had returned, it would shift the balance. Trinati was probably the best warrior among all the angel sworn, but not even she could defeat all the Morgarten on her own. And Azra was still weak. She could communicate to him through feelings, but she could not make him understand the situation fully.

The angel sworn were about to massacre each other.

She cupped her face in her hands, trembling with all the fraught feelings. Her mission, her purpose, had been to save them. Even with Jodocus's change of heart, would the Morgarten listen to him or to Darcia?

Enmity. Just as Iddawc had warned her about. The enmity between the two factions would lead to further bloodshed. Would perpetuate the cycle of revenge and hostility. She wanted to stop it. But she could do nothing chained to the floor. She was helpless.

There had to be a way.

"The pain from the snake bite is intense," Jodocus murmured.

"I think it's going to kill me. My heart is beating wrong. It's been getting worse."

"I wish I could help you," Cimree said, rubbing his back. "But I'd need a grafting wand."

The magic was draining her. She was on the verge of unconsciousness again.

"I have another one," Jodocus whispered. "In my boot. I've always kept a spare. Just in case."

Like his father. Cimree felt a glimmer of warmth.

"If I graft you to a serpent, it will provide you with immunity to the venom," she said.

"I hate snakes."

"Your affinity for birds means the grafting will be difficult. But there are other benefits, not just immunity to venom. Which boot has the distaff?"

"The right one. On the outside."

Cimree shifted her position slowly, keeping watch over the golem as she moved casually, trying to protect Jodocus from her power. He was resisting the urge to stare at her.

Carefully, she slipped her fingers into the cuff of his boot and found the rounded end of the distaff. He had a little sheath put there, a little leather wrapper. She slowly reached for it and curled her fingers around the end of it, leaving it in the boot. Sensing a serpent was easy. So many had gathered to the city of Koa, and they sought the warmer places like the hilltop where the fortress stood. She used the distaff's magic to draw a serpent to her. It was a rock viper. It undulated soundlessly toward her and Jodocus.

Cimree breathed slowly and started to sway, falling asleep mid-thought. She stiffened her resolve and invoked the grafting magic to bond Jodocus to the snake. Oh, it resisted! It wanted to bite him, but it obeyed because of her affinity, and the connection was made. Jodocus would feel the resistance through tingling sensations in his limbs.

"I'm feeling...better," Jodocus said in surprise. "Although it's unnatural."

"It isn't any more unnatural than me bonding with a goat," Cimree said. "Serpents are not evil. They are living creatures like any other. You can respect an eagle's talons but not a serpent's fangs?"

Her body began to sway again, and she planted her hand on the floor to keep from collapsing. The heavy weight of the cuff and chain caused her to droop even more.

"Keep the distaff," Cimree said. "Stay bonded as long as you can. You might be able to sneak out. Free the others. They deserve a chance to live as well."

"How can I get them out?" Jodocus said with frustration. "There aren't enough grafting wands anymore. After you stole some, I had the rest taken away. We are all helpless here, and I won't leave to save myself and let the others perish."

"Find a way, Jodocus. You have to. Only use short, careful slides, then be still and blend in with the stone floor. Get moving."

"And what about you? How will you get out?"

"I'm working on it. It's more important to me that we stop further bloodshed among our people. I can't get out because of the chain. But you can."

"I don't deserve your help," he muttered angrily. "I tried to kill you."

"You were blinded by loyalty before. Your eyes are open now. Get away while you can. As soon as I faint, the golem is going to rage. It might even kill you. Go."

Her vision faded, or was it that night had come? The patches of sunlight on the floor were gone. Twilight had arrived.

She watched with her serpent vision as Jodocus shimmied carefully away from her, accompanied by the rock viper. Then he was gone, the sense of his heat vanished.

The golem swayed in ecstasy.

She cut off the magic and slumped onto the ground.

"More!" it pleaded, ending on a surprised hiss when it noticed that Jodocus was gone.

The golem raged around the entire room, and the sounds it made were terrifying. But darkness swallowed her thoughts, dragging her toward unconsciousness. However, she was awake, just enough, to feel a human hand grasp hers. A warm hand.

The magic of the Tay al-Ard yanked her, causing a dizzying feeling in her stomach, and carried her away.

Twenty
The Coliseum

A strident, malodorous scent roused Cimree from her unconsciousness. The strain of using the medallion so much had taken its toll on her heart and body, but her mind clung to the memory of the Tay al-Ard's grip on her before she'd fainted.

It couldn't have been Azra who had taken her because she would have sensed his proximity. As she tried to rise, a hand steadied her shoulder. She heard the noises of hammering and chisels against stone and felt the recurring beats thrumming in her bones.

"Sorry for the rude way of waking you," Theo said as he stuffed a glass vial into his pocket. They were in a darkened stone chamber lit by a swarm of fireflies, it seemed.

"Where are we? This is not Koa." She felt a prickle of anxiety. The room smelled of dust, old paper, and the residual aroma of the fluid in the vial. Her sense of Azra was even more distant and in a totally different direction than when she'd been in the serpent-filled city.

"We're at the coliseum in Vaud," Theo said. "It's in the same region as Ecbatana. The kobolds are in the process of destroying it."

"Jodocus believed you'd gone far away after you stole the Tay al-Ard."

She did not see the magical device, but she assumed Theo had concealed it.

"I left Koa, yes. But I came back to free you. If it weren't for you, Cimree, I'd be dead right now and my life's work destroyed."

"Your life's work?"

Theo still crouched beside her on the floor. "This," he said, gesturing to the room. "Let me help you stand up if you'd like. There's a chair and a stone bench in this room."

"The bench would be fine," Cimree said. She did require his assistance to make it back to her feet again. The chain from her wrist was gone, although her arm still felt different, and she suspected the golem had used its magic against her after capturing her, to remove her symbiosis with serpents from only that part of her. She rubbed her hand down her arm as Theo helped her to the stone bench. She spied rows and rows of stone bookshelves crowded with an assortment of leatherbound tomes. A stone table with several grinding bowls and a collection of tubes and stoppered vials were present off to one side.

The stone bench was long enough to lie down on, but she sat and steadied herself with her hand.

Theo was wearing the glass disks to protect himself from her curse.

"You do seem rather worse for wear as they say," Theo declared sympathetically.

"The golem beat me," Cimree said, still sore all over from her bruises.

"I'm referring to the markings on your face. They are thicker at your throat but now they extend up to your cheeks."

"Do you have a mirror?"

"Of course!" he said proudly. "They are quite helpful in my studies." He walked over to the worktable, secured a rectangular mirror in a frame, and brought it to her.

Cimree gripped it and gazed at her reflection and was shocked at how much the vine tattoos had spread. They'd infiltrated her entire neck, traced along her jawbone, and had even spread over her temples, mingling with the serpents crowning her head. She felt sick as she observed herself, at the transformation that resulted from overusing the medallion's power. The warning from the Book of Secrets rattled her, that using the medallion would make her susceptible to dark impressions, especially her eyes and what she looked at. Dejectedly, she lowered the mirror, and Theo reclaimed it as he sat down next to her, setting it down on the bench beside him.

"I'd noticed the markings before, but now they've spread. Do I assume correctly that the medallion you're wearing is the cause?"

"Yes. It's called the Tanaquil amulet."

"Fascinating. I should like to learn more about it. But at present, there is a more urgent need."

"Yes. I need to rescue the angel sworn that are stranded in Koa."

"Ah, yes, well...that's not what I meant. And I'm not going to hand the Tay al-Ard over to you lest you steal it from me. I believe I have a very strong chance of surviving now with it. I can take you somewhere, of course, but I can't let you have it."

"Theo," Cimree said firmly. "The people are dying. I need to save them."

"And I'm sure you will do a wonderful job at that. But I've made records, I've written all these books, and they need to be preserved, or the knowledge I've acquired will be destroyed. And that is of more paramount importance to me than anything else. Especially the lives of the angel sworn with the repugnant way they treat others."

A flash of anger and impatience stung her chest, but she curbed it. It was the impulse of enmity. It would be wise to listen to Theo instead of arguing with him. Knowing his motivations would possibly help her find a way to bridge their competing needs.

"You've written all of these yourself?" she asked, glancing at the symmetrical rows.

"Yes. I'm an autodidact. I'm fascinated by knowledge of every sort. Knowledge is like stone blocks that can be built upon to create a tower. It is my duty, my life purpose, to preserve knowledge that it may be useful for future generations to build upon. The problem is the abundance of war, of strife, so much so that safeguarding knowledge has become incredibly difficult. I was yanked away from the coliseum by an angel sworn who took me captive and brought me to Jodocus. I was forced, against my will, to serve his aims—not my own."

Cimree could hear the little tone of resentment in his voice as he explained.

"No one wants to be in bondage," Cimree agreed. "It must have been very harrowing for you."

"Indeed. I've been worried about these books. This room is hidden. But the kobolds and their slaves are meticulous. It's only a matter of time before they find this room. And then they'll destroy the books. I cannot allow that. I need to transport them to a safer place. That is my highest priority."

"What did you have in mind?"

"I'll honestly admit that I'm inspired by what the angel sworn built on Montheron. But my vision is grander. I should like to find an island inside a vast lake. And I intend to build a city there. One with towering walls and protected docks. A fortress that could withstand any siege. I've even considered a name for this place. Just as Montheron was named after the breed of bird that roosted there, I would dedicate this city-island to the preservation of knowledge. I would name it Kenatos. In Ecbatanan, it means *the death of knowledge*."

He spoke with enthusiasm and vision. He had an ambition that was a source of unquenchable fire inside him.

"I seek to gather specimens. Perhaps that is the *wrong* word. I don't mean prisoners. I wish to gather people of all races and cultures. To preserve the idiosyncrasies of each. I wish angel sworn to live there too. As equals, not as overlords. I want gardens like they had in Ecbatana that held every fruit suitable for the climate. But no monsters. I wish to study metamorphistry in order to undo it. I might not be the one who succeeds, but the knowledge I've gathered would be passed down until someone, in the distant future, learned enough to figure it out."

"Have you found such an island yet?" Cimree asked.

"No. But I will keep searching until I do. I can see it in my mind. A hub, like that on a wagon wheel, with spokes reaching out to pockets of peoples who also seek to achieve my vision."

His idea made her think of the marshlands she'd visited that Azra had taken her to. She remembered how even the deer hadn't been threatened by her presence since they had no instinct to warn them that she was dangerous. And Azra had told her of a lake and an island there. And places to quarry stone. The memory whispered to her.

"I know of such a place," Cimree said softly.

Theo winced. "If you're trying to deceive me, Cimree—"

"I'm not, Theo. I'm only trying to help you. Azra knows of it. He's my...companion. And he's very sick and in great danger. So are the others gathered at the caves. But he told me of such an island in a vast lake."

"Just think of it. What if I could discover a way to cure you?" Theo said. "But I need time, and time is hindering my dream right now. I need the Tay al-Ard to remove the books from here to a safer place."

"Let's move them to the tunnels, then, in Tirich Mir."

Theo was silent a moment. "You mean well, Cimree. But your little band is no match for the Morgarten and the other angel sworn warriors that have been sent to vanquish it. After they've won, they'll search for me again. I need to move my books to a safer place, a place in which they won't be disturbed or damaged by moisture. Caves would not do." He grumbled to himself. "This really was an idyllic place to keep my library. The lords of Ecbatana used this coliseum for gambling on blood sports. It was protected, but now it's doomed. I wish I could help you, Cimree, but I have too much to do."

"I understand your motives, Theo. I also have a book, one that was engraved on a tome made of gold. It's called the Sefer Raziel, the Book of Secrets. It contains history and knowledge about the spirit creatures that inhabit this world. The book is hidden in the caves, and its knowledge must be guarded. I stole it from the Queen Mother."

That piqued his curiosity. "Truly?"

"Yes, Theo. And I have knowledge that can help you right now. I can help you protect your books and keep them safe from the kobolds. There is a rune that I can carve in the stone here that will keep them away. It will stop them from destroying the coliseum and drive them off."

"How? Nothing frightens these despicable creatures."

She was confident in her plan, and she spoke with conviction. "You will see. I will use my knowledge to help preserve yours. The kobolds will go away and leave this forsaken place. Azra has been to the island I told you about. He can take us there with the Tay al-Ard. He has all of Wegner's knowledge of building cities and fortresses. Wegner was the master architect of the angel sworn. If we help each other, we can accomplish so much more together."

He hesitated, the look of indecision on his face indicating that he was not sure whether to believe her.

"Theophrastus von Weissenau, the one they call Paracelsus, what could be worse than if we *all* fail? Time will eventually break down these walls. The earth will swallow up this coliseum, and new trees and shrubs will grow atop it. If we fail in Tirich Mir, then there is no future. You cannot multiply and replenish the earth on your own. You need us and we need you. Only together will we survive." She put her hand on his shoulder, her touch connecting them person to person.

He sat stock still for some time, concentration wrinkling his brow as he appeared to weigh everything she had told him.

Eventually he spoke. "You were the one they told me of who was chosen to be the Tyrant Queen. The one Lord Roque tried to destroy. I think I realize why the king chose you."

"Oh?" she asked.

"Because he trusted you. That if you were offered all that power, *you* would not abuse it."

With a sigh, he reached into his robes and drew out the Tay al-Ard. And he handed it to her.

"You saved my life. And you helped Jodocus escape even though he was your enemy. This belongs to you anyway. I have to trust that you will do as you promise."

Twenty-One

One Last Web

Azra clenched the hilt of the fated blade, squeezing it hard until the design on the handle imprinted into his skin. The venom from the spiders had robbed him of his health, but he was grafted with the stamina of a mountain goat, the cunning of his firavun faresi, the patience of an egret, and the savage fury of a snow leopard. Their combined attributes swirled inside him, causing pinpricks all across his body, from his toes to his scalp, as he returned from outside, where he'd performed the graftings.

"You are not healthy enough to do this, Azra," Trinati declared forcefully, grabbing him by the arm as he walked deeper into the caves to commence his search.

"And you're too exhausted from the journey here," he shot back. It had taken all of Trinati's incredible skill and ferocity to make it back into the caves alive after escaping Koa. She'd fought several of the Morgarten, all of whom were fresh, and had defeated them, but she was wounded and weary. While she had related to the other members of the high council the details of her ordeal in Koa and about Darcia's betrayal, he'd slipped away to put a plan into action.

"Let me join you!" Trinati pleaded. "Together we stand a better chance than you going alone. You are sick!"

"And Cimree is unconscious and was taken to another part of the world! We've suffered all of this because of Darcia's treachery, and I'm going to put an end to it right now." He jerked his arm from her grip.

"Azra—"

"This isn't your choice to make," he said. "It's mine. With this blade, I will know her weaknesses, her thoughts, and I will take them into myself. She's already done enough damage here. She's already caused enough harm."

"And what if she takes the blade and kills you with it?" Trinati warned. "How much more dangerous will she be then? Think this through, Azra."

"I have," he replied. "She won't defeat me."

"You don't even know where she is."

"I will find her, Trinati."

The boom of drums began to thrum inside the tunnels. The tempo firm and fast. The war drum signal, the indication that one or more of the entrances were in danger.

Trinati put her hand on his shoulder. "We need you, Azra."

"She's ordered an attack against us," Azra answered, shaking his head. "She's reacting to us now. I'm going after her."

"You're the most stubborn man I've ever known," Trinati growled.

"This is your fight, Trinati. Defend Tirich Mir like you defended Montheron. Seal the tunnels."

"But what about Cimree and Uorsin and Avari and all the others trying to get here?"

"The Tay al-Ard can get them back. That's our chance. We can't let the Morgarten overrun the tunnels. Close them off."

Another set of drums had begun. From a different part of the tunnels. "I don't like this," Trinati said with concern creasing her brow.

"Get back to Odeon," Azra said, reaching and squeezing her shoulder. "It's time to seal the tunnels."

Trinati gave a reluctant smile and let go of his shoulder. She drew her mirror blade and stalked back to the main corridor, drawing her grafting wand with her other hand.

Though the tingling sensations were uncomfortable, he was used to pain. Pain could be ignored. He summoned one of the spirit messengers.

It appeared as a whorl of blue light. "Find Darcia and lead me to her. Get as many others as you can to help in the search. I need to know where she is before we get overrun." With his words, he added his impression of need. The villagers had gathered in the tunnels. They were a warrior tribe, and they'd fight with courage, but the angel sworn were better soldiers, especially with animal graftings that made them much more powerful. Better to close off the caves and prevent bloodshed.

How many angel sworn were rallying against them? How many had his son, Jodocus, persuaded to join him?

From what Trinati had revealed, there were many angel sworn captive in Koa still. He couldn't think about them. He had to stay focused on the task at hand.

"Azra!"

Andrin jogged up, wearing armor and carrying his blade in hand. "Odeon put me in charge of defending Jackal's Gate. Where are you going?"

"I'm going after Darcia."

Andrin looked troubled. "You're too sick."

"I can do this," Azra said, feigning more confidence than he felt. "And so can you. It will be like when the Vikander attacked Montheron."

"We fought side by side back then," Andrin said, smiling at the memory. "Everything's in chaos inside. Perreta is gathering the children. They're frightened."

"Their father is a brave man," Azra said. "Tell Odeon to have the entrances sealed, Andrin. We've waited long enough."

"I will." They hugged briefly and broke apart. Azra rushed against the flow of men preparing to defend. A third set of drums had begun. The attack was happening from multiple entrances. Of course. But they had prepared for such an outcome. Uorsin had rigged stone barriers in some places. He'd created levers that held back nets of stones, which, when pulled up, would release the stones in a controlled avalanche to block the attackers from penetrating farther into the cave tunnels.

A rush of blue light approached. He felt it buzzing with urgency. The spirit creature had found Darcia, and she was close by.

Azra squeezed the dagger again, preparing for a fight that would end in his death or Darcia's.

Show me, he thought to the spirit creature guide, then followed it against the tide of defenders. The men of the tribe had gathered too, brandishing weapons like slings, staves, and daggers. A few had scimitars. Memories barged into his mind and trampled his feelings, of when the Queen Mother's angel sworn had arrived at the village and destroyed everyone. He stared from face to face as he passed them, reliving the awful moments when he'd watched his tribe get slaughtered. The wails of mothers for their husbands and sons before they too were put to death. Only the youngest children were spared, those too young to take up weapons.

His wife had been killed.

The Dryad's kiss brought all the feelings back in their fullness. He couldn't let such an atrocity happen again. Tears pricked his eyes, and he ran the back of his hand across them. He slowed his breathing, allowing the memories to pass through him, allowing the feelings to come. He thought of Cimree, of how she had first visited him when he was chopping firewood. Many years had passed. The grief had never fully left. The pain of such a loss ebbed and flowed. Cimree had healed his heart. Had given him a purpose once again.

Focusing on her helped soothe his pain as he followed the trail of the blue light. Calming breaths. Focus. Discipline. It was just another battle. Another foe. He'd never seen Darcia fight before, so he didn't have any knowledge of her style, but she had a dirk, and he imagined it would be slathered in venom. Few creatures were faster than a firavun faresi. His reflexes would prevail.

He passed one of the stone statues with glowing eyes, one that provided heat in the bowels of the caves. The face was from a man of Ecbatana, a statue they had brought to help provide some comfort. Azra had watched Cimree carve the rune of the Qodes Adonai under the man's bearded chin.

The blue light shot down a side tunnel, drawing his attention away from the statue. Azra registered that it was the tunnel where Andrin's family lived.

It felt like Uorsin had just punched him in the stomach. For an instant, he couldn't breathe. Darcia knew she couldn't defeat Azra herself. She knew his anger, once roused, was relentless. His weakness she already knew.

Azra followed the light into the gap in the stone. He knew the way perfectly, knew already in his heart what he would find. Hostages. She'd have waited, watching the cave for Andrin to be summoned to defend the entrances from the angel sworn. Darcia had chosen the family that Azra would protect at all costs.

He rounded the corner and found Perreta bound in silken ropes, her mouth gagged, her body limp. Edwina lay prostrate on the floor, unconscious, feverish. Cyrill was also comatose. And there was Darcia, talking softly to little Blanka, who sat blinking frightened eyes on a little wicker stool. A single druid stone illuminated the room.

"They'll be fine," Darcia said, stroking Blanka's hair with one hand. Her other held her dirk. "Just sit quietly a little longer. Hold very still or it will bite you."

He spotted an inky black spider on Blanka's hand. A black widow.

Then Darcia turned her neck and observed Azra in the corridor. No doubt her spider sentries had alerted her of his arrival.

"So you've spun one last web," Azra said, coming closer.

Darcia rose. She wore hunter leathers that would help to protect her against slashes. Another dirk was sheathed in her belt, which she drew. "You expected me to do no less, Azra. Now put down the fated blade. And back away. Children are especially vulnerable to spider venom."

"You're not going to hurt her," Azra said. His stomach squeezed, but he kept his voice unconcerned. He showed no fear.

"Let me speak plainly, Azra. And quickly since we're running out of time. If you hand over the blade, I will allow you to take the children and Perreta outside unharmed. All the villagers are going out too. The caves are for the angel sworn. And you, sir, are a fallen angel. You were once the great Azrael. I don't intend to fight you. I know you want to kill me. If you kill me, they will all die. So you see, it's really on your hands. Now put it down or the spider bites. If you care about this family, put it down."

"Azra?" Blanka called fearfully, her voice trembling.

"You can trust him," Darcia said soothingly. "He won't let the spider bite you."

"Let me speak plainly now, Darcia," Azra said coldly. "We are not leaving these caves. You are." He took another step closer.

Darcia stepped around the stool and brought the dirk to Blanka's neck. "There is no fruit that can bring someone back from the dead. Don't make me, Azra."

"You cannot do a thing and then blame someone else for it," Azra said, shaking his head. "Not even the Queen Mother would have threatened to kill a child. You thought you knew how to control me. You trusted I'd do whatever you said to save them. But I believe you won't kill her because that's not the kind of person you are. I'm your prey. This is between us."

Azra felt Cimree rouse from her unconsciousness. She was awakening. He buried his emotions. Tamped down his fears for her into the amulet and invoked its power to grow the fear inside of Darcia.

He took another step closer. Then another, his eyes locked on Darcia's, his peripheral vision testing to see if her wrist moved. He increased the terror inside her.

He'd called her bluff.

A spider ran across his throat. He felt the sting instantly.

Darcia flashed a victorious smile.

Twenty-Two

Return to Clairvaux

The magic of the Tay al-Ard dragged Cimree back to the valley of her childhood. Deep snow had settled all around. The familiar roar of the Wilderswill waterfall could be heard but not seen through the frigid mist. Seeing the rugged cliffs of the valley walls sent pangs of memory through her. All her past lives cascaded in her mind, all the times she had visited the sacred source of the angel sworn's immortality. But the Gallows Tree was nothing more than a charred hulk of broken limbs. Its life, and the life of its Dryad, were snuffed out years before.

The cold of the snow penetrated her boots. She wrapped herself in the cloak she wore. Theo had gotten it from a chest in his hidden room of treasures of knowledge. He would await her return, trusting that she would come back. She had carved the runes of the Qodes Adonai on all four walls of the room, and the power of the Oldknow had descended on the space, creating a warding magic that caused any who approached it to experience a fear of entering. The magic would drive the kobolds away.

She sensed Azra was in trouble. She knew a great battle was being waged in the Tirich Mir. Azra's pleading feelings beckoned her to help against the stronger foes assailing them. Even though their feelings were entwined, they could not communicate directly in words, so she didn't know what to expect. It was a desperate hour.

In the sanctuary of Theo's vault, she had pondered several courses of action. Angel sworn were still imprisoned in Koa, and she could return there and bring Uorsin and others back to the caves. But Uorsin was wounded. And they did not have weapons or grafting wands. Nor were there many to spare within the mountain tunnels, so it seemed unwise to gather them when there wasn't a practical way to use them.

She thought about trying to find Jodocus and seeing if he could call off the attack. But reason persuaded her that the Morgarten were loyal to Darcia. If they believed she had been named the Queen Mother's successor, then they would fulfill their mission with the same steadfastness they'd done for the original. Those Morgarten had been willing to burn down the Gallows Tree and destroy it rather than let the fruit fall into enemy hands. Their singlemindedness would make it nearly impossible to reason with them.

Of course, she could use the Tanaquil amulet to drive off her enemies. But she was still emotionally exhausted from trying to sate the golem's demands. If she used it too much, she would faint again and become helpless in their presence. Azra was sick and weakening fast. She could tell he had succumbed to spider venom again by the helpless feelings he'd previously displayed.

It all came down to her.

And an idea she'd had before. What if she loosed the Fear Liath on the Morgarten? They would not be expecting the creature that had terrorized Clairvaux to suddenly reappear at Tirich Mir. She did not want to kill them, but Darcia and her machinations had upended events. The common people and the refugee angel sworn had gathered and permitted all to join them. Darcia wanted to drive out those who were not loyal to her. Thus the runes of the Qodes Adonai would not save those loyal to Darcia from the advancing dangers. But she believed if she were in the caves, the runes would stop the Fear Liath from entering them.

Her heart wrestled with the decision she needed to make. Could she bring the Fear Liath with her? Would it attack and try to kill her? All she needed to do was touch it to take it with her to a place outside the caves. The statues with glowing eyes would protect those inside. And the Fear Liath could pick off those outside unless they fled. It felt like the sort of plan that Azra would make. But she worried she might not be deft enough to avoid the monster's claws. She also wasn't sure exactly where to go, and time was crucial.

So she'd knelt in Theo's vault and offered up her heart to the Oldknow, seeking wisdom and insight of what she could do to save her people, those who had trusted her despite her curse. Those who had followed her across the world. Could she withstand the Fear Liath? Could she tame it with the medallion?

The answer she received penetrated her heart and dispelled her confusion. The answer didn't arrive as a forceful scream or a stinging admonition. Yet it felt like a burning poker had been stabbed into her breast with a conviction so strong, so indelible, that she knew she would remember the words for the rest of her life.

Perfect love casts out fear.

And she realized that she and Azra shared that kind of love. It was a love of purity, of innocence, of shared tribulation, of having their hearts welded together.

She didn't need the medallion to tame the Fear Liath. It was a creature that was drawn to fear. One that fed on it. If she had none in her heart, it would not attack her.

Cimree had pleaded with the Oldknow to help her find the Fear Liath quickly. The idea of the ruins of the Gallows Tree had flitted through her mind. She didn't know whether it was there, or if that was where she should begin her search.

She marched through the snow, approaching the remains of

the tree. A hitch of sadness stung her heart. The Dryad who had lived there was Chrys's mother. Cimree had met the Dryad in person, and the Dryad had begged her to find a husband for her before it was too late. In that very spot, Jodocus had been bound and his memories snatched. Azra had fulfilled his duty, and then his memories had also been removed.

The skeletal flame-ravaged branches were thick with snow. She sensed Azra's anguish in her mind, his concern for what was going on. She tried to comfort him that she was coming and bringing help. All she could do was urge him to be patient.

When she reached the tree, she peered into the mist made by the waterfall. An urge to go closer to the falls spurred her forward. Snow clung to her boots, and fresh dots of white landed on her cloak as she maneuvered up the slope. The Silver River continued to flow away from that spot, the moving water refusing to freeze. She imagined the waters were absolutely frigid.

Carefully, she climbed the steeper part of the mountainside, which held pockets and caves. She paused on an icy outcropping of rock amidst the billowing mist surrounding the cascading waters. She'd once dropped into the waters from the top, and the journey down had shattered her body. If she'd not already eaten an entire fruit, she'd have died from such a foolhardy plunge.

Knowledge kept trickling into her mind. The Fear Liath was in the caves. It was vulnerable to daylight. That was why it fled into shadowy places during the daylight hours. Mist protected it from rays of sunlight. Clairvaux was a perfect dwelling place for such a creature. It had claimed the valley as its own.

Come to me, she thought to it. *I will not harm you. Come and see.*

Cimree waited, her senses dulled by the roar of the falls. Her feet were becoming numb from standing in the cold. She clutched the cloak to her, the cowl trapping in the warmth. Her serpents were lulling into torpor from the conditions. She could feel her own pulse as she watched the falls.

The world felt colorless. The rock, the frozen ice, the ironclad sky above.

A shadow passed through the waterfall, seemingly immune to the force of its weight. The Fear Liath hunched forward on its paws. The gray-white eyes and toothy snout were truly horrifying, but she felt not even a flinch of concern. It did not roar or even snarl. It stared at her through the mist, its body fading in and out of focus as the shifting tendrils wove around it.

Come to me.

Was it the Qodes Adonai carved into the medallion on her breast? Was it her utter lack of terror or troubling thoughts? She focused on her love of Azra, of hoping he would make it but realizing that whatever happened, he was for her and she for him.

The Fear Liath lumbered down the boulders at the base of the falls, each rock having sheared off from the heights to roll down before crashing into the forest floor. Evidence of similar impacts were within her sight.

The monstrous creation approached her, head low. She had the idea that the creature's eyes were its weakest sense. It wasn't totally blind, but it could not see her fully. And like other magical incarnations, it too was immune to her powers. Dew clung to its pelt. The long, razor-sharp claws clicked against the stone as it settled facing her. The absence of fear filled her with confidence. She trusted all would work out well, even though she had no idea what was going to take place next.

I need you. Enemies attack us at the Tirich Mir. Disperse them. But do not venture past the stone statues. That is forbidden you.

The Fear Liath uttered a snuffling sound. Its breath fogged from its snout. A predator by nature, it understood her meaning, and the idea of hunting angel sworn appealed to it.

Come with me. Frighten away the soldiers who seek to destroy us.

It snuffled again, swiping at the stone with its claws. The noise was a shrill tone that sent a tingle of apprehension down her spine.

The creature was powerful. But even it had been subservient to the golem.

Cimree reached out and caught some of its ruff in her fist. Her fingers felt like ice. The pelt was not warm, nor was it cold.

A spasm of anguish shot through Azra. His life was in peril. He believed he was going to die.

Cimree bowed her head, gripping the Fear Liath's pelt with one hand and the Tay al-Ard in the other. She invoked its magic to bring her to the main tunnel entrance. While she could have chosen any of them, starting at the central location felt right. Giving the Morgarten an opportunity to flee was important to her. And she believed the shadowy overhang at the mouth of the tunnel would offer the monster some protection.

The magic tugged her again and the Fear Liath with her. After a steadying breath, she looked around at the tunnel entrance and saw that the fortifications had been shut. No angel sworn were there.

She released the Fear Liath, and its snout inhaled the mountain air. A growl began to build inside of it.

And when it let out its fearsome roar, the stones in the tunnel trembled with the force of it. She watched the creature rush away from the cave, bounding on all fours. It was snowing outside, so the sun was veiled.

Cimree watched it go and heard shouts of terror from outside the entrance. Where was Azra? A surge of hope had come when he realized she was nearly there. She sensed she was close to him, and when she thought about it, she imagined the distance to be no farther than Andrin and Perreta's chamber. She made sure her cowl was shielding her and imagined herself in that corridor, appearing there only a moment later.

"Azra!" she called out.

"He's dying, Cimree," little Blanka said with tears running down her cheeks.

"Cover your eyes, Blanka."

Cimree marched forward, wondering what had befallen them. She found Blanka kneeling by Azra's body, her chubby little hands covering her face. She found Perreta, Cyrill, and Edwina trussed up with ropes, unconscious and pale with sickness.

Azra lay on the ground, blood blooming from cuts in his chest and arms. He was unarmed.

Cimree rushed to him. His pulse was struggling.

"She has...the fated blade," Azra whispered in despair. "Stop her!"

Twenty-Three

Enmity

Cimree laid her hand on Azra's chest. His muscles quivered uncontrollably. She noticed the bite marks on his throat, multiple livid wounds caused by spiders. Although he was highly tolerant of pain, she could feel his suffering intimately through their bond.

"I need to help you first," she told him, smoothing hair from his brow. Sweat bulged from his pores.

"I'm dying, Cimree," he panted. "I was already too weak. Help our people. Turn the others to stone if you must."

"Blanka," Cimree said to the little girl. "I'm taking Azra somewhere. When I am gone, you need to find help for your family. Can you do that?"

"I'm scared," Blanka said. "I don't want Azra to die."

Cimree felt at peace. Whatever happened would happen. She could only do so much. "I know you're scared. Edwina and Cyrill need you. Your mother needs you. Please find help."

Azra put his hand on top of hers. "Go, Cimree. Go. The blade whispers in the mind. Only our bond prevented it from ruining me. You have to kill her."

"I have to save you."

Azra grimaced. "You did save me, Cimree. I can't even stand up. I'm too heavy for you to carry. And no fruit from the Gallows Tree to heal me."

She leaned down and brushed her lips against his forehead. "Your daughter can heal you," she whispered. "I'm taking you to the tree."

"Cimree..." he lamented, shuddering in agony.

"Now isn't the time to be stubborn," she said, entwining her fingers with his. Then she gripped the Tay al-Ard. "Now, Blanka. Find help."

With a thought, she and Azra vanished and reappeared by the little sapling hidden in the crags above the empty village.

Reaching up, she lowered her cowl and instantly felt the flood of salt in her mouth when she stood.

"Chrys," Cimree said. "Your father needs you. Please heal him. He's already suffered so much."

Behind her, a statue of stone crashed into the rocks and broke into dozens of pieces. The angel sworn had been hovering in the air when he'd seen her and plummeted after his transformation. He hadn't even cried out in warning. Stone fragments littered the snow.

"Chrys," Cimree pleaded. "He doesn't have much time."

She felt a prickle at her neck and discovered Chrys kneeling in the snow by her father. "I will bring him to the river," Chrys said to Cimree, her face somber.

"What river?" Cimree asked in confusion.

"In a garden far away," Chrys said. "So he may rest."

Cimree's heart clenched in pain. "Will he die?" she asked, choking up.

"Death is only temporary, Cimree. It is your life that is like a dream. All is well."

Chrys touched Azra's chest, and a feeling tickled Cimree's eyes, which made her blink. The two of them vanished, leaving only an imprint of Azra's body in the snow. Not even their bond remained, and Cimree felt the void keenly.

Another gush of salt in her mouth. She whirled and saw one of the Morgarten in the midst of his transformation, his mouth open with horror, a longbow in his hands and arrow nocked, which turned to stone as well. Cimree walked toward him, expecting others. The Fear Liath roared again, the sound echoing off the rugged mountains. Rivulets of snow began to trickle down from the heights. An avalanche had been triggered.

She passed the one she'd cursed and saw another one who had just pulled out his grafting wand. He glimpsed her, and before he could react, he'd turned to stone as well. How many of the Morgarten were guarding the sapling of the Gallows Tree? How many were attacking the caves?

A stab of anguish struck her heart. Without sensing Azra, she felt alone. He was the only one who could look at her. He trusted her and she trusted him. Had Chrys taken him far away, farther than the chain of magic could link them? Or had he died, as Chrys implied he would.

It was not the time to grieve. What they had shared was special. He had loved another. And he had endured her loss by turning to anger. Cimree wouldn't do that. She heard signs of living things by the little tree, so she decided to return to the caves and go after Darcia.

Where to start?

She lifted her cowl, bowed her head, and used the Tay al-Ard to take her to Azra's room.

THE SMELL of the room nearly brought her to tears. It was dark, uninhabited, and she lit the druid stone slightly in order to see better. But with her serpent vision, she'd seen no one else hiding there.

Exhaustion from all she'd been through threatened to overwhelm her, but she continued to press on. That's what Azra would have done. She spied the fragment of red silk poking out from beneath the pillow on the stuffed mattress. Her emotions surged at the memory of the Ecbatanan garb. She didn't smother them with the Tanaquil amulet. Instead, she breathed slowly and let them pass through her. She focused her thoughts on the matter at hand. Finding Darcia.

If she began a random search through the tunnels, she might cause more harm among her people, turning them into stone unwittingly. She had to be cautious and deliberate.

As she headed toward the tunnel leading out, she observed the statue of Chuq poised there, eyes glowing and the stone providing warmth. The painful memory of that day stabbed her heart, but she had come to terms with the accident. As she passed, she touched the statue's head fondly, remembering the boy's grin. With the connection to the stone, she felt magic ripple inside her, and her awareness traveled along an invisible connection from Chuq's statue to another one. She could see through the eyes of the other statue into a different part of the network of tunnels and caves.

She'd carved the rune of the Qodes Adonai in every statue. Through one of them, she could watch from the others. Had this always been the case? Or was the power of the Oldknow responding to her presence in the tunnels. Did she have some kind of authority she hadn't realized before?

Cimree began to follow the invisible line from one statue to another. She had set up each one, so she knew where they all were. Through one set of eyes, she found a chamber where Setara was trying to comfort the women and children waiting there. No able-bodied men were there, but the sick and infirm ones were. Another statue looked upon the fighting. Some of the attackers had gotten inside and were clashing with the defenders. She found Andrin fighting alongside Odeon, their mirror blades held defensively as they parried attacks against them. They were outnumbered but were able to hold off against the larger force in the confines of the cramped tunnel, preventing the enemy from penetrating deeper.

Cimree shifted from statue to statue. Where was Darcia? An impression came to her mind of one of the side tunnels that was sealed off by a stone door Uorsin had made. From the statue's eyes, Cimree spied Darcia bent over the locking mechanism and working to open it. A dead angel sworn, Xarla, lay sprawled at Darcia's feet, blood staining her neck.

Light appeared, and Cimree saw Trinati approaching with a bare mirror blade clenched in her hand. Cimree wondered if it were possible to hear through the statues as well.

At that thought, the magic pulsed, and suddenly Cimree could hear the sounds in that other tunnel as if she were there with them.

"You killed *her* too?" Trinati said with fury. "How many corpses must there be to get what you want, Darcia?"

Darcia rose and turned to Trinati. Cimree was shocked at the look of madness she revealed. All friendliness had gone. If not for the medallion's bond, that could have been Azra. Her heart suffered another pang before she returned her attention to the woman who had hurt him and so many others. Darcia gripped the fated blade in her left hand. Cimree had never realized that she was left-handed before.

"At least one more," Darcia promised. "The Queen Mother knew you'd betray her in the end. She knew you couldn't be trusted. You were always too ambitious, Trinati."

Cimree had never been to that particular entrance before. And so she knew the Tay al-Ard would not be able to take her there. It must be one of the statues Azra had placed after she carved the rune into it. If she could have, she would have appeared behind Trinati so that Darcia would have glimpsed Cimree and received the brunt of the curse herself. If she managed to get the tunnel open, another phalanx of angel sworn would get inside. How close could she get to that place? If only she had all of Azra's or Wegner's memories.

"I am ambitious," Trinati declared. "I see that in myself now. Which is why I *choose* to serve Cimree. And I will never serve you. And she is here in the tunnels. Right now."

Cimree observed a twist of Darcia's lip and a mixture of cold fear and hatred in her eyes. "Then I'll have to kill her too. One nick of this blade and she's gone, and all her knowledge will be mine. Yours too, Trinati. Everything the Queen Mother shared with you, every secret she told you, I will know. This blade has power you don't understand."

"It's driven you mad," Trinati countered. She began to advance, swinging her blade in circles.

"You, and anyone else who crosses me, will fall before it. I know your weaknesses, Trinati. I've learned where you are vulnerable. Your feelings for Odeon. Feelings you've always failed at hiding. And now you've waited too long. Now it's too late to tell him."

Darcia was goading Trinati. To provoke her into an attack of rage. Enmity would overwhelm them both, and perhaps they'd kill each other. Cimree didn't want that.

Where was the serpent Iddawc? He would be in the thick of such a conflict if he was back.

"I don't need to kill you," Trinati said fervently. "I just need to keep you here. Keep you trapped in this corridor. You won't persuade me to act rashly. You aren't nearly as provoking as Cimree. So keep talking. It won't work on me."

Cimree felt so proud of Trinati in that moment. That she hadn't taken the bait. Cimree still had time to get there.

She lifted her hand from the statue of Chuq and could no longer witness the confrontation or hear it.

In her mind, she reached out with her affinity for the only other serpent in the caves.

When I stare at the night sky, I see a kaleidoscope of stars. Each star is a sun, like ours, only further distant. Therefore, there must be other worlds and other races and peoples. And just as there is a sun over this earth, which is the source of heat and light, able to be seen by any who have sight and felt even by those who do not, there is an Eternal Sun, called the Oldknow, which is the source of all wisdom, and those whose spiritual senses have awakened will observe that sun and be conscious of the Oldknow's existence. Those who have not attained spiritual consciousness may yet feel this power by an inner faculty called Intuition. The purpose of gaining wisdom is but to awaken oneself to a reality never before perceived. Awaken, Dreamer.

— The Hermetic and Alchemical Writings of Paracelsus

—The Hermetic and Alchemical Writings of Paracelsus

Twenty-Four
The Garden

Azra walked hand in hand with Chrys through a scorching desert. It felt like every breath he took filled his chest with fire. The heat from the sun was intolerable. His memory of how they had arrived at the desert was vague. The Tirich Mir was still shrouded in snow. In Azra's many journeys on the Long Patrol, he had seen vast deserts before and had grafted with birds to pass over the dunes. There were no birds. No animals of any kind.

"Where are we going again?" Azra asked his companion, his daughter.

"To the garden," she answered simply.

That made no sense to him. It also made no sense that there were no shadows of them in the sand. The sun was directly overhead and had not changed position even after what felt like hours of walking. Strangely, he didn't thirst. And it didn't feel like he was sweating, which was an alarming situation too. It meant his body was short on moisture, a situation that would kill him.

He didn't feel his muscles aching either, even when they climbed one side of a dune and trudged down the other. Nor was there any soreness in his feet. In fact, the only sensation he did comprehend—other than the oppressive heat from the blistering sun—was the feeling of his daughter's hand in his own.

"How much farther is it?" he asked. "To the garden?"

"We will get there when you are ready," she said.

"Ready? For what?"

"You will know."

Her words did not make sense to him. None of it made sense. He felt the urge to go back.

"Stay with me, Father," Chrys said, as if she'd heard his thoughts. "Don't be afraid."

Was he afraid?

The impressive heat seemed to increase with each rise of the dunes. Breathing hurt. But it was a different kind of pain. A torturing pain.

"Can we go back?" he pleaded.

"No. We must go forward."

"Why? I don't understand."

"I know. And you will. Once we get there."

Azra desired to turn his head and look back where they'd come from, but it felt...uncomfortable doing so. It felt wrong. Like something terrible would occur if he did. He buried the urge and plodded on.

Step after step. Hill after hill. The heat intensified. He saw someone ahead, a figure standing at the crest of the next rise.

Talking became painful. He tried to lift his arm and wave to the person at the hilltop, but his arm wouldn't rise. As they drew closer, he could tell the unmoving figure was a carving. His first instinct was to believe it the statue of someone who had glimpsed Cimree. But the stone it was made of was white. The visage and form were those of a woman with a cloak, her hand clutching at her throat to hold the fabric there, the other hand lifted to brush hair from her face. She was gazing down at him, although her body faced the other way. He understood in a way he couldn't comprehend that the figure was made of salt, not stone. And her face seemed familiar to him.

"She turned back," Chrys said dejectedly.

"What was she looking for?" Azra questioned.

"Her old life. Her past ways. They were too precious to her."

Azra reached the statue, studying the crystalline features of her face, the orbs of her eyes, the frown of longing or loss on her mouth.

And he *recognized* her.

It was Delara. His wife.

Azra whispered her name, the pang and shock of recognizing her churning inside him.

"What happened to her?"

"She stopped. The pain became too great. She tried to go back and she couldn't go forward. You must let her go, Father. You must let it all go."

Azra wasn't sure he understood. He'd reconciled himself to Delara's death. But was his daughter talking of Delara or Cimree? *You must let her go. You must let it all go.*

He stared at Delara's face, his heart churning with anguish for her. The heat became even more oppressive. It was hardening him. It reminded him of the white-hot heat of Uorsin's forge. It was transforming him. Into what?

He squeezed Chrys's hand and continued down the slope of the dune. As he continued onward, he noticed other statues along the way, all frozen in an attitude of retreating. Azra firmed his mind on the matter. He would not go back. Whatever he had to strip away from himself to move onward, he would. Pride? Gone. Anger? What use was it? He realized that what he needed to divest himself of wasn't anything he carried with him. Actually, he couldn't even perceive his body very well. What he had to slough off, like a serpent, was the skin of his old self—his particular combination of worries, resentments, and attitudes. He did so willingly, realizing that they had only been extra weights on his journey.

Movement became faster. Climbing the next range of dunes had become more effortless. Fear was one of the most difficult parts of him to shed. His fears about Andrin and Perreta and their family. Of the villagers who had joined them to seek protection from the angel sworn. He'd taken so much on himself. Had tried to foresee every situation and prepare a counter for it. Worry was the sister of fear. He discarded them both.

And after climbing another hill, practically running up it, he saw at last a view on the horizon that wasn't a continuation of the dunes. A series of snow-capped peaks jutting across the skyline. He'd traveled all over the world and had never seen such peculiarly shaped peaks in a row. And below, he observed a forested land thriving with wildflowers. Butterflies and birds abounded.

Relief flooded him.

"We're almost there," Chrys said proudly.

Down into the valley they walked, still holding hands, until they arrived at a wall bedecked with flowers and vines. The wall wasn't made of wood but animal antlers. The sharp tips made it appear like a wall made of thorns.

"I cannot go into the garden with you," Chrys said. "You must go alone."

A sparrow flew past him. He wished he could fly on its back.

"Why can't I stay with you?" he asked her, aching at the thought of parting from her, grateful that she had guided him through the desert.

"We will see each other again. I'm so proud of you."

His heart swelled. He crouched down and hugged her, and she clung to him and then kissed his cheek. And then, like a vapor of mist, she vanished.

Azra straightened and walked to the antler-wall, then followed it to the right. That was the direction he'd felt impressed to go. The journey was easy, the ground thick with foliage that smelled of mint and lavender. The flowers jutting from the ground were of every color imaginable. Bees droned lazily in their midst.

At last, he reached an opening in the wall in the form of a gate, where he found a man in tunic and trews waiting for him, holding a crooked staff. The fellow was middle-aged and had a slight paunch from overeating. Tufts of gray curled above his ears.

"Ah, you've come at last!" The fellow greeted him jovially. "I was told to wait for you at the entrance."

"Are you the Gardener?" Azra asked curiously. The arch of thorns was wide enough for them both to stand side by side. A ladybug flitted by and landed on the man's tunic above a distaff protruding from his belt.

"Are you angel sworn?" Azra asked after noticing it.

"I am not," answered the man. "My master, Ilyas, asked me to greet you. We both serve the Gardener. The Oldknow." He extended his hand to Azra.

Azra knew the name. Ilyas was the one who had visited the Queen Mother and warned her about the pending calamities. His words had been engraved in the Book of Secrets.

Azra reached out and clasped the man, and his insides churned and rushed with magic as the other man pulled him through the gate. It felt like a vortex had sucked Azra through, a feeling not dissimilar to what he'd experienced with the Tay al-Ard. A ripple of thunder sounded overhead. The closeness of the sound shook him.

He was inside the garden, hand still grasped by the friendly man at the arch.

"You must be thirsty," the fellow said, releasing his grip and clapping Azra on the back. "The desert is scorching. A refiner's fire. I had to walk that way myself."

"Did you have a guide?"

"I did. Some *pethets* forsake their guides early on. And wander strange roads."

Azra wasn't familiar with that term, but it had the intonation of someone worthy of derision.

There were so many different kinds of trees in the garden. And there were animals too. Tame ones that weren't bothered by their intrusion. The tranquility of the place made him forget about the troubles he'd endured. How he longed to just lay on the turf and fall asleep. If only Cimree were with him!

The man took him to a burbling brook that appeared ahead of them. A massive tree stood within the brook—no, the brook erupted from its network of roots. Day lilies grew at the banks.

The fellow knelt down, scooped up water in his hand, and drank from it. Azra did the same, and the pure, cool water refreshed him. Once he was satisfied, he wiped his mouth on his arm.

"My master has instructed me to have you anoint your eyes with the mud from the river. And wash them."

That did not make sense to Azra, but he didn't object, rather he immediately obeyed, remaining on his knees from his drink. He stuck two of his fingers into the wet earth abutting the brook and slathered the mud against his eyelids until he had covered them both.

"Bathe your face in the river," his mentor said, touching Azra's shoulder to steady him.

Azra leaned forward and used both hands to scoop water and splash it on his face, but he still felt residue on his eyelids.

"Again."

Azra repeated the action and was instructed to do it again, a total of seven times. The fellow patted him on the back.

"That is enough. The number seven, *sheva*, is a symbol of perfection, completeness. It is the number of the Qodes Adonai. It symbolizes holiness. You will see things you did not see before."

Azra wiped his face on his sleeve and lifted his head. He opened his eyes and saw that the birds and insects and animals had all transformed into other creatures. The pelts, plumage, and wings glowed with unfamiliar varieties of color, and it made him gasp in astonishment. There were creatures he'd never seen before. Cats with forked tails and horns. Deer with gems embedded into their breasts, the antlers made of gold. Azra began to weep at the beauty of the creations, of the strangeness and awe.

The fellow rose to his feet and helped Azra stand. "I wish Cimree could be here," he murmured. "Would these waters... would they heal her curse?"

"No," his companion said, shaking his head. "But Ilyas told me what will. You must bring her here, friend. To the garden."

He drew the grafting wand from his belt and handed it to Azra. It was the same distinctive style as the one the Queen Mother had held. Though different in subtle ways. Knowledge whispered to him. It was the distaff of Lan.

"But first there is another place we must go. A labor you must perform."

Twenty-Five

The Banishing

Cimree found Trinati lying on the ground next to the cold dead body of another angel sworn, Xarla. The mirror blade was gone. Cimree's heart lurched but settled when she saw heat radiating from Trinati's body. And then she noticed the swarm of spiders scuttling to and fro, wrapping her in a cocoon of silken threads. Cimree summoned the power of the Tanaquil amulet and commanded the spiders to flee. Power surged inside her, filling her with determination. The spiders immediately began to depart, leaving Trinati with evidence of bites on her skin and a dazed expression on her face. She'd been paralyzed with their poison.

Rushing to her side, Cimree knelt down and felt for a pulse. Her heartbeat thudded slowly, but it was still there. Miraculously, there were no other wounds. Darcia had had the opportunity to kill Trinati, but she'd chosen not to. Was that because of a spider's instinct to save a meal for later?

"Trinati, can you hear me?" Cimree asked, breaking the strands that were covering Trinati's body. Had Azra been bound up in such a way?

"Nnnngh," Trinati groaned. Her eyes closed and opened but otherwise she was uncommunicative.

The presence of a serpent snagged Cimree's attention. Iddawc slithered up.

"Where have you been?"

Spiders prey on serpents. I didn't fancy the idea of having my insides turn to goo.

It seemed the venom from these spiders were more of a paralytic kind. She didn't know enough about spiders to recognize the danger, but a bite was enough to render Trinati powerless. In a cramped tunnel, Trinati's own affinity would have been counteracted.

"I'm glad you are here. I need you to find Darcia."

That is too much work. I think I'll take a nap.

"Iddawc, this is not the time to be difficult. I can't wander around the tunnels trying to find her."

You don't have to. Drive away all the spiders, and she'll lose her grafting with them.

"If I try to summon enough power to send them all away, I'll faint."

Of course you will. Use the statues. They will obey you. Just as you drove all the bats away. You don't have to do this all on your own.

Cimree thought the advice was wonderful. However, she couldn't leave Trinati in such a state, so she grabbed Trinati's wrist and drew out the Tay al-Ard.

"Come with me," Cimree told the snake.

I suppose so.

The serpent writhed his way onto Cimree's thighs. She summoned the magic and brought them back to Azra's room. Because of the armor, it was difficult wrestling Trinati's body onto the bed. Her pulse was even more erratic when she checked it again. Iddawc curled up on a pillow.

"I'm glad Darcia didn't kill her," Cimree said in relief.

Her fear of you made her flee.

"What do you mean?"

You really do need to think more like a snake sometimes, Cimree. Spiders are especially vulnerable to your power.

"Why would that be?"

Spiders have eight eyes. They cannot close them. When Darcia is grafted to them, she cannot blink. It would be incredibly difficult to not look at you.

Was that why Darcia had never sought out Cimree since her transformation? Had that instinct for survival dominated Darcia's decisions ever since?

"She's afraid of me?" Cimree blurted out.

Most people are afraid of you instinctively. Except for that mortal you like to be with.

"Do you know where Azra is?"

Yes.

"Tell me."

No. I'm not allowed to. He's no longer in this mortal world.

"Is he dead, Iddawc?" Her heart heaved at the thought, a spasm of pain careering through her.

I cannot say more. Now, about driving all the spiders away. It might be a good time to do that.

Passionless, pitiless Iddawc.

Cimree shuddered with another ripple of dread before putting away her concerns for Azra to focus on the situation. The serpent was right. How many spiders had infiltrated the caves, acting as a web of spies to give Darcia knowledge of their plans and weaknesses? She rose from where she'd been sitting at the edge of the bed and walked over to Chuq's statue. Laying her hand on its crown, she bowed her head. Swallowing, she summoned the medallion's power once again as she had in the tunnel and sent a command to scatter the spiders and compel them to leave the tunnels through the cavern with the waterfall. In her mind, she imagined this message going to all the statues throughout the network of tunnels.

To her surprise, she discovered spiders all through Azra's room, which she hadn't even noticed until their path to freedom revealed them. They were very tiny and scuttled away hurriedly. But many were transformed into pebble-shaped stones. Her command had pressed them into action, but in doing so, they could not avoid her curse as they passed her in the doorway.

And she will feel compelled to leave as well.

"But what about the gate blocking it? Can she get through it?"

Do you care so long as she's gone?

"If she leaves with the fated blade, what will happen to her?"

You already know. You saw it happen in Ecbatana.

"The blade will drive her mad and she will kill herself."

Yes. And whoever claims it will suffer the same fate unless, like you, their emotions are protected. The memories of those past lives will resurface. It is a diabolical weapon.

Cimree felt tremors on the ground coming from the tunnel. She lifted her hand from the statue's head and drew her dirk. The approach was hesitant. Then she heard a voice.

"Cimree?"

She was relieved when she recognized it as Ramesh's.

"I'm in here," she said. "Are you alone?"

"Yes. Someone said they might have seen you, and Captain Odeon sent me to find you. I thought I'd start here. We weren't certain you had returned."

"I've only just returned. Tell Odeon that Trinati was attacked by Darcia. She's poisoned and lying here on Azra's bed. She needs to be tended to. I'm going after Darcia. The exit with the waterfall. Tell him that is where I'll be."

"Azra is missing too," Ramesh said. "Our warriors are falling. I've been helping with our wounded. The angel sworn are ordering us to lay down our weapons or they will slaughter us all. And there's a monster raging outside. The roars are terrifying."

"If we surrender, they will still banish us from the caves," Cimree answered. "We have to keep fighting."

"We're outnumbered, Cimree! Isn't it better to survive and go somewhere else? Whatever is outside is killing people!"

"We have nowhere else to go," Cimree said. "This is our last defense. I brought the creature. I set it loose. Tell Odeon to hold. I will destroy our enemies if I must, but the monster, the Fear Liath, will not enter the caves. This is our home. And the other angel sworn will not take it from us."

Ramesh sounded troubled. "I will find him. The defenders have been pressed. They're giving up hope."

"Tell them I'm coming. Retreat deeper into the caves. The monster cannot reach us."

"I will tell Captain Odeon at once," Ramesh promised. "He'll be glad to hear it!" She listened to the slap of his sandals as he rushed away.

Cimree went back to the bedside and stared down at Trinati. How long before the poison wore off? Trinati's strength and prowess were needed. It seemed as if everything they'd done to save themselves had been upended by Darcia and those loyal to her.

The emptiness she felt without her awareness of Azra deeply troubled Cimree as well. Memories of Theo stirred in her mind and the arena he was trapped in. Uorsin captured. The citizens of Koa chased and bitten by flying serpents. The Fear Liath wreaking havoc outside.

Had there been a situation more hopeless than this when all chance of survival seemed to dangle above a precipice?

She stared back at the statue of Chuq. A little boy who had lost his life merely by looking at her. But his death had served another purpose. He and the other statues had become sources of light and warmth. And they were driving away all of Darcia's spiders. Such a small little power. Seemingly insignificant. Yet even in death, good had grown from it. And if Azra had died, would his death also have meaning greater than what she could understand at that time?

You mortals are so maudlin. You may as well blame all your troubles on Lan for choosing to taste a mouthful of fruit that began the decay. You were made of dust anyway. Why does it startle you that you will end up so?

Cimree faced the serpent. "Is that all we were meant for, Iddawc? To go back to the dust again, to rise no more?"

So has every mortal wondered when they dwell somberly on their fate. But those of us who have seen beyond the dunes know of a garden there. And light and joy incomprehensible. Do not grieve for the dead, Cimree. Death is but the portal to a new existence.

"Why can we not see it, then?" Cimree asked. "Why do we only see prey and predator? A never-ending cycle of violence?"

You cannot see now in the dark, when only the moon and the stars give us their meager portion. Wait for the sun to rise. And then you will see it all clearly. You will see what truly is. And you will no longer weep that you spent a flicker of your existence in the dark.

Somehow the serpent's thoughts steeled her courage. Whatever she would face, she would face it bravely. She would confront it. She would triumph over it. If death was not the end, she could hope for something better in a life to come.

"Shall we face it together, you and I?" Cimree asked, moving to the cushion where Iddawc lay coiled.

To the end of days, my dear. To the end of days.

Cimree bent down, and Iddawc slithered into her arms. She took a steadying breath. She'd witnessed the fall of Montheron. Of Ecbatana. In the end, the people had turned on each other. When survival was at stake, violence seemed like the only answer. But it wasn't. She gripped the Tay al-Ard, and it felt warm to the touch, a warning that even it would fail if used too much.

She squeezed the jeweled device and thought about the cave where Wegner had died. And she summoned herself there.

Darcia knelt by the gate, clawing at the stone with the fated blade, the scraping noise grinding. By the light shining from Wegner's eyes, Cimree watched spiders scuttling like a river through the bars, fleeing into the cavern beyond. Her mouth tickled with salt as a myriad of spiders suddenly died in her presence, their tiny bodies turning to pebbles.

Darcia gasped in shock, her head jerking up. But she did not face Cimree.

"No, no, no, no!" Darcia began to whine in terror. She bent down and covered her head with the cowl of her cloak.

Cimree wondered if the fear was real or a ploy. She kept her vision focused on the fated blade. Knife fighting was Cimree's specialty. The risks in this situation were great, but Cimree's power would decide the encounter. All the spiders were running away, depriving Darcia of her affinity creature.

"We end this now," Cimree declared. "Leave the blade and I'll only banish you."

Instead of answering in words, Cimree heard Darcia laughing. Wild, hysterical, terrified laughter.

Twenty-Six

Destroying Angel

Azra stood on an outcropping of stone on a hilltop nestled with olive trees. What he saw filled his heart with wonder and ominous possibilities. From his position at the grove's edge, he stared at a walled city with heavy fortifications. A city besieged by an army the size of which he had never beheld before. There were hundreds of thousands of soldiers encamped. The susurration from it, even at that distance, sounded like an eerie wind, and the constant motion and activity below made the army appear like one swollen, writhing beast.

"What is this place?" Azra asked in wonderment. "Where have you brought me?"

"It doesn't seem familiar to you?" asked his mentor, leaning on his crooked staff.

"No. I've traveled to many lands and seen many things, but not a fortress like this nor an army so vast."

"When we passed through the stone arch in the garden, we arrived in another world. This one has several names. Where I come from, the world is called Idumea."

"Idumea," Azra repeated.

"My master, Ilyas, was from this world. He became a wayfarer, one who travels between worlds." He stretched out his hand toward the walled city. "This army has already destroyed many kingdoms. The brutality they inflict is beyond imagining."

"I have seen the worst that mortals can do to each other," Azra said, grimacing with pain from what he had seen in his childhood.

"No—you have not. This world was the most depraved, the most violent, the most wretched of all the Oldknow's creations. In every land this army conquered, they beheaded their enemies and stacked their skulls into pyramids. They impaled the heroes on spikes and carried off the remainder to become their slaves in distant lands. When the nobles and elders of the people begged for mercy, kneeling in the dust and pleading, 'If it please you, kill us! If it please you, spare us. If it please you, do what you will to us!"

Azra's stomach twisted with disgust. "And they were slaughtered still?"

"Yes." The nestor's wizened face bore an expression conflicted with grief. "Idumea was the worst of the worst. It violated every stricture of the Oldknow. Not just the laws but the meaning of the laws. Is it not written in the Sefer Hamalakh, the Book of Lore? 'And what doth the Oldknow require of you—but to do justice, to love mercy, and to walk humbly.'"

He sighed.

Azra felt his heart stinging at the words. He knew of the Sefer Raziel, the Book of Secrets. But what was this tome that was spoken of? He wanted to learn more about it.

"And this city?" Azra asked. "Will they also be destroyed?"

"Come with me," the man said. "We must enter the city and visit its king."

"How will we get there? I've never seen an army that large."

"How?" quipped his mentor with a smirk. "You are angel sworn. You have a grafting wand. Take us into the city. They will not observe us. I will cloak us with a word of power to stop them from seeing us. You will take us both to the king's fortress up there."

Azra swallowed his apprehension and drew the distaff of Lan. He spotted two shrikes in the grove of olive trees, and with a summons, he bonded with them for himself and his companion, and the birds willingly submitted to him. He didn't even feel any prickles in his shoulder blades at all. The grafting was effortless. They lifted off the edge of the hillside. Azra heard the man utter a word under his breath, and the two of them became translucent, void of color but still tangible to Azra's new vision. He followed the fellow as he swooped easily along the currents of air toward the walled city. The defenders' armor was different from any style Azra had seen before. Their soldiers were spread out upon the walls, staring down at the besieging army with ashen faces. Their terror was palpable. A cacophony of noise burbled up from the invaders' camps. There were siege ladders at the ready. Battering rams. The attacking soldiers had braided beards with beads interwoven in them, conical helmets, and were laughing and celebrating amongst themselves. They were brim with confidence.

Azra and the nestor floated along the current of air, and Azra was guided to the king's palace, which appeared powerfully built, but it was nothing compared to Montheron. They soared to one of the upper balconies and landed there. Azra peered down into the city. The streets were empty. People were undoubtedly hunkering down in fear, waiting for the impending attack. He felt pity for them.

Then he noticed a rectangular structure with tall gold-wrapped pillars and a fiery altar out in front of it. Men in bloodied cassocks were offering animal sacrifices on it. The smoke from the altar trailed into the sky. Everything about the place felt foreign and strange to him.

The spell of concealment was revoked, and the fellow grabbed the handles of the balcony door and entered, eliciting a cry from a man in an ash-stained tunic that was torn down the front from his collar, exposing his chest. The fellow was middle aged and looked destitute.

Azra's companion muttered another word, and this time, Azra heard it clearly. *"Xenoglossia."*

The man in the grubby clothes scooted away from them in terror but then stopped, blinking in surprise. "M-Maderos?"

"Why are you scuttling about on the ground?" answered Azra's mentor, Maderos. "Have you lost a coin?"

"I've been praying," said the man desperately. "Pleading with the Oldknow to help us."

"I know," Maderos said. "And I have brought you help." He gestured to Azra.

The man looked confused, still on his knees. He studied Azra in confusion. "You brought *one* man?"

Azra felt wholly surprised by the introduction. Butterflies began to flutter in his stomach.

"You were expecting an army, Ezekias?"

"I was hoping for a miracle. When they attacked the northern kingdom twenty years ago, they scattered the people...who knows where. They mixed with the remnants. They are half-breeds now. Pagans. And if we are destroyed, the same will happen to us. Please, Maderos. I'm trying to cling to my faith, but they will soon destroy us just as they destroyed every other kingdom they've conquered."

"And what did Yesa tell you?" Maderos countered. "What did he promise your kingdom?"

"His promises are riddles!" stammered Ezekias, who Azra suddenly realized was the king of the besieged people. His ash-stained tunic, his unkempt appearance would never have signified he was royalty.

"Riddles, you say? Did you not understand them?"

"I don't understand *how*. Not a single arrow will be shot inside the city? That they...they will leave voluntarily without payment, without tribute?"

"What does your name mean, Ezekias?"

The king's shoulders slumped. "I know what it means."

"Then stand up. Fear has many eyes. It always seeks what was and what may be and not what *is*. Focus on now. On right now. Not tomorrow. Not the past. Now."

Azra watched the king slow his breath. Then he stood and looked at Maderos pleadingly. "I will do as you say. I will trust, even though my knees tremble."

Maderos embraced him. "Good. This is Azrael. He is one of the angel sworn."

King Ezekias pursed his lips. "I've seen you before. You were with the cloaked woman."

Azra started in surprise. He hadn't been to this place before. And the cloaked woman...Was that a reference to Cimree?

"Ah! Ah!" Maderos exclaimed vigorously. He turned and motioned to Azra, then fixed his attention back on the king. "They came seeking the *Nehushtan*?"

"Yes," the king said somberly, confused. "I destroyed it when they brought it back. The people worshipped it. They take everything good and seek to twist it."

"When was this?"

"Last...year? I think? Before I stopped paying the tribute. The staff was in my treasury."

"Excellent...excellent! I discern now there is more than one reason we were meant to be here."

"You've arrived just in time. Earlier today, the chief cupbearer came forth and yelled to my people, in our own tongue, that we would fail. That we would fall. He proclaimed that the Oldknow had commanded them to destroy us. That our soldiers were doomed to eat their own dung and drink their own piss for defying them. It caused a panic in the city, Maderos!"

"He's a *pethet,* Ezekias. Nothing more. An empty threat. I have brought you help. This is Azrael. He is the *destroying* angel."

Azra turned to Maderos, shocked by his announcement.

King Ezekias gawked at him in fear and then fell to his face with a groan. "Forgive me. Forgive me. I spoke amiss. I spoke from fear. Please spare us. Please!"

The reaction was so sudden and visceral that Azra could only look upon the prostrate king, mouth agape. He glanced back at Maderos, this time in confusion. What had prompted such a reaction?

Maderos knelt by the frantic king and soothed him. "Do you not remember, old friend? Do you not remember the covenant of *hesed*? You have helped this people turn back to the Oldknow. And the Oldknow will not forsake you in your hour of need. Yesa knew it too. He told you to believe. They will depart. Not an arrow will be shot into the city. Your people are spared. Remember this, old friend. Remember to trust."

Maderos rose and put his hand on Azra's shoulder. "We must go."

Azra nearly balked, but he retreated to the balcony with Maderos. The connection to the shrikes was still strong.

After vanishing temporarily, they flew up the height of the rectangular temple and landed on top of it. A haze of smoke obstructed their view of the scenery. It smelled like a cooking steer.

"I am a fallen angel," Azra said to Maderos firmly.

"You are Azrael. In every world, an angel is chosen to mete out the Oldknow's justice. The Oldknow is patient, longsuffering, and merciful. And it has already provided a way for Ezekias's people to escape this calamity."

"How do you know this?"

"Because this is a story from the Sefer Hamalakh. This moment is from my past. We are seeing it, living it, but it happened long ago." He put his hand into his tunic pocket and produced an iron key like the one Cimree had found in Ecbatana.

"My master, Ilyas, let me borrow his voided key to bring you here. With it, we can travel in time as if time were a river. Time flows forward, but the voided key allows us to go against the current."

Azra felt his mind grasping with this knowledge. "He remembers seeing me earlier because to him it was the past but to me—"

"To you, it was the future."

"My future? Our future?"

"Yes. Ilyas has shown me times in Idumea. Moments that I could experience for myself. I cannot alter events that have already passed away. I am here to witness them. But *you* are here to impact them."

"And what am I supposed to do, Maderos? Destroy the army? By myself?"

Maderos cackled. "By yourself, hah! The seed was already planted. The sapling grows. By yourself. Hah! The smallest seed can become a towering tree rising even higher than this temple or these walls. I could show you trees that would astonish you. But it all begins from a tiny seed. A tiny action. A tiny thing. By the small and the simple are amazing things done. I will demonstrate to you the power contained inside the tiniest flea. By yourself. Bah! This is the Oldknow's battle. You are here to prove to these mortals how weak they already are."

Twenty-Seven
Plague

Maderos brought Azra into the thick of the besieging army, and they wandered the cramped camp without notice. Maderos had taught Azra a word of power—*mareh*—that rendered them both to appear like members of the invading army. Their disguises were obvious to Azra, for having anointed his eyes with the clay from the river, he could see everything as it really was. But as they mingled among the soldiers, no one paid them any attention at all. Maderos led the way with his crooked staff, searching from tent to tent. Azra heard the scrape of whetstones against metal blades, the guffaws of comfortable soldiers, and smelled the dung of animals thick in the air.

"What do you see?" Maderos asked him, glancing back as they walked.

"There must be tens of thousands," Azra said. "The baggage of gear and supplies alone suggest they are well provisioned."

"Look smaller," Maderos advised. "Study the ground as we walk."

Azra did so. It amazed him how such a simple word, spoken in the tongue of the Oldknow, had made infiltrating the army so effortless. And from another word of power, he understood the language they spoke. They were excited to plunder the fortress. To ravish the women. To carry off slaves and to execute whomever they felt inclined to harm. They were drunk on their formidable strength. And they mocked the religion of the people they were on the verge of destroying.

Azra peered at the ground, seeing puffs of dust as they walked. How rapidly the grasses had been trampled and destroyed. What was he supposed to find? What was he supposed to see?

The sun was failing as the day waned. He roved his eyes from tent wall to tent wall, searching for some evidence of what Maderos wanted him to see. A few dead rats littered the area, probably trampled by the press of bodies as they slunk between tents foraging for food.

Maderos stopped abruptly. "Listen. Do you hear?"

Azra noticed the moans, and coughing, from several tents ahead of them.

"This way," Maderos whispered, waving with his staff for Azra to follow.

They veered in a different direction, following the sounds of distemper. Azra noticed more dead rats along the way. One was in the agony of dying, its gray fur and limbs twitching as it contorted in death throes.

Maderos paused at a tent, the source of the coughing. Men were speaking inside the fabric walls. The smell of vomit and defecation were strong.

"Two dozen more fell sick today," a man said worriedly. "Fourteen died. We have to tell the captain! It's spreading."

"The captain isn't a patient man," said another person.

"But surely he's noticed how unfit some of the soldiers are?"

"He thinks they've been drinking too much—"

"They're dying!" The declaration interrupted the other man.

"I know. I know. I will tell him in the morning. After we've counted up the dead. How many do you think there will be?"

Azra heard a sniff and silence. He gave Maderos a look of curiosity. It seemed like these were healers supporting the army.

"I can't say. But after the symptoms appear, some are dead within a day. Others have lingered for two."

"Ishtar save us!"

"Prayers will do no good," the other quipped. "This is a plague. A punishment from the gods."

A terrible voice groaned. "I need water. Please...water!"

"I'll help him. You have to tell the captain. It is spreading too quickly."

"I don't feel well myself," said the first. "I'll tell him tonight."

"May he answer with patience."

Azra heard the tent flap rustle, and then the remaining healer poured a drink and tried to comfort the suffering patient.

"This is the interior of the camp," Azra whispered to Maderos. "The men on the front don't even realize what's going on here."

"And neither do the healers," Maderos said softly. "They do not understand the source of their misery."

"What source? Is it the rats?"

"No. The rats are also the victims. Look closer. One was dying over there. Did you see it?"

"Yes," Azra said.

Maderos retraced their steps back to the twitching rat. Its movements had become even slower. Its breathing was shallow.

"Closer," Maderos said.

Azra dropped to one knee. He peered at the common rat. And he noticed the dark flecks on it. Fleas feasting on the rat's blood.

Azra squinted up at Maderos. "Fleas?"

"One of the tiniest of the Oldknow's creations," Maderos said. "The fleas are sick. The plague is rotting in their gut. They thirst but cannot be sated. And with their bile, they spread the illness to the rats, who die from it. And when the rat is dead, they seek the blood of another kind."

"They've bitten the soldiers," Azra affirmed. "All this suffering...from a flea bite?"

"Yes. The rats have followed the army, seeking free food. The destruction commenced weeks ago, killing the rats first. Rat to rat. Then rat to soldier. Little whiskers sniffing. Ignored because they were insignificant. And a flea even more so. The men, coughing in the tent, spread the disease farther, to all who breathe their spume. It will come faster now. Faster and faster. Dead stacked on dead. The Oldknow prepared for the deliverance. But tonight is the night they are saved. And you will perform it."

"I will?" Azra asked in confusion.

"You are the destroying angel. The captain they spoke in fear of already knows of the illness. Many captains have heard of it. They're terrified but put on brave faces. If they do not abandon the siege now, they will all become corpses. They don't yet understand about the fleas, nor do they suspect the rats feeding on their grain and souring their milk with their dead bodies when they perish."

"But this has already transpired," Azra said, his mind bursting with confusion. "This is the past. You already know how many will die."

Maderos clasped his hands together. "I was told by my master to bring you here. At this day. So that on this night, you may cause the retreat. One angel sworn to defy the most terrible army in Idumea at this moment. Prepare yourself. At midnight, you will chase them away."

Azra had never grafted with lions before. The raw power he felt surging down his arms and legs was thrilling. The region also contained an abundance of buzzards, who were drawn to the army and the natural death that occurred among them, as well as the corpses that had been secretly removed and piled into ditches.

The buzzards provided him the power of flight. He had two swords, one in each hand, the metal heavy, gleaming, and polished. He'd spent an hour sharpening them each to a deadly edge.

The angle of the moon in the sky was as Maderos had described, which meant it was nearly midnight. The myriads of stars were different from the night skies of his world. Maderos had taught him several patterns, including a series that led to a single star that always pointed north. King Ezekias had provided a hauberk of chain mail and a helmet to protect Azra's skull.

He stood atop the city's main gate, which had been cleared by the king. The city's soldiers had been commanded to gather and prepare to defend from beneath. Azra waited, biding his time. Maderos was with the king in his chamber, joining him in prayer.

The time had come.

Azra did not feel the tingles of the grafting magic, even though he'd been holding the connections for several hours. He felt strong, confident. Memories of the siege of Montheron bubbled into his mind. Andrin was not there this time to guard his back. But Andrin had his own desperate post to defend in his world.

Azra bowed his head and offered a prayer to the Oldknow. Then he leaped from the wall, soaring above, transfixed in the sky. With a thought, he made the druid stone embedded in an amulet around his neck shine with radiance, brightening the midnight sky in a whorl of blue. He remained poised in the air, blades in hand, drawing the phalanx of attackers on alert at the front to watch him. Gasps from the soldiers began to ripple.

Then Azra rushed down with a lion's roar and flew into the forward troops. He heard his own cry echoing off the stone walls. His blades spun and severed his enemies' heads and limbs, and instantly, gasps turned to shrieks of dismay and horror. Azra pierced through the front ranks, cutting down anyone who stood in his way. The fear from his midnight raid caused dismay to erupt from within the camp. Horns began to blare, rousing the sleeping masses.

Azra sliced through the enemy, and when a wall of foes armed with spears rallied to face him, he took to the sky over them, securing howls of astonishment. He thudded to the ground at their rear, shifted, and savaged their ranks from behind until the hastily gathered cohort spilled off in alarm.

The druid stone burned from his chest, revealing their contorting faces that gazed at him with fear. Their enemy could fly? More soldiers were being rallied by commanders. They were coming at him from all quarters, but they were hastily arranged and struggling against the brunt of their fleeing companions.

Azra made the most of the confusion, brandishing the blades as though they were lion claws. The dead and wounded dropped around him. There was no forfeit of energy as he attacked. Even his breathing remained calm.

"Band together! Attack from all sides!" The shouted command came from a warrior leader.

Under the aegis of the word of power, Azra understood the order and flew again, heading directly to the commander and stabbing him through. Many soldiers began to peel away and flee, but others were determined to face this threat with courage. Maderos had said this army had never lost a conflict. They had razed innumerable cities and butchered their foes.

Azra spun around and cleaved through another man, then stuck his blades into the body, hilts up, and faced the rush with his bare hands.

Blue flames surged into his fingers, and he let loose the fireblood on the charging foes. Stretching his arms out to either side, he spun in a circle, becoming a wheel of death. Tents caught fire, creating dazzling light and the roar of flames and prompting moans of despair.

The enemies hurled down their weapons as they all fled from him. Fear cracked like a whip over their escaping heads as they scattered. The siege was broken. The people in the walled city would awaken in the morning to find charred ruins and corpses littering the land. And the plague already unleashed would continue to destroy the army as it fled, depleting its forces further.

Helmets lay scattered about Azra's feet as he walked a few steps forward, searching for any who would challenge or fight him. Swords and spears lay haphazardly around. But no one opposed him. No one dared.

The shouts and screams issuing from the devasted camp burned in his ears. Azra lowered his arms, quenching the flames in his hands and the light from the druid stone. But the fire from the tents would continue to burn. Mayhem would prevail. He didn't know how many he'd killed that night. But it was over. With the sickness ravaging the army and their morale broken, the threat had ended.

Azra took up his two blades and flew into the sky, a shadow against the night.

Truly, death is the midwife of very great things. It brings about the birth and rebirth of physical forms a thousand times improved. One species of rat can be improved upon, generation after generation. One serpent can become a thousand over time. Ignorance, more often than not, begets confidence and not knowledge. It sires rigid beliefs. Those who know little, not those who know much, are the ones who assert that this or that problem cannot be solved by observation and study. In death, we see rebirth in countless ways. In death, we learn patience. In death, we transform to higher orders. Death is the highest mystery of the Oldknow.

— THE HERMETIC AND ALCHEMICAL WRITINGS OF PARACELSUS

Twenty-Eight
The Reckoning

"Put the blade down," Cimree said more firmly, unnerved by the frantic edge in Darcia's erratic laughter.

"I'm supposed to just believe you?" Darcia grunted, stifling her laugh.

"Have I lied to you, Darcia? Have I been disingenuous with you? Banishment is merciful, considering what you've done."

Darcia's laughter died out. "*You* betrayed the Queen Mother. You stole the fruit of the Gallows Tree."

"The Gallows Tree didn't belong to *her*. Its fruit was always a gift from the Oldknow. Lilith was never supposed to remain in Clairvaux."

Darcia hissed, "You are unworthy to speak her name." Cimree realized Darcia's graftings had ended when she turned from the gate to face her with eyes shut tight, which added to her look of torment. Darcia leaned back against the bars of the gate, the fated blade still clutched in her hand.

Her mind is splintering, Iddawc mused. *Better to just kill her. Would you like me to bite her?*

No, Cimree thought back. *I want to provide her a chance to walk away freely.*

Compassion can be a fault, you know.

"You are not the judge of my worthiness," Cimree told Darcia. "And your spiders have all fled, so you cannot send them to bite me."

Darcia's face twisted with disgust. "You have no idea how many you've killed already. How many you've murdered."

"But spiders are prolific, are they not? Milena taught me that one egg sac can hold hundreds. I imagine you have many allies waiting to be born in the tunnels. Your own little army. But as you can see, they've been banished too. Please leave, Darcia. Or I will kill you."

"I can't get out," Darcia lamented. "I can't get past this gate."

"I will open it. But lay down the dagger. Kick it to me. Or you will end up just another statue down here."

Cimree watched the reaction her words provoked. Darcia was terrified of being turned to stone. She panted, gripping the bars with one hand, the dagger aimed toward Cimree with the other. There was a chance that Darcia would hurl the blade. But Cimree was ready for that, and her serpent reflexes and Darcia's lack of sight would make dodging it easy.

"And we're supposed to survive out there with the Fear Liath? Even the Morgarten fear it."

"This was your own doing," Cimree answered. "You all would have been welcomed here as brothers and sisters. But you wanted to rule."

"The Queen Mother *chose* me to rule."

"She also withheld information about the prophecy. She believed she was wise enough to prevent Clairvaux from falling. But she died."

"Part of her lives on with me. She was killed with this blade. I can still…feel her."

"When I found that blade, the previous owner had killed himself with it. He plunged it into his own heart. Your mind cannot handle this. Believe me."

"Why should I?"

Cimree stepped closer, quietly. She could grapple with Darcia for the blade.

"Why should I believe you?" Darcia repeated.

Cimree said nothing and took another cautious step. Then another.

"Cimree...don't..." Darcia's voice quavered.

Being so close to a threat, Cimree felt the tingle of venom in her mouth and fingertips. Her body involuntarily prepared her to strike.

Do it, Iddawc thought eagerly.

"All right, all right!" Darcia burst out. She dropped the dagger onto the stone floor, where it rattled as it settled. Then she gripped the bars with both hands, wilting with the suspense. Tears dripped down her pale cheeks. Her knees wobbled.

Cimree slowly, cautiously took the fated blade. She felt the jolt when she touched it, but the Tanaquil medallion protected her from its impulses. Then she sheathed it in her belt at her back.

"Oh shades, oh shades," Darcia whimpered, dropping down to her knees.

"Turn around and face the bars," Cimree said. "Head down."

"Don't kill me. Please don't kill me."

"I told you I wouldn't. I'm going to open the gate and let you out. But you must never return."

"Cimree! Please! I'm sorry. I'm so sorry. Don't make me go out there."

"Your choices brought this punishment, Darcia."

"What if I go back to Clairvaux? If I climb the Wilderswill, will you forgive me? Can I earn your trust again?"

Don't trust her. She is going to try and kill you once you've opened the gate.

"Trust is easily broken and difficult to mend. I can't promise anything right now, Darcia. It all depends on how sincere you really are."

"I'm sincere. I'll do any penance you demand of me!"

"Banishment is your penance. Now scoot away to the wall. I will open the gate."

Just kill her now. She will always be a danger to you and this people.

Cimree ignored the serpent's advice. "Move."

Darcia, on her knees, turned around and shimmied to the edge of the gate where it connected to the stone. Memories flooded Cimree's mind of when Uorsin put it in and taught her and Azra how to unlock it. Only members of the high council had copies of the wrench-key needed to unlock it. He hadn't revealed that to Darcia, which was why she'd been stranded there. The key wasn't to a lock but acted more like a lever to pull up the forked pin sunk into the stone. The only other way to get past the gate was to batter it down or pry loose the rivets in the walls. Noisy tasks.

Cimree removed her key from her pocket. Darcia was close still, but facing the wall, head bowed and weeping softly.

Cimree fit the key into the aperture and used a good deal of strength to push down, which swiveled the locking pin up. It took both hands and all her weight to get it to move. The latch reluctantly slid up, and Cimree pulled on the key to drag the mobile half of the gate toward herself.

That's when Darcia struck.

A fistful of sand hit Cimree in the face, the gravelly bits stinging her eyes painfully. A boot struck Cimree in the side, knocking her off balance.

Why don't you listen to me? Iddawc said disappointedly.

Cimree backstepped, rubbing her face to clear her vision. Thankfully, her serpents could observe perfectly well as their eyes had a hardened film on them as protection from dust and dirt. The sand hurt, but it wasn't fatal.

Darcia attacked fiercely but randomly, sweeping with her legs, trying to find her. Her breath rattled with fear, but she had become desperate.

Cimree blinked, grateful for the natural tears that helped rinse away the grit, although the water from the pool in the cave would be much better. Cimree switched sides, staying well out of Darcia's reach. Each punch and kick became more frantic as Darcia realized she didn't know where Cimree was standing. Opening her eyes would be fatal.

Darcia gasped in pain when she kicked the stone wall of the cave. She spun around in a circle then, pausing to listen despite her heavy breathing.

Cimree remained still.

"Fight me!" Darcia goaded.

With surefootedness, Cimree stepped over to the gate she'd partially opened. Darcia was on the side of the gate that didn't swivel. Cimree gripped the bars and then jerked on them to drag the gate against the stone.

Darcia lunged, aiming a punch that struck a metal bar instead. The gasp of pain that followed indicated that Darcia had likely broken her hand. She winced and pressed the injured hand to her bosom. Cimree used that moment of pain and shock to act.

She stepped around the gate and seized Darcia's uninjured arm with a grip and then twisted Darcia until she flipped over and landed roughly on her stomach. Cimree maintained her hold on the arm, controlled the wrist by applied pressure, and plunged her knee into Darcia's spine. It was an easy disarming and controlling move that Azra had taught her on their journey to Tirich Mir. She'd never been able to get Azra to submit to the hold—he always had an escape maneuver. But Darcia was helpless, panting, sobbing, and Cimree had lifetimes of memories returned.

Now can I bite her?

Cimree hesitated. She could not see the future. If she let Darcia go, would she seek revenge later and cause even more harm and heartbreak? Should Cimree be her executioner? Should she allow Iddawc to be?

Controlling Darcia with the hold, she listened for guidance

from the Oldknow. *Vengeance is mine. The day of calamity is at hand. Her doom comes swiftly. Send her away.*

Cimree swallowed, feeling sorrow at the premonition.

"I banish you, Darcia, from Tirich Mir. You must go into the world and survive the best you can for as long as you can. You will not find succor here. On pain of death, I warn you not to return. You are a fallen angel now, forbidden to taste the fruit of the Gallows Tree."

Darcia wept onto the stone in misery. Cimree hauled her to her feet, twisting Darcia's arm behind her back, and then shoved her through the opening of the gate. As Darcia fell on the other side, landing on her chin, momentarily stunned, Cimree gripped the bars and shoved the gate to close it. As soon as it had swung over the cut-out portion where the lever was seated, Cimree dropped to pull up on the key and locked it. Then she pulled the key out and backed away, raising the hood of her cloak.

Darcia was crying softly on the ground. All her plans had fallen apart. Cimree was grateful that Uorsin had not been there to witness it. It would have wounded him to understand that Cimree had killed her. So despite Iddawc's frequent urgings, Cimree had followed the guidance of the Oldknow and let Darcia's fate fall upon herself. Guards would be assigned to watch over the gate and make sure Darcia and her ilk never returned.

Long is the way—and hard—that goes out of sheol and leads up to light. I don't think she'll have the courage to climb it.

But she might, Cimree thought in reply, peering down at the little pale snake.

Oh, I rather doubt it. When Asmodeus was cast out of paradise, he was certain his unconquerable will, his lust for revenge, his immortal hate, and his courage to never submit or to yield would allow him, in time, victory over the Oldknow and to usurp the golden throne. It did not work out well for him clothed in a revenant's bones.

"Cimree..." Darcia pleaded. "At least give me some food."

"All the skills you need to survive were taught on our journey here," Cimree said. "And you can't convince me that a spider doesn't have the instincts for catching a meal."

Cimree scooped up Iddawc and started to walk away.

"Don't abandon me," Darcia moaned. "Please. I'll release all the prisoners in Koa. I promise."

As Cimree walked, the light of the tunnel was fading, and she felt a spasm in her leg. A familiar throb. Dread ignited in her stomach.

She stopped, listening, waiting. The muscle twitched again, stronger. Her bone began to ache.

The golem was coming.

A shudder went down her spine.

"Cim-reeee!" crooned the malevolent voice.

Darcia began to shriek in terror. "Turn me to stone! Please! Please! I beg you! Turn me to stone! *Nooooo!*"

Twenty-Nine
The Druid

Cimree's heart churned with anguish at Darcia's frantic cries. She wanted to run away, to clamp her ears and drown out the frightened, pleading sounds. But she cautiously returned to the gate to watch the events unfold.

Darcia's back was pressed against the bars. She cradled her injured wrist against her, gasping. The golem made its familiar clicking noise. Darcia shuddered.

Then the golem yanked her off the ground, causing additional shrieks. Cimree steadied herself against the wall, peering into the gloom of the cave.

Her connection to Azra was suddenly restored. He was outside the mountains, flying like an eagle toward her. No feelings of anxiety dwelled in his heart, just a determination to reach her. The golem was in the cave, however. It had power over the graftings of the angel sworn. She could not use words to communicate with him, but she warned him with her feelings that where she was, it wasn't safe. He didn't deviate in his resolve.

"No, no, oh no!" Darcia wailed.

Cimree edged closer, trying to decipher what was going on. The golem had Darcia dangling upside down by her foot from one hand. With the other, it wove a sort of magic conjuration upon her body. Words were whispered, harsh and sibilant. A feeling of foreboding, of unnatural magic, lingered. The golem spun Darcia, and white strands began to envelop her, rolling around her body until it was veiled in webs.

Darcia's moans quieted. Had she fallen unconscious from the terror?

Soon Darcia's entire body was shrouded in silk. The golem batted this cocoon, making gurgling noises, and then set it down on the cavern floor near the edge of the pool. No part of Darcia had been left uncovered. The golem had worked its magic on her body. Just as it had done to Cimree. What new abomination had it created?

She sensed Azra outside the cave, swooping down like a bird of prey.

Again she sent her worried thoughts to him. It was too dangerous! He would be in danger if he intervened.

His mood didn't alter in the least. If anything, he was even more determined to reach her.

Cimree crept closer to the bars and witnessed the golem hunkering down near the bundle of silken threads. It peeked over at her.

"More?" It came as a request. A plaintive one.

"What have you done to her?" Cimree asked solemnly. She knew the monster wasn't strong enough to get through the bars. But she didn't want it reaching through to grab her either, so she stayed back.

"More," the golem insisted, padding toward her.

"No more," Cimree answered, shaking her head. She sensed Azra's arrival at the tunnel at the head of the waterfall. The golem hadn't sensed him yet.

Azra, please. You can't come this way!

The golem lunged forward, grabbing the bars of the gate and throttling them. *"More! Cim-reee! More!"*

"No!" she shouted at it. "No more! Begone!"

The golem raged against the bars, but Uorsin had built them to withstand the creature's strength. The golem settled down, glaring at her, and then it swiveled its neck and a clicking noise sounded. Its nostrils wrinkled as it sniffed.

"Azra, it can smell you!" Cimree cried out.

With her heat vision, she saw him appear above the falls. He had a grafting wand in his hand. With a leap, he flew into the cavern, soaring above the pond.

The golem barked in anger and waved its deformed hand at Azra.

Nothing happened. Azra hovered over the pond. The grafting was intact.

The golem made the gesture again, grunting with impatience. Still Azra did not fall. The golem roared in rage and began to roam the edge of the pool. It snarled savagely at the angel sworn floating above.

Azra gave a flick of his wrist with the wand, and the golem howled as if struck by a painful blow. Then it began to keen noisily, in despair and defeat.

Azra brandished the scionwood wand again, and the golem leaped off its feet, as if stung. It scrabbled backward and raced to climb the walls, spiderlike, disappearing out the tunnel and splashing the half-frozen waters as it fled.

Then Azra floated down to the edge of the pond and landed. She spied an amulet around his neck with a strange sigil on it. He paused at the silk-shrouded form of Darcia, a pitying frown on his mouth, but then approached the gate.

She was so relieved to see him, so grateful that he was whole and healed. He smiled at her tenderly, and she felt the love pouring from his heart. He put the grafting wand in his belt.

"Let me open it," Cimree said eagerly, drawing the key from her pocket.

"Ephatha," Azra said in a language she didn't recognize. The

knob on the gate wrenched of its own accord, lifting up. He pushed on the gate's bars to open it, passed through, and shut it behind him. The locking mechanism slid back into place as he embraced her.

Cimree clung to him, amazed and confused and delighted. He held her tightly, wrapping both arms around her, and the warmth that suffused her with his return was like the sun breaking through the clouds.

He pulled back, taking her cheeks between his hands, and then he pressed his forehead against hers. What startled her significantly was that her serpents didn't feel any threat from him at all. The urge from them to strike him, the revulsion for his affinity—gone. In fact, it seemed like he had no particular affinity.

"I need to take you somewhere," Azra said. "I just returned from another world. A world called Idumea. The cure for you is there. A way to revoke the transformation and make you whole again. But let me finish securing the tunnels." He screwed up his face in concentration.

"Finish securing?" Cimree asked in confusion at his choice of words.

He patted the amulet dangling from his neck. "This is called a talisman. I've already summoned spirit creatures to drive out the attackers. They will send the Fear Liath away."

"I brought it here with the Tay al-Ard," Cimree said.

"I know," Azra answered. He traced the edge of her chin. "You've done so much. I have the distaff of Lan. And even the Fear Liath must obey it."

Cimree brightened. "Is that why the golem couldn't break your grafting?"

"Yes. I have authority over every creature, both natural and spiritual." Azra glanced down at Iddawc. "Even you, wise one."

His eyes are open. He's become a druid, Iddawc murmured. *I like him better now.*

Azra bowed his head to the serpent as if he too had heard the thoughts.

"There are injured and wounded," Azra said. "The sick and the poisoned. What we will bring back from Idumea will heal them all. There is a sacred staff there called the Nehushtan. We'll go together through the Gallows Tree. I'll take you through the desert to the garden. Someone is waiting for us there."

"I'm so relieved you're safe," Cimree said, brushing her fingers through Azra's hair. "It's been so hard. Everything we've gone through. I thought I was going to lose you."

He nodded in understanding. "But your courage and resilience prevailed. We are going to begin over with this world. All of us here in the Tirich Mir. We're going to bring everyone to settle in that land you and I visited. The pristine land that was never settled. I've seen a glimpse of the future, Cimree. Of the changes that are coming. The changes that you and I will make." He slid his hand into hers, bent down, and kissed her mouth gently.

A muffled groan from the cavern alerted them that Darcia had revived. Cimree saw that the silk threads were rupturing. She began to lift her cowl to cover herself, but Azra caught her wrist.

"She's one of the golem's creations. She's immune to your power now," he said.

"How do you know she's immune?"

"I'll explain that later but understand that I see the world very differently now. I know her for what she truly is. The same as Iddawc. And you. This is her punishment."

Cimree stared past the bars and watched as the silk wrapping was shredded away. Darcia's upper torso and arms were as they'd always been. She lay on her stomach, hair spilled over her arms. But her bottom half had transformed. Cimree nearly gasped when she looked upon the bulbous lower segment and eight huge hairy, tarantula-like legs. Her body from the waist down had been morphed into that of an enormous spider.

"W-What's happening?" Darcia moaned, lifting her head. She

tried to rise, but the legs weren't all cooperating. As they unfolded from the binding strands, Cimree shuddered in horror at the sight of the half-woman, half-spider the golem had formed with its twisted magic.

When Cimree had awoken after her transformation, she hadn't realized what had been done to her. She gripped one of the bars of the gate.

"The golem changed you," she said to Darcia. "It transformed you too."

Darcia rose on trembling spider legs. Each one was about as large as her regular leg, but they were sheathed in hair, jointed into segments, and attached to a bulbous, swollen nether region.

"It made me into this?" Darcia exclaimed, looking down at herself in loathing. "And this is my doom? This is what's to become of me?"

"I didn't want mine either," Cimree said. "It wasn't my choice."

"But this is too much. I can't be with other people. If they discover me, they'll try to kill me. What am I supposed to do, Cimree? How can I live like this?"

"I can't answer that," Cimree said with pity. She reached for and squeezed Azra's hand. Even with her curse, she knew she had Azra's love. But Darcia had no one. Not even Uorsin, whose feelings she'd manipulated and trampled.

"I can look at you now," Darcia said, advancing. Her voice sounded desperate. "I would rather be a statue of stone like Wegner than endure this."

"You waited too long to make that choice," Azra said. "Wegner chose to sacrifice himself before his transformation in order to save others. He listened to the whispers that came to him."

"What whispers?"

"The whispers that you heard as well." Azra continued. "The warnings. The premonitions. The Oldknow kept trying to reach you, but you went beyond hearing. You hardened your heart against his counsel. You were past feeling in the end."

"That's not fair!" Darcia said spitefully. "I didn't hear anything. I wasn't warned."

"You were," Azra said. "You heeded the call of your own ambition instead."

"I can't stay here," Darcia said, shuddering. "This place means nothing to me now. It's a tomb. A crypt. You are all going to die in here."

Cimree felt sorry for her, but Darcia would always resent her punishment. She would not learn from it. And she would destroy others.

"Then go," Cimree said. "The golem made you to kill people. But we will be safe in here."

"I hope I never see you again," Darcia said with hate.

And with those words, she scuttled over to the wall and climbed up its side until she reached the tunnel at the top of the waterfall. Cimree watched as her shadow slipped away.

"My curse doesn't feel as awful as hers," she murmured.

"It wasn't the curse but how you handled it," Azra said. "It helped you in ways it won't help her."

"Will we ever meet her again?" Cimree asked.

"I don't know. There is so much about the future I don't even understand. Come with me back to the tree. Someone you need to meet is there. An Unwearying One."

"A what?"

"You'll understand soon enough. He will take us to Idumea for the staff. The staff that will transform you back."

"I wasn't sure it was even possible," Cimree said. "I thought I would stay like this forever."

"No," Azra said, stroking her cheek. "But some things *are* meant to last forever."

She pulled the Tay al-Ard from her belt, and they joined hands over it.

Thirty

The Garden of Mirrowen

Cimree and Azra walked the dunes hand in hand. The give of the sand beneath her boots felt pleasant, and a cool breeze stirred the air. The sun was high overhead, never changing its position as they walked, which was curious but not alarming. The rays of light felt luxurious against her skin.

"This place is beautiful," she said to him. "I've never been in a desert before."

"It wasn't this pleasant when I crossed it," Azra said with a chuckle. "I thought I was going to die."

"And Chrys made the journey with you?"

"Yes. She was my companion until we reached the garden."

"I never knew a Dryad tree could act as a portal," Cimree said. "Where we are right now...it doesn't seem like it's in our world, does it?"

"I don't think so. It might be a bridge world. It might be the world beyond the grave. I don't understand where we are, but I think the purpose is to unburden us from the toils we've suffered in life. My journey took a lot longer than this. A more painful journey. But I can see the mountains already."

"They're magnificent," Cimree said, gazing at the snow-peaked crags on the horizon.

"What's strange is I passed statues made of salt. They were each staring back at the dunes, not looking ahead. I haven't seen any this time."

"I wonder why?" Cimree mused.

"I think they were burdens from my life. Things that I hadn't resolved. One of the statues was of my wife, Delara. Chrys said I needed to release that burden, or I wouldn't be able to move on either. It felt highly symbolic."

"Indeed so," Cimree said, wondering why there were no statues of salt for her.

Perhaps she had already shed the burdens of guilt previously. Like turning Chuq into stone. Or Khaf. Azra had warned her that the desert would be difficult, hot and arid, but to Cimree, it had been pleasant. Soothing even. Was this because she was already at peace within herself?

After tramping down another sand dune, she spied a wall of antlers ahead with a prolific garden beyond it.

"We've arrived," Cimree said with interest.

"Maderos will be waiting for us at the gate."

Squeezing Azra's hand, Cimree increased the pace. The long trek through the dunes hadn't wearied her at all. Azra had told her that time seemed to stand still in this place, that their journey away from the Tirich Mir would not have changed in their absence.

They followed the perimeter until they arrived at the arch Azra had mentioned. A man stood there, someone whom she didn't recognize, though he felt familiar to her. He wore a long tunic, one that nearly reached his knees, and held a twisted staff in one hand and a chalice in the other. The chalice had pictures sculpted into the sides.

"Ah, welcome back, old friend," Maderos said to Azra. His eyes fell on Cimree next. She had no fear of him and he had none of her. She knew in her heart that he would be unaffected by her magical curse.

"Maderos," Azra said respectfully. "This is Cimree."

"Hello, sister," Maderos said, inclining his head to her. "My master, Ilyas, spoke of you often."

"I've never met your master," Cimree said. "But I have read his words."

"Indeed so. My master is a harbinger, one who sees the future, the past, and the present. I am a humble learner. A seeker of wisdom. He is teaching me to take his place, although I lack his special gifts."

"I'm grateful to meet you, Maderos," Cimree said.

"Welcome to the garden," he said. Then he wagged the cup at Azra. "I found this in the enemy camp after the army fled. In the cupbearer's tent. The man who had threatened the city with destruction. This is the king's cup. I offer it to you now."

"I'm no king," Azra said, shaking his head.

"Even still, the cup is yours. For thus the whispers tell me."

His choice of words intrigued Cimree. She had, for a long time, experienced the Oldknow's will through whispered thoughts.

"You have heard them, lass," said Maderos. "You hear the whispers from the garden. And you trust them."

Cimree blinked in surprise. "You…you can hear my thoughts?"

Maderos shrugged. "That is my curse, Cimree. And a hunger for good food. For pleasant company."

"Those don't sound like curses to me," Cimree said. She felt comfortable with him. Like he was an old friend.

"There are many gifts of the Oldknow. And to some, they can feel like curses. But mine is rather unique. But has not the proverb said…'And thou, Oldknow, hast searched me, and known me. You know when I sit down and when I rise. You understand my thoughts afar off. You are acquainted with all my ways. Where shall

I go, or can I flee from your presence? If I ascend up into heaven, you are there. If I make my bed in sheol, behold, you are there.' Is this not so, Cimree? Did you not hear the whispers even in your darkest hours?"

"There were many times I felt alone," Cimree answered truthfully. "But I was never truly alone."

"You carried your burdens," Maderos said to her knowingly. "But it's time to have them lifted from you. Welcome to the Garden of Mirrowen."

"DRINK FROM THE CUP," Maderos instructed after he'd led them to the tree that was in the center of the garden and from whose roots the rivulets of water emerged.

Azra handed Cimree the cup that Maderos had offered him before they crossed the threshold of the arch. He had taught Azra how to assist someone in coming through, so Azra had been the one to help Cimree to cross.

Cimree took the cup and knelt by the stream. She filled the cup and drank from it. The water was cool and clean, and she felt reinvigorated after tasting it.

"The cupbearer's chalice you will bring back with you," Maderos instructed. Cimree handed it back to Azra. "The Oldknow has placed a curse on it. A blight. When a mortal holds it in their hands, it will fill with a silver liquid. Drinking that liquid will cause a pestilence to infect that person. There are many plagues contained within that cup. Ilyas has told me that those plagues impact the future of your world. They will cause diseases upon your posterity until the dregs of the cup have been drunk. This is in the future."

"Then we must be careful of it," Cimree said, her heart lurching. "I've seen enough suffering in my lifetime."

Maderos gave her a knowing look. "You will see more, little sister. Pangs always precede the gift of life. You may as well ask the sun to be veiled in shadow as to wish for troubles to pass away. If the sun were veiled, everything would perish in time. Night and day. Day and night. Both are needed for life to flourish."

"So I must bring this back into the mortal world?" Azra asked.

"Aye, little brother. There are purposes to be fulfilled. You both will watch these events unfold. Or so Ilyas tells me."

"Will I get to meet Ilyas someday?" Cimree asked.

"When your time as an Unwearying One is finished," Maderos said.

"What does that mean?" Azra asked in confusion. "My daughter told me that *you* were an Unwearying One."

"I am," Maderos said. "I've just begun and am but a lad, and the people hate me. My master said that I will eventually pass the mantle to another. Then he and I will be reunited in Idumea."

"You must pass your cloak?" Cimree asked in confusion.

"My calling. My ordination. My fate. There is but one way to kill an Unwearying One. And then my responsibilities will pass to another. The cycle of life and death must end at last. You are chosen, Cimree and Azra. You were called and you answered. You came when summoned."

"What does it mean to be an Unwearying One?" Cimree asked. She felt totally unprepared for such a shift in fate.

"It means you will live through the ages of this world and watch the Oldknow's plans unfold. It means you will be taught the mysteries of time, the traditions of the ancient ones. And you will teach them to others who heed the whispers and follow them. You have the voided key, Cimree. The voided key that was entrusted to Lan and Havah. With the authority I will bestow on you, you will both be able to visit the past with the Tay al-Ard. You will learn the truth of this world, whence it started and its ultimate destiny. I used the voided key from Ilyas to visit the past in Idumea. That is where we will find the Nehushtan and remove the sign of the serpent from you. After you have healed your people, you will return here, and I will teach you the mysteries of the ancient ones. And you will rule on this world from the Garden of Mirrowen until the end of all things."

Cimree felt humbled by Maderos's words. Feelings of inadequacy blossomed. "I don't think I'm prepared for this. I'm just a healer."

"And I was just a pig keeper," Maderos said with a shrug. "You were called, Cimree. You were chosen, Azra. You will teach these mysteries to the mortals. And in time, they will forget them. They will defy them. They will forsake them. But there will be others who will heed the whispers from Mirrowen. And they will seek you in the garden. I must go away after this. You will remain as stewards. As seneschals."

Cimree noticed the troubled look and the scowl on Azra's face. But he complied, and she felt she should do the same.

"If we can do it together, I think I could bear it," Cimree said.

"You must do it together. Neither of you has the strength on your own. Teach the ones you have saved. Follow the premonitions that come from whispers. You will do well enough."

"So what must we do?" Azra asked. "How do we retrieve the staff that can heal her?"

Maderos untied the voided key that dangled from his belt and handed it to Azra. "This key is yours on loan. You have been to the holy city. You've met King Ezekias. Now you will return and go back to a time before the enemy invaded their lands. He will give you the staff to borrow that those injured may be healed. Then you will put it back in the treasury."

"Who made this staff?" Cimree asked.

"That is a story for another time," Maderos answered. "There was one man, long ago, who hearkened to the whispers of the Oldknow. The people were unruly and unbelieving. A curse of serpents arose to afflict them. The Oldknow commanded the staff to be made to heal them. The serpent is a manifestation of the Oldknow. A type of it. The serpent is a symbol of regeneration. Or new life."

He lifted his finger and touched Cimree's forehead. "Hail, Serpent Queen."

THIRTY-ONE

THE NEHUSHTAN

The magic of the Tay al-Ard transported Cimree and Azra to another world. They arrived at dusk, moments after the sun had set. The disorientation Cimree felt suddenly standing on the balcony of a palace overlooking a majestic city made her knees wobble. But the vista was beautiful, and the smells rising from the busy streets reminded her of the souk in Ecbatana.

"This is Idumea, the world of the Oldknow," Cimree said, staring across the scene of rooftops, palaces, and fortress walls.

"A time in its past," Azra corrected her. "When we came here, Maderos brought me to that hill over there. Do you spy the olive trees?"

"Yes. It's a pretty scene."

"He said a matter of some significance will take place there in the future. Didn't share what. But on those hills, as far as you can see, an invading army had gathered to besiege this city. Hundreds of thousands of soldiers had encamped all around."

"What is that building over there? The one with the smoke rising from it?" Cimree pointed to it. "It's quite lovely."

"It's a holy site," Azra said. "They offer animal sacrifices in the courtyard during the day."

Cimree studied it closely. She could feel magic radiating from it, similar to the statues she'd imbued with power. "I feel the Qodes Adonai. The rune is engraved there somewhere."

"Interesting," he said. "It's so different from when I was here before, which is only a few months from now. The invading army is already making its way here because King Ezekias stopped paying tribute to the overlord."

"And he's the one we need to see?"

"Yes. I need to invoke a word of power so that we can understand each other. But he told me that he recognized me from an earlier visit and that I'd brought a woman with me. It was surely you. But you'll need to cover your head until we get the staff."

Cimree's heart wriggled with nerves. "I want to believe what Maderos said, but I'm still frightened it won't work."

Azra faced her. "It will. I understand it the same way I knew I could see you without harm. Whatever power that artifact possesses exceeds everything we know. It's powerful enough to overturn the golem's curse."

His reassuring manner and intent face comforted her. She put her hand on his chest, nodded, and then raised the cowl of her cloak.

"Xenoglossia," Azra said, invoking the word of power.

She felt the prickle of gooseflesh down her arms as he said the word. But no other outward manifestation happened. "How do we know if it works?"

"I suppose we shall see. Let me speak to Ezekias first."

Azra went to the balcony door and twisted the handle. He went in but left the balcony door ajar. Cimree crept to the edge to peer inside, where she saw torches illuminating a royal bedroom. A man was kneeling at the bedside, head bound, hands clasped together in the attitude of prayer.

"Ezekias." Azra spoke his name softly.

The kneeling man wore a colored tunic with a luxurious vest and sandals, similar to what she'd seen in Ecbatana. He was bearded, wore necklaces, and had decorative bracers affixed to his forearms. His beard had no streaks of gray in it.

The king found Azra standing behind him and bowed his forehead to the ground. "Are you an angel?" the king whispered in awe.

"I am of the angel sworn," Azra said. "I seek the Nehushtan. I have need of it to heal someone."

"I am unworthy to be in your presence," the king murmured.

"Stand. We are fellow servants of the Oldknow."

The king looked up slightly, and with a reassuring nod from Azra, he stood up. "The Nehushtan is in the treasury. I had to hide it from the people, for many worshipped it as Adonai."

"I need to borrow it for a brief season," Azra announced. "Then I will return it."

"It is not mine to give or to withhold," the king said. "Do with it as you please. I will send for it." He strode to another door and opened it. "Amaryahu!" he called out.

Cimree heard another man's voice, but it was too muffled to distinguish the words. Then Ezekias returned from the doorway.

"My servant will bring it promptly."

"Thank you."

"You are not from this world," Ezekias said. "I can sense something different about you. And your garb is strange to me. What is that stick you have in your belt?"

"My distaff," Azra said. "With it, I can control animals."

Ezekias gaped in surprise. "Do you have a flaming sword?"

"A mirror blade? Yes."

"I've always wanted to behold one. Do you have any other messages for me? Our enemies are gathering. The northern kingdom has already been destroyed. Yesa has told me not to fret. That we will be preserved. But I am nervous."

"Trust your friend's counsel," Azra said. "You and I will meet again in time."

Cimree waited, listening to the subdued conversation, but she sensed the approach of a deeply magical presence. The feeling was palpable as the tremoring footsteps thumped down the hall. Her heart quickened with eagerness. She sensed the rune of the Qodes Adonai again. The servant returned, bringing with him a rugged staff, the wood pale gray and thick. The wood seemed almost petrified with age. But a serpent carved of copper or bronze was wrapped around the upper portion of the staff.

As soon as she laid eyes on it, she felt the core of herself wrenched apart.

It happened so powerfully, so suddenly, that she fell to her knees, her strength sucked out of her. The image of the coppery snake sizzled in her mind. Power went down her arms, her legs. The injury she'd sustained in the catacombs of Ecbatana, the one that had broken her bone, was healed utterly. The strange sensation that she'd often had, that alien ache, was gone. She sensed the presence of serpents and found a dozen around her on the floor. They were no longer attached to her head, no longer part of her. She sensed them with familiarity, with friendship. They had been part of her curse, but they were living things, and they were their own again. She experienced not only her own relief but theirs as well. She was still grafted to them, but it wasn't through compulsion.

The door of the balcony opened and Azra stood there, holding the ancient staff. She lifted her head and met his eyes wonderingly.

His smile was endearing. "Your hair is back," he said, dropping to his knee. He slid his fingers through her dark hair.

"It worked instantly," Cimree said. She tried to stand, but her legs were still weak. Azra helped her rise and then offered her the staff to support herself with. When her palm touched it, she felt its power rushing through her fingertips. Energy and healing filled her.

"Another angel sworn?" Ezekias said, looking her over with an expression of wonder, but then he noticed the serpents on the balcony and flinched.

"They will not harm you," Cimree said. She observed a young man near the door and assumed he was the servant who had brought the staff.

"Forgive me, my lady," Ezekias said, bowing. "A double honor to be in both of your presences. You are welcome to abide with us."

She could feel Azra's emotions brim with joy at Cimree's transformation back to herself. Her curse was gone. The power of the Nehushtan had reversed the metamorphistry. Just as she suspected, she found the rune of the Qodes Adonai engraved on the copper serpent's tail. Cimree had sloughed off her old self and was renewed.

"We must return to our people," Cimree said with gratitude. "Many have been bitten by serpents. Many are dying of venom."

"By all means," Ezekias said with a humble bow. "Your need is pressing." He bowed to Azra. "Until we meet again."

Azra took Cimree by the hand and brought her outside.

"We'll go back to the garden?" she asked him.

Azra declined. "I'd like a moment just to be with you," he said. "Let's go down to the city and walk among them. I want you to remember what that's like. To know that you never have to hide your face again."

"But they'll see the markings from the amulet. I'll stand out."

Azra shook his head. "The markings are gone. On both of us."

Her throat clenched as tears stung her eyes. If only she had a mirror, but she believed Azra. And she saw with her own eyes that his patterns were gone. She stared down at the snakes and released the grafting. They were free to go, to scatter into the countryside, which seemed a perfect climate for the heat-loving reptiles.

Azra drew his new distaff and bound them to two doves roosting on the palace roof. Hand in hand, they floated off the balcony wall. Night had settled over the ancient city, and they landed in an empty street at the edge of the souk. He released the doves.

Cimree gripped the staff and listened to the noise from the festivities with anticipation. It would not take long before she'd had enough of the crowd, but being with Azra in that moment, sharing it with him, was pure bliss.

"Are you ready?" he asked her.

She was and the two walked forward. The crammed vendor stalls were set amidst well-worn paving stones. City walls and arches towered overhead. Torches lit the expanse, and everything flashed with dozens of colors. There were fabrics, garments, baskets of multihued fruits. As they walked amidst the crowd, she could understand the speech and listened in on a hundred conversations. Many were tormented by news of the approaching army, though a few believed it would be destroyed before it ever reached them. Some haggled over prices of beaded necklaces or amethyst stones.

Many glanced at Cimree and past Cimree, and there was no rush of salt in her mouth. Some wrinkled their brows in confusion at her strange outfit. The women, it seemed, wore tunics that reached their feet and had their hair covered in scarves. Others looked at her askance. But they could notice her and not die, and it made her wipe away tears of gratitude.

Surging feelings swelled in her chest. A couple of vendors noticed the staff and asked where she'd purchased the replica of the Nehushtan. Food sellers offered samples of their wares, whether a marbled skinned fruit called a date or a skewer of cooked lamb with savory spices. Spritely music drifted on the air, and Cimree tugged at Azra's hand and led him to a place where dancing was taking place.

"Is that similar to the dances the Pashmir do?" Cimree asked after watching the small group dancing in a circle in the street. Young men danced in rings together and the young women danced separately. Both sets eyed the other as they did so.

"The men and women dance together. It's joyful to watch. But it has the same energy as this. The same enthusiasm. When I was here, the streets were all empty. They can't even imagine what is coming to their walls."

"We didn't know that either," she said, turning to face him. "Azra, I don't want to be parted from you again. I don't want to have a separate room. I don't care about the Queen Mother's traditions or her prohibitions. I want *you*."

Azra smiled at her suggestion. "I think the Oldknow's tradition is the best. I don't want to leave you either. I don't want to spend another night alone. Maderos mentioned a marriage rite. I don't think I can wait for a village ceremony. Let's go back to the garden. We can ask Maderos to marry us."

"You are asking *me* to marry you?" Cimree said with a smirk.

"We'll break every tradition if we have to," Azra said. "I saved that red silk kiyafet. I want to see you wear it again." He leaned over and kissed her mouth. In public. In front of everyone. Since there was no urge from serpents wanting to strike him, she gently bit his bottom lip.

"We must be patient," she told him. "We must rescue and heal the others first. Then we go back to the garden. All right?"

He bent to kiss her again.

And they were still kissing when the Tay al-Ard swept them away.

Thirty-Two

The Rising of Kenatos

With the Tay al-Ard in one hand and the Nehushtan in the other, Cimree summoned herself and Azra to the area in Koa where the angel sworn prisoners had been kept. Where once it had been the site of a fledgling escape plan, it had become a scene of suffering and despair. Many of the canvases used to block out the sun were in tatters and flapped in the warm breeze. Moans from the dying could be heard throughout the encampment. Cimree didn't see any angel sworn guarding the prisoners. It was the middle of the day, and the sun was chasing away all evidence of winter.

She had brought them to the tent where Cimree had talked with Salisha. The rip in the tent was still there and the noise of suffering inside wrung her heart.

"Cut it open," Cimree told Azra as she stuffed the Tay al-Ard back into her belt. Azra drew his dagger and slit the tent wide open, then stepped in followed by Cimree. Inside they found a bandaged Uorsin tending a feverish angel sworn—Salisha—whose pale face and sweating body revealed that she'd been bitten by the serpents.

"Azra!" Uorsin blurted out, having grabbed a sturdy mallet as a makeshift weapon. The blacksmith seemed exhausted and had purple bruises over his face, a half-swollen eye, and other signs of violence on his body.

"Hello, my friend," Azra said as the two men embraced.

Uorsin did a double take when he noticed it was Cimree who entered behind Azra, his initial startled response transformed into a relieved sigh when he realized that she had transformed back to herself.

Cimree knelt by Salisha and felt for her pulse.

"She was bitten only yesterday," Uorsin said with a mournful countenance. "She's lasted longer than many of the others. But the bites are fatal, and there's no fruit of the Gallows Tree to save her."

Cimree reached out and gripped Uorsin's arm. "I'm just grateful you're still alive."

Uorsin grimaced. "Many others died during the revolt. But I couldn't leave and go back to the caves. Not with Darcia still there."

"She's gone," Cimree said with sympathy, feeling a mixture of the pain Uorsin carried in his heart. "The caves are ours again. We'll bring the rest back. Just as I promised."

"Even if we had enough grafting wands, they are too sick, Cimree. There are just too many who cannot even stand up."

"I know, Uorsin." She glanced at Azra. "We brought help from Idumea." Then she tried rousing Salisha from her lethargic sleep. "Salisha. It's Cimree. Can you open your eyes?"

Salisha lay still, but after some further prodding, she began to revive. "C-Cimree?"

Cimree shook her again. "Open your eyes."

"Wouldn't that...kill me?" Salisha asked confusedly.

"I've been cured. The curse is gone." Cimree smoothed the hair from Salisha's forehead.

Salisha blinked, her wearisome expression mingled with pain. "It's too late for me," she whispered. "Try and rescue the others."

Cimree brought the staff into view. "Look at this, Salisha. Look at the Nehushtan. It will cure the snakebite. It will heal you."

Salisha lifted her eyes to the coppery serpent figure wrapped around the top of the staff. Cimree felt power radiate from it, and Salisha's pallidness transformed to vibrant health, as if she'd taken a bite of the fruit of the Gallows Tree. Her expression shifted from one of suffering to enjoyment.

"I-I'm healed," Salisha said, sitting up without help.

Azra reached for her hand and pulled her to her feet. Uorsin looked awestruck.

"Anyone who has been bitten by the serpents will be restored if they stare at this," Cimree said, rising. "I'll go tent to tent. Azra, can you help the survivors graft to any birds nearby? We need to get everyone back to the caves."

"I haven't seen any of Jodocus's guards," Azra said. "Where are the Morgarten?"

"They all left," Salisha said. "Except for Jodocus. He's here in the camp. And he's also dying from the bites."

Cimree glanced at Azra in concern and then turned to Uorsin. "Where is he?"

"Come with me," Uorsin said, wincing as he rose.

"I'll help spread the word," Salisha offered.

They left the tent, but they could hear Salisha shouting out to others, inviting any who could walk to join them and be healed. Uorsin led Cimree and Azra through the crowded maze of tents, their boots kicking up plumes of dust. Cimree felt the staff thrum in her hand as she walked and realized that its healing power had been invoked again. And then again. People were emerging from their tents in droves and seeking her and gazing at the copper-colored serpent fixed to the staff.

"He's in that one," Uorsin said, pointing to another tent farther on.

Azra raced ahead and flung open the tent flap. When Cimree

arrived, she found Azra kneeling by a makeshift pallet on the floor where Jodocus was shivering with fever, his breathing troubled.

"Hurry, Cimree—he's nearly gone," Azra urged.

"Revive him," Cimree instructed. "He needs to look at it."

"Jodocus, my son," Azra said with emotion. He had tears dripping from his eyes. Jodocus continued convulsing. Azra pinched a bit of skin between his thumb and forefinger.

Jodocus hissed and began to writhe. "Just leave me. I'm a dead man."

"Open your eyes. You will be healed," Azra said.

"I deserve to die. Just go away. There is nothing anyone can do to save me."

"I will not leave you, my son."

"Who are you?" Jodocus asked in confusion.

"Your father."

"My father is dead. He was slain by someone I trusted."

"I am he," Azra assured him.

It was an obvious struggle, but Jodocus opened his eyes and stared at Azra's face. He grimaced with emotion. "It's my fault she's gone. It's my doing. I didn't know...I didn't understand..."

"Shhhh," Azra soothed. "Cimree is healed. And she'll heal you. Look, my son. Just look and you will be healed."

Cimree ventured closer and held the Nehushtan before her. "It will heal you, Jodocus."

Jodocus closed his eyes and faced away. "I cannot be healed when so many died because of me. Because of my pride."

"You blame yourself too harshly," Cimree said, remembering the words Azra had used after she had severed her connection with him and run away. Guilt was its own special torment. "Darcia has been banished. We are in control of the caves. The Morgarten are scattered."

"I expected too much of them," Jodocus said with anxiousness.

"My son, open your eyes. Be healed."

"I don't *deserve* it!" Jodocus moaned.

Azra hooked his hand around Jodocus's neck and lifted him up and embraced him. "I spent years hating the Queen Mother for what she did in this land. For the injustice of it. But that hatred festered. And so will your guilt. We are trying to save as many as we can, angel sworn and anyone else who will come. It's a choice, Jodocus. Choose to join us. We could use you."

"I'm unworthy of forgiveness," Jodocus whispered.

"So was I," Azra said. "But you are worth saving."

Jodocus lifted his head. He noticed Cimree and peered at the staff, and once again, the power swelled within it. The healing was instantaneous.

"Father," Jodocus breathed.

"Son," Azra said chokingly and embraced him once more.

THE TAY AL-ARD swept Azra and Cimree to the crumbling ruins of the arena at Vaud. The corridor smelled dank. When she had gone there before with Theo, he had taken her to his hidden study where he kept his shelves full of the writings of the discoveries he'd made. She had promised him that she would use the Tay al-Ard to help bring him and his records back to Tirich Mir. Before leaving, he'd led her to the corridor outside so that her sudden arrival wouldn't startle him or turn him into stone.

Azra turned and sniffed. "I can't smell the gévaudan."

"They should be gone," Cimree said. "Theo's study is behind that stone wall."

They had successfully begun the evacuation of the remnants of the angel sworn and the survivors of Koa back to the caves. Most of the Morgarten had fled from the Fear Liath, but some had chosen to join the safety and protection of Cimree's people, and when Jodocus had arrived and demonstrated loyalty to her, a few more had returned.

"It's so quiet," Azra said. "Why aren't the kobolds breaking it down?"

"I carved the Qodes Adonai in Theo's room," Cimree answered. "It drove them away." She reached the hidden door that Theo had shown her and used the Tay al-Ard to knock on it.

In a moment, the door began to slide open. She saw Theo in the gap wearing the glass eyepieces to protect himself from her defunct power.

"I'm healed, Theo," she said, noticing his surprised expression.

"Come inside," Theo beckoned nervously, gesturing for them both to enter. They did so and Theo shut the door, removing his eyepieces with his other hand. Cimree noticed that the books had been removed from the shelves and stacked in even rows of matching heights. His instruments had also been packed away in hidebound chests.

"I was getting nervous about whether or not you were going to return," Theo said to her, giving Azra a wary greeting.

"This is Azra," Cimree said to introduce the two men.

"I know who you are. And your reputation," Theo said humbly. "You also have the fireblood. Very interesting. I should like to talk to you about it sometime. It can be difficult to control."

"And I wanted to thank you for saving Cimree's life," Azra said. "If you hadn't stolen the Tay al-Ard from Jodocus, things would have been much worse."

Theo shrugged off the praise. "I would like to think of it as a mutually beneficial exchange. Is there a place prepared in Tirich Mir for my books? It needs to be exceptionally dry, as books don't fare very well with excessive moisture."

Cimree enjoyed Theo's manner of speech. He'd always been a prodigious thinker and observer of the world.

"There are several that will be suitable," Azra said. "But having fresh water to drink is important to staying alive."

"Ah. Of course. I didn't seek to complain."

"You weren't," Azra said. He walked around the room, examining the stacks of books.

"And I can bring my entire collection?" Theo asked. "It will require multiple trips, naturally. But anything we can do to preserve knowledge will benefit future generations. I'll admit I'm intensely curious about that island you mentioned, Cimree. The one in the middle of the lake."

Azra pursed his lips, turning an inquisitive look to Cimree.

"The land you brought me to," she said by way of explanation. "Theo wants to build a city like Montheron."

"Only much larger," Theo said, holding his hands apart and widening them. "I want to preserve every scrap of knowledge we can find. Unfortunately some knowledge has been lost permanently. Like the Cruithne, for example, the race that the revenant made to construct Ecbatana. They're extinct now. It's a shame really. They would have been helpful in constructing Kenatos."

"Kenatos?" Azra queried.

"He's already named the city he wants to build," Cimree said.

"I'm very ambitious," Theo said humbly. "I have this burning urge to save knowledge. I would not discriminate between races and cultures. All would be free to dwell safely in Kenatos."

"The land has more than enough space for many kingdoms," Azra said. "There are rich veins of stone perfect for quarrying. No one has ever settled there before because the ground is too marshy."

Theo snorted. "That's a simple matter to resolve. With ditches and dikes, we could divert the water away from the lowlands, and it would become very fertile. I'm excited to visit this place. When can we go there?"

"When we know it is safe to," Cimree answered. She peered at Azra again, sharing a knowing smile. "When the whispers tell us we can go."

Those who dwell in the caves of the Tirich Mir have come to call our haven by a new name—Mirrowen. Named after a certain garden in a between place that bridges other worlds. I find this vastly interesting. The caves are full of statues from the Queen Mother's previous victims. The eyes of the statues glow, and they are a source of heat, light, water, and purification of food. None of the stored food has spoiled. And, interestingly, none of the baskets of grain or vats of oil have dwindled since we all arrived. I do not understand how these statues demonstrate such incomparable power, but it is a relief to have them among us, although I find the stone faces seem to leer at me from time to time. It's quite unnerving. From what I can understand, the statues act as an intermediary of sorts, bringing light from a part of the world where it is day. Bringing water from a distant stream. It is unclear how the grain or the oil is replenished, but I have some markings on the jugs to track the ebb and flow in the hope that I might understand the principle behind the magical production of food that sustains us during our sojourn here. As ever, I am eager to explore the outside world. The monsters the golem created continue to maraud the land. It is everyone's hope that someday their feral cries will be silenced for good.

— The Hermetic and Alchemical Writings of Paracelsus

Thirty-Three

The Ancient Rites

They crossed the desert once more to that place between worlds called the Garden of Mirrowen. The Tay al-Ard would not bring them there, even though both Cimree and Azra had traveled there already. Cimree clutched the Nehushtan, using it as a staff as they ascended and descended the dunes. Birds flew overhead, seen as shadows in the sky against an immovable sun. But no grafting magic worked there either. A special place between life and death. A place where time seemed to have halted.

They walked in companionable silence, holding each other's hand, enjoying the warmth of the sunlight. They had rescued the survivors of Koa and brought them back to the caves, some traveling through graftings and the more seriously ill through the Tay al-Ard. Those who had been stricken by serpent or spider venom had been healed by the staff they'd brought from Idumea. Cimree had gathered the high council and provided instructions to welcome the newcomers who had agreed to abide by the laws established by the Oldknow in the beginning. Not the customs of the angel sworn, but the eternal laws. Those unwilling to make an oath were invited to withdraw from the caves. Only a few had refused.

"I wonder how long we will live in those caves," Cimree said, studying Azra's profile.

"I think we'll stay until the world has been purged," Azra answered. "I've no idea how long that will take. But we have food. We have shelter. We have light. It is enough."

She squeezed his hand. "And we have a little pale snake that is trying to provoke everyone to get upset with each other."

"But the arguing has lessened. They don't take offense as quickly anymore."

"There's a feeling of gratitude," Cimree said. "So many were healed on the verge of death, they find solace in no longer being in pain. I'm almost reluctant to return the staff. Its power is truly wonderful. Even the Tay al-Ard wearies of transporting us. But the staff never diminishes."

"It was a gift and must be returned."

"I know. I'm just grateful we could borrow it a while."

"I think I spy the mountains in the distance."

Cimree peered ahead and spotted the snow-capped peaks she'd been awed by on their first journey, all hazy in the distance. They increased their pace and soon were at the antler-walls of the garden, finding Maderos awaiting them at the gate.

"The foundlings have returned," Maderos said with a chuckle. "Have all the little goslings been gathered into the nest?"

"All who were willing to come," Cimree answered.

"There are *pethets* on every world," Maderos said enigmatically. "So it will always be. Come! Hand over the staff. I must return it to the treasury."

Cimree glanced at Azra and then back at Maderos. "We would ask a blessing from you, Maderos."

"Oh? What blessing do you seek, little sister?"

Azra spoke. "In the Origin it says that Lan and Lilith were given in marriage in the Garden of Clairvaux."

"You seek the rite of the ancients," Maderos said, his brow furrowing. "The irrevocare sigil."

Cimree had no idea what he meant. "I've not heard of that before."

"Only because the Queen Mother never wrote it down and never allowed it to be performed. She abolished marriage among the angel sworn. You seek a different path."

"She said her law was a higher law," Cimree said. "But I don't believe the Oldknow intended it that way."

Maderos grimaced and shook his head no. "If I teach you the irrevocare sigil, will you allow others to practice it? Or will you guard the knowledge for yourself?"

"Whatever the Oldknow demands, we will do," Cimree said simply.

Maderos grinned. "Then take my hand, little sister. Enter the garden once more."

MADEROS HAD ESCORTED them into the center of the garden, where the stream emerged from the roots of the largest tree. He'd asked them to place the Nehushtan against the tree where they could keep it in sight.

"Now we need an altar stone," Maderos said thoughtfully. He uttered a word of power, and a tingle went down Cimree's spine at the sound. Then he leaned against his crooked staff and waited patiently. The birds in the trees grew excited as if anticipating a miracle. Cimree clung to Azra's arm. Maderos had spent about an hour teaching them about the history of other worlds and of evil primordial spirits that sought to destroy all living things. Her mind had been swallowed up in the imagery of his tale.

"Look," Azra whispered.

A boulder was floating toward them from within the garden. The rough stone was long and flat, with jagged edges and a broken piece cut out of one side, like a step. It would have taken twenty people to heft such a massive stone, but it hovered above the ground and approached them. Maderos pointed to a spot and the boulder settled there. The top surface held smooth ripples and reached about as high as their thighs. Puffs came up when it settled on the ground.

"Covenants are made at altars," Maderos explained. "Either crafted by man or crafted by nature. Kneel across from each other and take hands."

Cimree and Azra did so.

"You are certain you wish to do this?" Maderos added. "Once the irrevocare sigil is performed, it cannot be undone. You will be bound together forever."

"I'm willing," Azra said without hesitation. He looked at Cimree with excitement and love shining in his eyes.

With a gentle flutter in her stomach, Cimree squeezed his hand and smiled so big her face ached with it. "So am I."

Maderos chuckled. "So you've made your choice. I concede. Because you have both accepted the Dryad's kiss, you will remember the words of the oath and the covenants you will make to each other. You will remember it perfectly so that you may perform this ceremony for others. But it must be done in the most sacred of places. A place sanctioned by the rune of the Qodes Adonai. A place set apart within the caves that no person dwells in."

"Where should we build this place?" Azra asked.

"You will be led," Maderos explained. "You will need master craftsmen to build it. There will be guardians appointed to it, day and night, to keep out those who have not been initiated into the order of the druids. Let me explain the size and dimensions." He did so, offering specific measurements for the inner and outer sanctums.

"It will take time to build it, then," Cimree said, thinking about Odeon and Trinati and their growing affection for each other.

"It will not take as long as you think," Maderos said. "After I have bound you together by the irrevocare sigil, I will charge you to make several journeys. Cimree, you hold the voided key and so you have the authority to travel in this world. To visit times in the past. You will save the Cruithne from destruction, they who were slaves to the revenant and built his palaces. When the golem destroyed it, those remnants all perished for want of air. You will bring them to the mountains."

She looked at Maderos earnestly. "You mean it has already happened? In the past?"

"Yes, little sister. You will make the journeys you have already made."

"You mean it was Cimree at the Wilderswill?" Azra asked in surprise. "She was the one who told Trinati and Odeon to go back to Ecbatana."

"Now you begin to see, little brother," Maderos said. "But you will only go where the Oldknow bids you. You will intervene where commanded, not of your own will. You are a wayfarer, Cimree. An Unwearying One. Now squeeze each other's hands and let me perform the ancient rite. Remember it. Make your people worthy of it."

And Cimree and Azra turned to one another once more, and each stared into the eyes of the one they had chosen to be bound to forevermore.

Cimree stood within the ruins of Ecbatana once more, shrouded in a spell of invisibility. All the walls of the city had been breached. She'd passed through the forbidden gardens and had discovered that the remainder of the statues she'd created had been broken to rubble. The noise of hammers and chisels came from every direction. The iron fences had been broken loose and dragged away to who knew where.

She was amazed at the devastation and how so many fine

palaces had been brought low. She walked to the heart of the city, grateful that she and Azra had decided to lead the others to the Tirich Mir. If they'd tried to hold off the hordes of gévaudan, they would all have been slaughtered.

The king's palace was in ruins as well. The once elegant pillars and mirrored floors were littered with rubble and dust. She made her way to the interior and reached the spot where the vaulted doors had safeguarded the revenant's lair. Sunlight crept into every space that had once been dark, and the stale sepulchral smells had blown away. The doors were gone. Everything was in ruin.

She stood just inside the doorless portal and drew the Tay al-Ard out while gripping the voided key in her other hand. She realized that she was the one who had brought the Sefer Raziel to Ecbatana. Or...would be the one to bring it. It was no accident that she'd found it that day when she'd discovered the fated blade in the skeleton. At some point, she knew the whispers would guide her back to the Wilderswill to retrieve the ancient tome from the past, and she would take it to where she'd discovered it.

Cimree closed her eyes, bowed her head, and sought direction for how far into the past she should go. When had the golem destroyed the lychgate? When had the Cruithne suffocated?

A whisper came to her of a memory. Of a particular day when she and Milena had been tending the garden together at their little cabin in Clairvaux. Cimree could almost smell the herbs, feel the soil clinging to her fingers. Could hear Milena's patient voice as she explained the different plants and their purposes in healing. Cimree knew she had the power to go back to that moment. To see her friend and mentor. But she was not to go unless commanded. She was not supposed to avert events based on her will or wisdom. It required trust in the Oldknow's purposes.

Cimree remembered the day and used the Tay al-Ard and the voided key to bring her back to that same day and time while remaining in this place.

In an instant the scene changed. The chamber was plunged into darkness, save for hissing torches that ignited on contact with air. A feeling of rancid evil permeated the chamber. The malevolence struck Cimree to her heart and made her recoil at the terror and fear exuding from the stone walls. The doors were open, and men were gathered with a caged wagon at the threshold, the men wore the silk tunics and costumes she'd seen on Khaf and the others.

A cage sat inside the chamber and inside that cage, she saw the golem in abject humiliation, its wrists locked with chains. A thrum of pity struck her chest.

A shrouded figure with red sparks for eyes stood near the cage. "Take it to the arena at Vaud," the figure hissed at the men. "This is my new champion. It will destroy the angel sworn and I will rule for a thousand years!"

The men, the servants who arrived to haul the golem away, bowed submissively. There were twenty or so of them, some carrying spears, and others, swords. They all seemed terrified out of their wits. The awful smell of the place was violent to Cimree's nose. Though invisible, she stepped out of their path to remain unnoticed and watched as they fearfully entered the revenant's chamber.

"Ephatha!" the golem growled, invoking a word of power that unlocked the gate of its own cage.

Cimree recognized the word of power the golem uttered. The revenant turned in confusion as the chains around the golem's wrists burst open and it shoved the bars of the gate.

The men quailed in terror.

"Nimeos!" the revenant uttered another word of command, and the stone doors of the vault began to grind closed.

The golem launched at the revenant and smashed its cloaked form, scattering bones in every direction with the violence of its attack. The men tried to stab at it, but the golem swept aside their spears with a roar of rage. Cimree gaped as some of the guards were violently killed. The doors continued to drag closed, the gears and mechanisms moving to seal the vault again.

"Stop it! Kill it!" someone shrieked.

The golem scrabbled up one of the doors like a spider and then launched itself at the head guard, grabbed him, and threw him across the room like a discarded toy. Cimree could not help but be impressed at how effortlessly the golem scattered the guards, the remainder of whom fled with screams as they escaped.

The golem chuffed, waiting by the doors as they relentlessly closed. Then it sniffed. Its skin was translucent as she remembered, its horrid muscles bulging visibly to her sight. It smelled something that interested it.

The golem's head swayed back and forth. It sniffed again. Then it approached her. It kept searching with its eyes, but they did not focus on her.

Instead, it *smelled* her scent.

Fear wriggled in her chest. She squeezed the Tay al-Ard, readying herself to vanish. The golem had smelled her in the revenant's lair. And it had smelled her again at Montheron.

The golem hissed as the light began to dim. The vault doors were almost closed. A clicking noise bubbled up from its throat, and it bounded through the gap before the door shut with a menacing thud. The locks and gears clicked shut, sealing it closed. Not even Lord Roque had been able to open the doors after that.

Cimree's heart pounded with relief.

The sparkling torches would be extinguished when all the air in the room was gone. She began to search for the Cruithne. And she found them beneath a trapdoor made of iron that swung on heavy hinges. Down below, she saw the heat of dozens of bodies in cramped quarters.

They were short, muscled men, gray with soot, and had piercing eyes that could see in the dark.

"Xenoglossia," Cimree uttered, invoking the word of power to

enable her to speak to them. This race had been created as the revenant's builders. They'd constructed the catacombs and been forced to live down there in the dark.

"Come with me," Cimree called down to the mass of beady-eyed refugees. "The revenant, your master, is destroyed. I've come to set you free."

Thirty-Four

Henna

Setara painstakingly decorated Cimree's hands and arms with ink. Henna, as it was called, was a tribal custom, part of the marriage ceremony, one for which Azra had expressed a special fondness to her. Although Cimree and Azra had been married by irrevocare sigil by Maderos, they decided to adopt the local custom so that others might witness their union and the entire community could celebrate it. Cimree wore the red silk dress that Azra had saved for her. Many women and girls were in the chamber Cimree shared with her husband, who was with the men in a different part of the caves, participating in a ritual of camaraderie and storytelling as his hands and arms were also painted in the reddish-brown tattoos.

Trinati was there, looking slightly uncomfortable by the foreign tradition, but she merely watched without criticizing anything. Pereta and her girls, Edwina and Blanka, were clearly enjoying the activity. Pregnant Yasmin was there too, her belly swelling with new life as she made suggestions for the decorations to be done. Other Pashmir women were there too with their daughters. Cimree was comfortable with all of them, even though the room was a little too crowded and getting too rambunctious.

Setara, noticing Cimree's growing discomfort, encouraged the others to join the rest of the congregation that was gathering in the largest cave to celebrate the marriage.

Setara finished the decorations and then blew on the last dabs of ink to help them dry. The pattern on Cimree's hands and up her arms was intricate and vibrant with shades of red, ranging from a bright orange to a deep maroon. Patterns of flowers, snakeskin, and leaves decorated her fingers, hands, wrists, and up to the crease of her elbows. The ministrations had taken hours to complete, and Cimree and Setara had always enjoyed each other's company in carefree conversation.

"You look lovely," Setara said to her, tilting her head to one side. "I remember you don't enjoy crowded places. That you prefer to be solitary. But your people need to see you celebrate."

Cimree admired the artwork on her arms and hands. "I don't really think of them as my people. We have all gathered together to save ourselves. That is enough."

Setara was sitting on a cushion atop a basket, Cimree on the edge of bed. Setara made a solemn frown. "If not for you, Siyah Malkah, we all should have perished." She pursed her lips. "Now that you no longer rule from the shadows, I wonder if we should rename you. *Afei Malkah.* The serpent queen."

That does have a certain nobility to it, Iddawc whispered in her thoughts. The snake was coiled up on a pillow in a languid pose.

Cimree looked at the serpent, who was always trying to get a rise out of her. "I like the name you already gave me, Setara, but the title I prefer is 'healer.' Not 'queen.'"

"You healed my injured sons," Setara said. "You drove out the spiders. You humbled Koa and brought more refugees here. The food isn't dwindling. Truly, you are more than just a healer. Now, I suspect the men are growing restless and want the celebration to happen already. Your husband will desire to see you."

Cimree examined the serpentine pattern on her arms again and nodded, then rose from the bed as anticipation swirled in her stomach. Accompanied by Setara, she walked out of the room. The statue of Chuq had been moved to Ramesh and Yasmin's tunnel. As the two women left, Cimree quenched the light from the druid stone on the shelf. The thin fabric of the silk dress made her feel cold, and she had to consciously not rub her arms for fear of smearing the ink.

As they walked down the tunnel together, a cry rang out, causing a jolt to surge through Cimree, quickly released on a quiet laugh when she recognized it was a shout of joy.

"They're coming! They're coming! We can begin!"

An instant later, music filled the air. The light and airy sounds warmed Cimree's heart, and soon they arrived at the largest cavern. Druid stones illuminated the space along with light from the statues. Cimree's self-consciousness swelled as she became the object of everyone's attention. Claps and cheers filled the air. The number of people who had gathered for the celebration stymied her imagination. There were hundreds in the tunnels. Angel sworn, Pashmir tribesmen, and Cruithne had joined together for shelter. There were too many for her to have already learned all their names, but they greeted her and welcomed her.

She smiled shyly at the well-wishers and their admiring looks. And then the crowd parted and her eyes found Azra. He wore a tribal tunic made of the warm fabric, the sleeves rolled up to display the henna on his hands and arms. His pattern was different from hers, a series of flames denoting his fireblood as well as claws, feathers, and antlers—a tribute to his ability to hold many graftings at once no doubt. His eyes locked on hers, and their warmth and his slightly upturned grin were her proof that he approved of what she'd chosen to wear for the occasion.

Setara led her to Azra, where he stood by Andrin and his family.

Perreta beamed at her. "Cimree! You are so beautiful!"

Edwina squealed and gave Cimree a hug. "Can I have henna

when I get married?" she asked her parents after gawking at the designs.

Perreta laughed. "I think you're a little too young to be thinking about it right now."

Andrin provided Cimree a respectful bow, and then he clapped Azra on the back. "I'm so happy for the both of you," he said.

Cimree tried to ignore the commotion of the room, keeping her gaze fixed on Azra's face. Setara calmed down the assembly. Cimree had created a carving of a face in the wall at the entrance to the room using the Qodes Adonai that would impart xenoglossia on anyone who passed into the room. That made it a wonderful gathering place where all could communicate freely. But Cimree wanted to be alone with Azra again soon, and she endured the situation patiently, warmed by the sense of camaraderie.

The marriage ceremony was brief, and involved them joining hands and having a woven ribbon wrapped around and joining their wrists. There was no altar stone this time, no quiet burbling of the stream. Cimree had been "adopted" by Setara and her husband, and Azra had been "adopted" by Andrin and Perreta. The ceremony ended with a raucous cheer and then the music began in earnest. Cimree had received some lessons from Setara, and she and Azra had practiced the dance routine several times beforehand. But as the center of attention and giddy from the rite that revealed to the community her bond with Azra, it was more complicated than she remembered and she made mistakes.

The thrill of the dance spread to those assembled. The angel sworn were standing on the outskirts as observers, watching the festivities but not engaging in them. And then, to Cimree's surprise and delight, Trinati grabbed Odeon by the arm and dragged him into the dance. And once that had taken place, other angel sworn began to sheepishly join in.

Cimree and Trinati locked eyes, and Cimree gave her an

approving nod. A little blush came to Trinati's cheeks. But maybe it was just from all the dancing.

Cimree and Azra walked hand in hand, taking the time to roam the cavern and accept the well wishes from their integrated community. The Cruithne had already started working on an inner sanctum, a carved portion of the tunnel where the rites Maderos had taught them could be performed. It would take time, of course, to make it ready. The Cruithne had acted as servants when they'd first arrived, but Cimree had worked to overcome that and informed them that they were free to roam the tunnels. Everyone had a role to play in the community, and no preference was given to one set of people versus another.

As they passed the tunnel that led to the waterfall and pool, Theo was leaving it and approached the two of them, walking briskly and with a nervous glance back the way he had come.

"What's wrong?" Cimree asked, noticing the tension in his expression.

"The golem has returned," he said furtively, his voice low. "It's in the cavern with the waterfall."

Cimree had told Azra already about her journey back in time and how she'd been discovered by it even though she was invisible.

Azra touched the distaff in his belt. With Lan's grafting wand, he could send it away.

"What is it doing?" Azra asked with concern.

"It keeps calling for you," Theo said to Cimree. She hadn't felt it come. Her leg hadn't troubled her at all since she'd been healed by the staff. "Certain animals are disturbed by smells. I could concoct a potion that might send it off."

"We need Uorsin to repair the other gate," Cimree said. He had been working closely with the Cruithne to learn from them and to teach them his knowledge of forges.

"I'll drive it off," Azra offered.

"I'll come with you," Cimree responded.

After what it had done to Darcia, no one felt comfortable with it nearby.

"I'm perfectly fine waiting for it to be gone," Theo said with a shudder. "It is uncontrollable. I still have nightmares about it."

"Thank you for telling us. Would you go inform Trinati and the rest of the high council?"

Cimree had offered Theo a place on the council too. His knowledge had proven incredibly useful so far. All his books had been relocated to the caves—to the dryest part of them with engravings that dried the moisture in the air.

"I will, Your Highness," Theo said with a bow. "And before I forget. Congratulations."

"Thank you," Cimree said. She nodded to Azra and he drew out the Tay al-Ard. His only weapon was a dirk in his belt and the distaff. But the fireblood he possessed gave him a power others did not have.

"Are you sure you want to come?" Azra asked her.

"I'm sure I don't want you to go alone," she answered. "What we face from now on, we face together."

Azra held out the Tay al-Ard, she gripped it, and they both disappeared, reappearing together immediately at the gate. Two angel sworn with spears were at the ready, facing the iron gate that stopped the golem from entering the tunnels. All the other entrances were blocked as well.

"Cim-reeee!" the golem hissed as soon as she appeared.

"Glad you're here," one of the angel sworn said nervously. "It's been calling like this for an hour."

The creature quieted. It reached its muscled arm through the bars and began whimpering. *"More? Cim-reee.... more?"*

It wanted her to use the Tanaquil medallion. To feed it with the special combination of feelings it craved. It had changed since she'd seen it in the revenant's lair. Larger than its original incarnation. It had exchanged its own limbs for more powerful ones. But the essence of it was still the same. She felt pity for it, but it could not dwell among them. Its instincts had been forged by the revenant. It wanted to destroy, not build things. And she was loathe to bring back the markings that were no longer on her body.

"You must go," Cimree told the creature. "Your home is out there."

"More!" the golem demanded, grabbing the bars and shaking them. It wanted what it wanted. Its motivations were straightforward. And it would never tire from its demands. Never.

"Send it away, Azra," she said sadly. No weapon had been found that could kill it. It seemed to regenerate swiftly after any injury.

The golem began to keen, as if it understood what she'd said. *"Cim-reeee! Cim-reeee!"*

Azra drew the distaff. "Depart," he commanded, flicking the scionwood wand at it.

The golem screeched in anguish. Cimree felt the prickle of magic go down her arms, bringing out gooseflesh. The golem keened mournfully, released the bars, and scampered back into the cave. She watched it scrabble up the walls to the waterfall and then its shadow slunk away until it was gone.

One of the angel sworn gasped in relief.

Cimree's heart ached. She wondered whether the Nehushtan staff would have healed it, or maybe it no longer was the creature it had been when created if it had metamorphosed so many times its true origin was lost. She listened for a whispered answer to her query, but none came.

"What do you think it wanted?" asked one of the guards to her.

"I'm not really sure it even knows," she prevaricated. "But we must be vigilant and guard this gate. It may return. And then we will drive it away again. It is relentless."

"Yes, Queen Mother," said one of the guards to her.

His choice of title still rankled her. She felt she was nothing like Lilith had been. But she imagined that by giving her the title, he was seeking mostly to comfort himself.

"Thank you for doing your duty," she said to them both. "For missing the festivities."

"A small sacrifice compared to what you've been through," said the other guardian somberly.

She hooked arms with Azra and the two began to walk back down the tunnel.

"You don't really want to go back to the celebration, do you?" he asked her.

"Not really. I just want to be alone with you."

"That sounds...heavenly," he said. "We can go back to our room if you like. Unless the snake is still there."

"I have something else in mind," Cimree promised. They were alone in the tunnel, having passed the sharp bend, away from the attention of anyone else. She pushed him against the wall.

His fingers slid into her hair, and he began to kiss her with a passion that grew more and more pronounced. Her body responded to the fierceness of his kisses.

"We can go anywhere in the world," he whispered, drawing back for a breath.

"I know," she said, reaching in his belt for the Tay al-Ard. And she thought of just the place she wanted to take him.

Epilogue
The Scourged Lands

THREE HUNDRED FORTY-FOUR DAYS LATER

Cimree gathered the high council after Trinati returned from her scouting expedition. The stores of grain and fruit were dwindling, had been dwindling for several weeks. Earlier that morning, Cimree had helped deliver another baby to Yasmin and Ramesh in the caves of Mirrowen, which was the new name they had given their home, in homage to the Oldknow's power, which had protected them from the onslaught of monsters trying to overrun their defenses during their long incarceration within. Dramatic displays of thunder and lightning had been common in those days. Sometimes the mountain peaks had been wreathed in flames. And others, a gentle hoar frost descended and sheathed the land in silver crystals.

There had not been such an occurrence in months, but every time the high council had discussed sending out search parties, they'd all gotten an overwhelming sense that it was not the time and to forbear. Until recently. The first few forays by the angel sworn had revealed a total and utter devastation over the land. Koa had been leveled. Every building, every structure had been pulverized. Those who hadn't fled before the destruction were no more.

The additional scouting parties revealed no survivors anywhere. No encampments. No trails of smoke from cookfires. There were carcasses, fragments of weapons littering the earth, some poking up from the dusty remnants and sand. Nature swallowed everything eventually.

"You're lost in your thoughts," Azra said softly, gently touching her shoulder.

"Our rations won't last much longer," she murmured back to him. "And I still don't know if it's safe to leave."

"You'll know when it's time," Azra said confidently.

"Will I? The weight I feel for the safety of this people is...it's enough to take my breath away."

They were still waiting for a few others from the council to join. Other conversations went on in the chamber, illuminated by the light of the druid stones. Odeon could not sit still. He was chafing with impatience for the news Trinati had brought, but she would not speak until everyone had assembled. Uorsin was a solemn presence; though quiet, his counsel was always useful. Setara fidgeted with the beads on her necklace and made a remonstrative comment to her husband, who had likely said something in an attempt at humor. Theo had not yet arrived. Nor Andrin. Tolkeh, the Cruithne delegate, had a furrowed brow and gold hoops dangling from his earlobes.

Andrin and Theo arrived at the same time and took the last two chairs at the council. Cimree nodded to Odeon, who had taken Wegner's place as the administrator of the high council, and he rose.

"My apologies for being tardy," Theo said abashedly. "I was inspecting the waterfall chamber and Andrin had to find me."

"We're glad you're here. Trinati has returned with her scouts and is ready to report to the council," Odeon said. He gave Trinati a gesture, and he took his seat as she stood.

Trinati had softened her appearance since the integration of the tribe and the Cruithne into their community. She had adopted the clothing of the Pashmir. Rather than the severe edges of the former archangel's gear and clothing, she wore a tunic and boots lined with fur and beads. And she was often seen with a slight smile, especially when in conversation with Odeon, though at the moment, her face held an earnest expression. "I went farther than I ever have before," she reported. "Each of us pushed our speed to the limits, looking for any signs of life. It appears there is no one left. We are the last of humanity."

The room exploded in a chorus of gasps and concerned questions, but everyone fell silent at a sharp gesture from Odeon, and Trinati continued her testimony. "There are no signs of kobolds, gévaudan, grimalkin, bats, or flying serpents. No sign of the golem either. Natural wildlife has reclaimed the land. There are packs of wolves hunting small game. Bears catching fish in the rivers. Birds are plentiful. My scouts went in eight different directions, and all returned with the same report...that fruit is growing on the trees in the wild. One found a crop of wild asparagus. We all camped on the ground with no threat, no harm."

"Where did those monsters go, then?" Setara asked. "They can't have just disappeared."

"I can't answer that," Trinati replied. "But we've found no evidence of them out there."

"Those creatures the golem made," Cimree said, "seemed only to feed on our kind. What would an animal in the wild do if deprived of a source of food?"

"They would wander," Azra replied. "And ultimately starve to death."

"What if they can't starve to death?" asked Setara's husband in an atypically serious tone.

"They would continue roaming," Azra said with a shrug. "Or attack one another. Maybe they killed off their own kind."

"We can't know that for sure," Trinati said. "But food is

running out. I feel that it's time to leave the caves. We can rebuild the villages of the Pashmir. Grow crops."

Theo shot Cimree a worried look.

"I want to hear from everyone," Cimree said.

Theo lifted his hand timidly.

"Go on," Odeon said to him.

"What about that land west of Clairvaux? We've talked about going there before. Of making it more suitable for living. Why not go somewhere that has not been settled before?"

"It's a long way from here," said Tolkeh the Cruithne. "My people would prefer staying in the caves."

"If we are to survive," Setara said, "it would be wise to stay together. To band together. We'll need everyone's help if we are going to last more than a few seasons."

"I agree with Setara," Odeon said. "Unity is strength. We've learned that over this last year."

"Then we will abide the council's decision," Tolkeh said.

"Azra? You've been quiet." Cimree arched her eyebrows at him.

"The diminishing food is our sign that the Oldknow wants us to fend for ourselves now. The abundance we were provided was never meant to be permanent."

"So you think we should go?" Cimree asked.

"I do," Azra replied.

"I suggest a small search party," Trinati offered. "Use the Tay al-Ard to go to that uninhabited land. If it looks empty of threat, we could begin establishing a settlement there. Not everyone at first, to make sure that we do not leave a trail to follow. I for one should like to revisit the valley of Clairvaux as well."

"I would like to see what's left of Montheron," Odeon said.

"A small party," Cimree agreed. "A group of four. That has always been the standard size for a mission."

"You and Azra are inseparable," Trinati said with a teasing smile. "Do you count only as one?"

"I should very much like to go," Theo volunteered.

"I think we all would like to go," Trinati said, her eyes roaming the room. "You'll have to choose, Cimree."

Cimree saw the eagerness in all their faces. "Azra and I. Theo. And Setara. Trinati is in charge while we are gone. I feel it's time we ventured farther from Mirrowen. Are we agreed?"

The council voted unanimously in favor.

AZRA AND CIMREE walked along the shore of the island. She missed the colorful waters of Lake Beatriz, but there were mountains to the east and west. The island in the middle of the vast lake was larger than Montheron had ever been. In her mind's eye, she tried to picture what it would look like with fortress walls, stone buildings, cobbled streets.

Setara came walking up to them with excitement lighting her face.

"So what do you think of this land?" Cimree asked her.

"I've never known a place with so much water. So much life! I don't believe my people could even choose one place to dwell if they had to. We might be content to just keep roaming. This land is glorious!"

"We will all need to lend a hand and help build," Cimree offered as a reminder.

"Of course!" Setara exclaimed. "And we could always retreat to the fortress if there is trouble. I think my people will always prefer to be nomads. I am so excited to tell the others about this land."

Cimree agreed. After their confinement in the caves, it would be wonderful to be in open land again. Theo had climbed to the tallest peak on the island and was standing, peering out at the lake and surrounding lowlands. There were so many trees to provide lumber. Azra mentioned a helpful contraption Wegner's memories offered him of building watermills to grind grain into powder and to be used to saw the wood.

Chrys had revealed to her and Azra that the Gallows Tree would commence bearing fruit the next spring. A new beginning was dawning.

Theo shouted and began running down the hill toward them, but the distance made the words and even his intention unclear. Cimree looked at him and wondered what had disturbed him. Setara turned in surprise and stared up at Theo, who was rushing down the hillside at breakneck speed.

Azra scowled and began to search the horizon.

"I see people," Azra said in surprise. "They're flying over the waters, headed this way."

"Angel sworn?" Cimree asked. She spied the distant figures but could not make anything out.

Azra drew his grafting wand.

Theo approached breathlessly. "I s-saw them from the hilltop," he spluttered. "There's a structure over there," he said pointing west. "A watchtower. Those people rose from it, like the angel sworn. It could be a threat."

Azra summoned a falcon and grafted with it. A half-dozen individuals floated over the waters toward them. Not swiftly, instead, it was as if the air current were blowing them closer.

"What do you see, Azra?" Cimree asked.

Azra searched deeply into the distance. "They're not angel sworn," he said.

"I thought it would be safe here," Theo said in distress.

"Their style of clothing is unlike anything I've seen," Azra reported. "They have long dark hair. Black hair. They have swords in scabbards, but the hilts are very unusual."

Cimree did not feel any sense of warning, but she clenched the Tay al-Ard and prepared to whisk them away. As they waited on the shore, the six figures became clearer. Azra was right. Their outfits were flowing, silken robes with sashes instead of belts. And instead of boots, they were barefoot. The six approaching men appeared to be warriors, and each had a stern countenance. Their complexions were a light ocher coloring, and their eyes had an almond shape to them that was different from any she'd seen before.

"I've never seen such people before," Theo said with interest. "Fascinating."

"Nor have I," Setara agreed.

The six landed about two dozen paces away from them on the sandy shore. No weapons were drawn.

One of them had a silver tiara on his brow. When he addressed them, he spoke in a language that was baffling.

"Xenoglossia," Cimree said under her breath, invoking the word of power to translate languages.

"...and I am a prince among my people," the fellow said. He bowed to them in respect. "Do you understand me?"

"We do," Azra answered. He offered a bow in return.

The fellow gave a confused look. "How is it you understand our language?" he asked.

"It is a gift from the All Father," Cimree answered. "Did you build a tower in that forest?"

"Yes," the prince said. "We did not mean to trespass in your lands. We believed these shores were uninhabited."

"Where do you hail from?" Theo asked them eagerly. "From across the sea?"

The prince bowed again. "We are sojourners from another world. We seek to escape the ruthless Dragon of Night, the Jade Emperor who conquers all kingdoms with his magic and his dragons. We did not come by ship but through a mirror door. We seek a place of shelter. A refuge from the Jade Emperor who has destroyed and will destroy all who defy him and his queen."

The prince went down on his knees before them, and his five cohorts followed suit.

"I implore you, on behalf of my people, the Vaettir, to grant us sanctuary in your world. All who will not kneel to the Jade Emperor must pass the Death Wall and perish in his Grave Kingdom."

Cimree felt a tingling go down her neck. Gooseflesh riddled her arms.

I brought them here, came a whisper to her mind. *More will come. Protect them all.*

The Vaettir are an impressive people who strive to uphold principles of honor and duty. Their ability to float and hover in the air is not a result of grafting magic but is a gift from their gods in another world, a power obtained through eating a certain fruit native to that world, which they brought seeds of to this one. When they breathe in deeply, they begin to rise, as if the buoyancy of their bodies in air is different from ours. They are cunning artificers and skilled in making tools, carving stone, and shaping precious metals. They have claimed the forests on the northwest area all the way to the ocean and have named it Shiruban. In our tongue Silvandom. The Cruithne have claimed the eastern mountain ranges and called it the Alkire. There are plenty of caves there, which they prefer. The lands directly south continue to flood with each season, so there haven't been any settlements there, but to the southwest, the ground is higher and the mountains perfect for quarrying stone. The people who have settled there call it Stonehollow. Uorsin has made that place his home, and he is responsible for harvesting the stone blocks used for the city and dragging them with beasts of burden to the shores. Every group contributes laborers to help build Kenatos on the island, which Odeon and I are overseeing the construction of. Some have chosen not to live in the settlements at all. The Pashmir, for example, wander from place to place. This may cause problems as the population increases and others choose to carve out land for their own. Cimree and Azra often depart for Clairvaux and stay there in the quiet of the valley with that little pale snake they keep as a pet. We have certain spiritual creatures that we can send to summon them, and they return, of course, for the regular meetings of the high council. Cimree tells us that more people will come. More refugees. That others will follow the whispers of the Oldknow until they come here for asylum. And that she and Azra have been charged to bring them here for safety. Some have chosen to become disciples of Cimree and Azra and to wander, offering help and passing on knowledge of the land and its spirit creatures. And these are called the druids. When I have built Kenatos, I will spend some time among them to learn more.

— THE HERMETIC AND ALCHEMICAL WRITINGS OF PARACELSUS, FIRST ARCH-RIKE OF KENATOS

Author's Note

Thank you for joining in this imaginative journey that weaves history from our world along with a fantasy world partially inspired by my imagination. More on that later!

Of the many inspirations for this series, I have withheld one until now, the final book. In the class I teach called *The How of Creativity*, I reference that so many great ideas come as a mash-up between other ideas. Stephen King once said: "Good story ideas seem to come quite literally from nowhere, sailing at you right out of the empty sky; two previously unrelated ideas come together and make something new under the sun. Your job isn't to find these ideas but to recognize them when they show up."

The novel *Watership Down* was a key ingredient in coming up with this story. It's a story about a tribe of rabbits in England that are forced to leave their warren and establish a new one far away while dealing with the dangers of a world full of predators. I admire the culture of the rabbit world that the author developed, including its mythology. Astute readers will notice other similarities as well. Most of the villians in my novels have been people. I wanted a 'man versus monster' story, one that would create tension and against which our heroes would never fully prevail.

Ultimately, I decided that I wanted *Angel Sworn* to be the origin story for my *Whispers from Mirrowen* saga, which long-time readers understand was the genesis to Muirwood. That is why you've seen so many overlapping ingredients mingled together. And now that you've reached the end, you will notice connections to *Grave Kingdom* as well. I'm planning to write a sequel series to that as my next project and following a recent research trip to Japan. This will explain who the Vaettir are and how they are connected to the Bhikhu.

I have one more revelation to make which I've kept long before *Fireblood, Dryad-Born,* and *Poisonwell* were published. The story of *Whispers from Mirrowen* was originally a Dungeons & Dragons campaign that I created for my long-time friends Jeremy and Brendon and for our wives Rochelle and Gina. The twist from the campaign came, months into it, when they realized that their adventure was taking place in the world of Shannara based on an obscure paragraph from *The Sword of Shannara* that spoke of an ancient civilization that existed in the Four Lands. It was so fun to watch their shocked expressions when they realized that their campaign was happening in the world of Terry Brooks.

As a novice author back then, I secretly hoped that someday I might be able to persuade Terry into letting me add my "fan fiction" somehow, but then he decided to write his own prequel novels and there was no way that it was going to be approved. So I had to change everything and build my own world in which to tell the story.

I've shared this secret rarely and decided it was time to reveal the twist. It was *Elfstones of Shannara* that inspired me to start writing back in high school. And Terry Brooks has had some of the deepest influences on my stories since then.

Terry announced his retirement from writing in March 2025.

About the Author

Jeff Wheeler is a Wall Street Journal bestselling author of over thirty epic fantasy novels, including the *Kingfountain* and *Muirwood* series. His stories captivate readers with strong, moral protagonists, complex characters, and richly detailed worlds. Known for clean, compelling fantasy, Jeff's books explore themes of integrity, loyalty, and growth, with interconnected series that keep fans eagerly turning pages. A husband, father of five, and active in his faith community, Jeff draws on his life and history to craft uplifting tales. Discover his worlds at jeff-wheeler.com or through his online classes at Writers Block (writersblock.biz).

www.ingramcontent.com/pod-product-compliance
Lightning Source LLC
LaVergne TN
LVHW091142150826
845672LV00005B/1017

* 9 7 9 8 9 0 0 4 3 1 5 4 3 *